双语 精华版

心灵鸡汤

[女性系列]

U0133165

聆听花开的声音……

韦 虹 张 洁 张楚武 译

Hearing the Voice of the Flowers

Jack Canfield & Mark Victor Hansen 等 著

Chicken Soup for the Soul

安徽科学技术出版社
Health Communications, Inc.

图书在版编目(CIP)数据

心灵鸡汤:双语精华版.聆听花开的声音/(美)坎费尔德(Canfield, J.)等著;韦虹,张洁,张楚武译. —合肥:安徽科学技术出版社,2007.9
ISBN 978-7-5337-3882-2

Ⅰ.心… Ⅱ.①坎…②韦…③张…④张… Ⅲ.①英语-汉语-对照读物②故事-作品集-美国-现代 Ⅳ.H319.4:Ⅰ

中国版本图书馆 CIP 数据核字(2007)第 129496 号

心灵鸡汤:双语精华版. 聆听花开的声音
(美)坎费尔德(Canfield,J.)等著　韦虹　张洁　张楚武译

出　版　人:朱智润
责任编辑:付　莉
封面设计:王国亮
出版发行:安徽科学技术出版社(合肥市政务文化新区圣泉路 1118 号
　　　　　出版传媒广场,邮编:230071)
电　　话:(0551)3533330
网　　址:www.ahstp.com.cn
E - mail:yougoubu@sina.com
经　　销:新华书店
排　　版:安徽事达科技贸易有限公司
印　　刷:合肥晓星印务有限责任公司
开　　本:889×1100　1/24
印　　张:10
字　　数:202 千
版　　次:2007 年 9 月第 1 版　2007 年 9 月第 1 次印刷
印　　数:10 000
定　　价:25.00 元

作为原生于美国的大众心理自助与人生励志类的闪亮品牌,《心灵鸡汤》语言地道新颖,优美流畅,极富时代感。书中一个个叩人心扉的故事,充分挖掘平凡小事所蕴藏的精神力量和人性之美,真率倾诉对生命的全新体验和深层感悟,字里行间洋溢着爱心、感恩、信念、鼓励和希望。因其内涵哲思深邃,豁朗释然,央视"百家讲坛"曾引用其作为解读援例。

文本适读性与亲和力、故事的吸引力和感召力、内涵的人文性和震撼力,煲出了鲜香润泽的《心灵鸡汤》——发行40多个国家和地区,总销量达一亿多册的全球超级畅销书!

安徽科学技术出版社独家引进的该系列英文版,深得广大读者的推崇与青睐,频登各大书店及"开卷市场零售监测系统"的畅销书排行榜,多次荣获全国出版发行业的各类奖项。

就学英语而言,本系列读物的功效已获广大读者乃至英语教学界的充分肯定。由于书中文章的信度和效度完全符合大规模标准化考试对考题的质量要求,全国大学英语四级考试、全国成人高考的阅读理解真题曾采用其中的文章。大学英语通用教材曾采用其中的文章作为精读课文。

为了让更多读者受惠于这一品牌,我社又获国内独家授权,隆重推出双语精华版《心灵鸡汤》系列:英汉美文并蓄、双语同一视面对照——广大读者既能在轻松阅读中提高英语水平,又能从中感悟人生的真谛;激发你搏击风雨、奋发向上的生命激情!

CONTENTS

目 录

目录

目　录

The Interview
面　试

Dreams are powerful reflections of your actual growth potential.

Denis Waitley and Reni L.Witt

梦想能充分反映你成长的真实潜力。

丹尼斯·维特力，瑞尼·L.维特

The job of a lifetime,that's what it was,secretary for the district attorney.I couldn't wait for my interview.This was the kind of position I'd dreamed of,what all those years of college and entry-level positions were for.

The night before my interview,I spent two hours going through my closet to pick out just the right outfit.What would I say to him?I curled up into my pillowy bed and stared at the ceiling,unable to sleep.How should I act?　Nervous,I shut my eyes and tried to get some rest,but I kept tossing and turning.

去当地区检察官的秘书，那可真是我愿意做一辈子的工作。我迫不及待地等着面试。这是我梦寐以求的职位，是我多年大学学习和下层初级职位辛勤努力的目标所在。

在参加面试的头一天晚上，我花了两个小时搜遍衣橱，寻找适合穿戴的全套行头。我对他说什么好呢？我蜷缩在柔软的床上盯着天花板难以入眠。我该怎么做呢？我很紧张，闭上双眼想歇息片刻，但却止不住地辗转反侧。

Finally,the alarm clock woke me.I tried to open my eyes,but something was wrong.My face felt stiff,strange.My hands flew to my cheeks.

"No! "My lips were unable to open all the way.

I ran to the bathroom and looked at myself in the bathroom mirror, horrified.My face was contorted like a stroke victim's.My eyes were misaligned.I couldn't move the right side of my face.I could barely recognize myself.What was happening to me?What nightmare did I wake up into?

My mother came into the room,"What's wrong?"Her eyes bulged as she withdrew in terror.

"What's happening to me?"I slurred to her.

"I'll take you to the emergency room,"she finally gasped.

We were rushed in.The nurse took one look at me and called in a specialist.There,under the blazing white lights,my mother and I waited.

After several hours of tests,the doctor finally explained,"You have Bell's palsy.It is a condition in which your face muscles tighten because of stress.You need to get plenty of sleep,and in a few days your face will return to normal."

"But I have a job interview this afternoon,"I sadly remembered.

"I'm sorry,"the doctor said,concerned. "You should reschedule, maybe for later in the week."

During the long car ride home,all I could think about was how bad it would look to reschedule.Certainly,that would dampen my chances. Nobody reschedules with the district attorney.All the other applicants would have the advantage then,I concluded.

I looked at my watch and made the decision,"Mom,drop me off on Jacob Street.I'm going to the interview."

"Honey,I don't think you should.You look…strange,"she said,ever so gently.

I knew she was right.He probably would take one look at me and

最终，闹钟唤醒了我。我想要睁开双眼，但是发现什么东西不对劲了。我的脸感觉僵硬，好奇怪。我飞快地把手伸向脸颊。

"不！"我的双唇怎么也张不开。

我冲进浴室，惊恐万分地看着镜子里的自己。我的脸就像中了风的人脸一般扭曲着。双眼变形了，右边的脸也不能动了，我简直认不出自己了。我怎么了，一觉醒来跌入了怎样的梦魇？

母亲来到房间，"怎么了？"她吃惊地后退时眼睛瞪老大。

"我这是咋回事？"我向她含糊不清地反问。

"我带你去急诊室，"她最后喘着粗气说。

我们一路飞奔。护士看了我一眼，然后叫来了专科医生。就在那刺眼的白炽灯下，母亲和我等待着。

经过几小时检查，医生做出最终解释，"你得了贝尔氏麻痹。它的症状是你的面部肌肉因为紧张而绷紧。你需要大量的睡眠，过几天以后你的脸就恢复正常了。"

"但是我今天下午就有个应聘面试，"我难过地想起这事。

"我很抱歉，"医生关爱地说道，"你应该另外约个时间，也许是本周末。"

在坐车回家漫长的路上，我所想的就是重新约面试时间有多糟。那当然会让我的机遇渺茫。没人能和地区检察官重约见面时间。我想那样的结果只能是让其他所有的申请人获得优势。

我看了一下表做出决定，"妈，在雅各布街把我放下，我要去参加面试。"

"宝贝，我认为你不该去。你看着……怪怪的，"她像以往一样温和地说。

我知道她说得对。他很可能就只看我一眼，然后凭我此时的相

judge me by my appearance rather than by my experience and talent.I probably shouldn't go.But if I didn't,I'd always wonder if I could have gotten my dream job.

"No,Mom,take me there."

Reluctantly,she took me where I wanted to go.I walked right into the formidable office with the mahogany furniture and pillars of white marble,not letting my own self-consciousness or any disease stop me.Not now,not when I had worked so hard for so long to be given this opportunity.

I went to the woman sitting behind the front desk and said,as well as I could,"Nicole Jenkins to see Mr. Robertson."

She stared at my face."He's expecting you.Go right in."

I entered the room to her right and saw a gray-haired man sitting behind the large desk reading a file.

Suddenly my nerves got the best of me,and I had to sit.I took the chair in front of him.

"Hello,"he said."Miss Jenkins?"

"Yes.Please excuse me.I'm having a Bell's palsy attack.My doctor explained to me that it would last a few days.I came right from the hospital."

"You're very dedicated to come when you're not feeling up to speed,"he responded,after a pause.

"Yes,sir."

He spent a few minutes looking over my application."Is everything on here correct?"He held it out to me.

I glanced over the paper,"Yes,but I failed to mention I type seventy-five words per minute."

"Wonderful,"he smiled. "Out of one hundred points,you had our highest score on the application test.You scored well above average on grammar and computer programs."

貌而不是我的经历和才能给我下个结论。我也许不该去。但是如果不去的话，我将永远幻想能否得到我梦寐以求的工作。

"不，妈，把我送到那里去。"

母亲极不情愿地把我带到了我想来的地方。我径直走进那间令人生畏、有红木家具和白色大理石台柱的办公室，没有让自我暗示或任何病痛妨碍我。它们现在不能，决不能在我努力工作了这么久就要得到这份工作的时候妨碍我。

我走到坐在前面桌子后头的女人那里尽可能清晰地说道，"妮克乐·简金斯拜见罗伯逊先生。"

她盯着我的脸，"他在等你。进去吧。"

我进了紧靠她右边的房间，看到一个灰头发的男人正坐在一张巨大的桌子旁边读一份文件。

我突然一下子自信地鼓起勇气，我要坐下去。我坐在了他面前的椅子上。

"你好，"他说，"是简金斯小姐吗？"

"是的，请原谅。我意外地得了贝尔氏麻痹。医生说这病会持续几天。我是从医院赶来的。"

他迟疑了一下，很快说道，"你在感觉不宜参加面试的时候还能前来真是有毅力。"

"是的，先生。"

他把我的申请表翻着看了好几分钟，"这上面说的都没错吗？"他把申请表递给我。

我扫了一眼说，"没错，但是我没提我一分钟能打75个字。"

"那太棒了，"他微笑着说，"在这次100分的申请人考试里，你得了最高分。你在语法和计算机程序上的得分也超过了平均分。"

"It comes easily for me,"I honestly replied.

"Well,you are certainly qualified.You have an impressive background with related experience.I see here you worked for the navy."

"Directly with legal affairs,"I reiterated.

"When are you available?"

"Two weeks."

He gazed down at his desk calendar."The 27th then,be here at 9:00 A.M.."

I gasped."You're hiring me! "

"Yes,you're perfect for the position."

I stood."Thank you for believing in me.I won't let you down."

"I know,"he smiled,rising from his desk to shake my hand. "Not only have you got the skills I'm looking for,you also have the character."

Nicole Jenkins

as told to Michele

"Screech" Campanelli

"那对我都很容易，"我老老实实地回答。

"那么，你肯定是合格的。你的相关经历背景给我们的印象很深刻。我看到这里有你过去给海军工作的介绍。"

"那是与法律事务直接相关的，"我重申道。

"你什么时候可以上班呢？"

"两周后。"

他朝桌上的台历看了一眼。"那么27号吧，上午9点到这里来。"

我呼吸困难了。"您雇佣我了！"

"是的，你是这个位置的最佳人选。"

我站了起来。"感谢您信任我，我不会让您失望的。"

"我知道，"他微笑着站起来与我握手，"不仅是因为你有我所要的各项技能，还因为你的性格。"

尼科勒·詹金斯
米歇尔·坎普奈利整理

Love and War

People always want to know who won.

When I tell them my husband and I met when we were opposing attorneys on a case,that's always their first question.

"Who won?"

"You decide,"I say.Then I tell them the rest.

I was an aggressive young associate,newly hired by my law firm and anxious to prove myself.John was a seasoned pro who worked for another law firm in the same building.When I found out he was opposing counsel,I was nervous.I'd seen his name on countless appellate decisions and knew he was far more adept at this type of case than I was.I decided that what I lacked in skill and experience,I would make up for with hard work and bravado.

I devised a campaign of daily badgering:discovery requests,legal motions,correspondence,phone calls.If I wasn't satisfied with how quickly he responded,I walked down the hall and pestered him in person.I was relentless—a terrier yipping at his heels.My client and my boss loved it.

But somewhere along the way I started to like him.Maybe it was the way he overlooked my obvious lack of sophistication and treated me like a serious adversary.Maybe it was our verbal sparring that often left me walking away with a stupid grin,as though we'd been flirting instead of arguing.Whatever the reason,after a few months on the case,I decided my adversary was a decent guy.If we'd met under difference circumstances,I might want to see where the flirting could go.But since we were opposing counsel,ethics prevented us from becoming personally

爱情与战争

人们总是想知道谁是赢家。

当我告诉他们我和我丈夫是在担任一个案件的双方代理律师时相识的时候，这总是他们要问的第一个问题。

"谁赢了？"

"你们到最后定吧，"我说，然后我就告诉他们剩下的故事。

我那时是个很年轻很有进取心的陪审员，刚刚被一家法律事务所聘用，正亟待在那里证实自己的才能。约翰是个很温和的律师，在同一座楼里为另一家法律事务所工作。当我得知他正提出与我相反的主张时，我紧张起来。我在数不清的上诉决议上看到过他的名字，知道他远远比我更擅长办眼前这个案子。我决心用努力工作和虚张声势来弥补我在技术和经验上的欠缺。

我想出每天纠缠他的一整套策略：请他告诉新发现、诉讼动态、来往函件、电话等。如果我对他的快速反应仍不满意，我就径直走过大厅，亲自登门去烦他。我毫无顾忌，成了一个不住地给他找麻烦的人。我的当事人和老板都很喜欢我这样。

但是不知道为什么我开始喜欢他了。也许是因为他忽略了我明显不够老练世故的表现，却把我当做一个很认真的对手来看待的态度。也许是因为我们双方争论时所说的话，这些话常常让我从他身边走开时还带着憨笑，仿佛我们是在调情而不是争论。不管什么原因，在这桩案子进行了几个月以后，我认定对手是个不错的家伙。如果我们能在其他场合碰上，我倒真想看看这种调情能带来什么结果。只是因为我们双方意见太悬殊，道德的力量阻止我们个人情感

involved.Romance was out of the question.

One Friday afternoon John left his office without giving me a set of documents I needed to review over the weekend.I tracked him down at home and demanded he turn over the materials to me that day.

"All right,"he said,"I'll have them at my house tonight."

Skeptical,but not wanting to back down,I said,"Fine,I'll be there at 7:00."

That night changed everything.

Some people claim an instant familiarity with a place or a stranger, convinced they must have been there or known each other before.Walking into John's house,what I felt was not déja vu,but more a sense of how things could be.I felt instantly at home,as I never have any place before or since.

The house was small,with wood floors and walls decorated with a strange combination of quilts and antlers.The furniture looked lived-in without being shabby.The place was modest,warm and comfortable—not at all like some of the palatial showcases I'd seen other lawyers strut through.

Seeing him in that environment,I felt more comfortable around John,too.Even though it was his house,it felt like neutral ground.I didn't have to act so tough anymore.I sank onto his couch and felt myself relax.

"So what's your story?"I asked,and he gave me a brief sketch of his life.

My answer to the same question was much briefer:"Work. That's all I do."

"I used to be like you,"John said. "Trust me—it can't last. You need other things."He told me he was happiest when he was backpacking or sailing,running the power tools in his workshop,or simply puttering in his vegetable garden on the weekends.What a curious idea.I had always thought weekends were for more work.

的卷入。所以浪漫是不可能的。

一个星期五的下午，约翰离开办公室时没有把一些文件交给我，而我那个周末正需要查阅这些文件。于是他回家时我一路跟踪，并要求他那天将材料交付于我。

"好吧，"他说道，"今晚在我家里会有。"

我很怀疑，但又不想放弃，于是说，"好吧，我7点钟去。"

那个夜晚改变了一切。

有些人声言对某一个地方或某一个人一刹那间就熟悉起来，坚信他们一定是在这之前就到过那里或者熟知彼此。走进约翰的房子，我没有感到记忆错位，而更多的是感到事情原来可以这样美好。我立刻感到如同在自己家里一样，就像我以前或者有史以来从没有去过别的地方。

房子很小，木质的地板，墙上用棉被和鹿角装饰成一幅奇特的组合画。家具看着像用了很久但并没有用旧。这个地方简朴，温暖而舒适，一点也不像我看到的其他律师所炫耀的那些像陈列橱窗似的富丽堂皇。

看到他身处那样的环境，我感到在约翰身旁也很自在。尽管这里是他的房子，但我的感觉这里是一个中立场所，我在这里不用再惹是生非了。我坐在他的长沙发上，感到非常放松。

"讲讲你的经历吧？"我问他。于是他简单地概述了他的人生。

对他提出的同样问题，我回答得更加简洁："我所做的全部就是工作。"

"我过去也像你一样，"约翰说。"相信我，这样坚持不了多长时间。你还有别的需要。"他告诉我当他背上背包旅行或者去航海，摆弄他车间里的电动工具，哪怕是周末在他的蔬菜园里做些琐碎的工作他都很快乐。多让人好奇的想法。我过去总是以为周末就是要做更多的工作。

I wished I were there under other circumstances.I wanted to talk longer.I wanted to know him better.But eventually duty called.I stood and held out my hand for the papers.

"I don't have them yet.Let's take a ride."

He drove me in his nine-year-old Honda station wagon(more bonus points—a modest car)to a house a few miles away.

"Come on,"John coaxed.I followed him to the door.

John's client answered.It's hard to say who was more shocked,the client or me.

"You know Elizabeth,"John said.His client raised an eyebrow,but politely shook my hand.Then he handed John the papers I'd wanted.John handed them to me.

Years later John confessed that what he'd really wanted to say when his client opened the door was, "Look! I have captured their queen! "

And it was true,he had.

My way had always been to rush into a relationship then see it flame out a month or so later.That couldn't happen this time. Being on opposite sides of a case forced me to get to know him slowly.I had the chance to see his character in action—his integrity,loyalty,honesty.By the time our romance began,I was already sold.

We had two choices:Wait until the case was over to pursue a relationship,or plunge ahead.If we weren't going to wait,one of us would have to withdraw from the case.

The next day I told my boss.He promptly fired me.

John's client still swears he paid John to date me,just to get me off the case.He says they both knew I was trouble.

Another lawyer took over for me and eventually the case settled.By then John and I had already been married three years. Good thing we didn't wait.

我真希望我还能在其他时间待在那里。我想跟他交谈得更久。我想了解他更多。但是最后使命召唤我。我站起来伸手要文件。

"我还没有拿到。我们一起开车去拿。"

他用他那部开了9年的本田客货两用轿车（一种小型轿车——可以赢得额外加分）带着我来到了几英里外的一家住屋前。

"来吧！"约翰哄着我。我跟着他来到了住家门口。

约翰的当事人开了门。很难说当时我和他谁更吃惊。

"你认识一下伊丽莎白，"约翰说。他的当事人扬起眉毛，但最后还是彬彬有礼地握了握我的手。然后他递给约翰我要的文件，约翰又转交给我。

几年后约翰承认，他的当事人开门时他真正想说的是："瞧！我俘虏了他们的女王！"

是的，他确实做到了。

我做事的方式一贯是一下子闯入一种关系网，一个月或者稍后再看看它是否会突然冒出火焰。但这次不行。我们处于同一桩案子对立方的事实迫使我缓慢地对他进行全面了解。我有了解他做事性格的机会——他正直、忠诚而可靠。等我们的罗曼史开始时，我已经不能忠实于我的当事人和老板了。

我们只有两种选择：等这场官司终了再发展关系，或者继续发展。而如果我们不等的话，我们两人中有一人必须要退出这个案子。

第二天我告诉了老板，他迅速地解雇了我。

约翰的当事人后来发誓说他花钱让约翰同我约会，目的是为了让我脱离这桩案子。他说他们两个都知道我是个麻烦。

另一个律师接替了我，最终那案子了结了。那时约翰和我都已经结婚3年了。我们没有等真是明智。

John and I have been married ten years now.We still live in the house where I felt so at home that night.There are still quilts and antlers on the wall,and we've only just now replaced the couch where I sat one Friday evening and wished I could know this man better.I still badger my husband at times,and he digs in his heels when I'm wrong.Ours is a marriage of negotiations and compromise,of flirting when we seem to be arguing.A worthy opponent,it turns out,makes a wonderful spouse.

So who won?

No doubt about it:I did.

Elizabeth Rand

约翰和我现在结婚10年了。我们依然住在那个夜晚让我感觉如此自在的房子里。墙面上依然有被子和鹿角,我们现在只换掉了那个星期五晚上我坐过的长沙发,并且当时还希望更好地了解这个男人。我仍然不时地来纠缠我的丈夫,我不对的时候他依然决不妥协。我们的婚姻充满谈判与妥协和解,我们两人似乎总在争论中调情。看来,可敬的对手才能成为最佳的人生配偶。

那谁是赢家呢?

毫无疑问:是我。

伊丽莎白·兰德

"It was a purely professional decision, Harris. I hope
my firing you won't affect our marriage in any way."

女性系列／聆听花开的声音

Getting Away

I don't get out much.Like most moms,I'm too busy doing mom stuff to take time for myself.

It wasn't always like this.Before I had kids,I had a career. Though I spent more hours nurturing my professional image in those days,it still seemed there was time left over for me.I'd make time to rejuvenate at a spa or unwind on a daylong shopping spree. Relaxing was a crucial component to the corporate image I was polishing.

Now,the only thing I polish is the furniture.

Having swapped the corner office at work in order to write from the corner bedroom at home,I now consider a trip to the grocery store without the kids to be a getaway.The business lunches I enjoyed at fancy restaurants were so long ago that the navy blue business suit I'd worn to them has gone out of style.I've cashed in the career and all the perks that come with it.

Oh,I'm not complaining.This is exactly where I want to be. So you can imagine the emotional tug-of-war I felt when my literary agent phoned to say that the publisher of my first book was sending me on an all-expense paid publicity tour from coast to coast!

At first the whole idea of a business trip seemed almost scary to me.The last time I was away from home all night I was giving birth.It's been a decade since I've gone anywhere without stuffing Goldfish crackers and an Etch-A-Sketch into my bag for the ride. I'd have to step out of my comfortable role as mother and step into the role of—what?—businessperson?Out of my Reeboks and into heels?Out of the laundry room and into television studios?Can I pull that off? I wondered.Won't

出逃

我不常出门。就像大多数母亲一样,我有太多母亲的活要忙,没有时间留给自己。

过去可不总是这样。在我有孩子以前,我有自己的事业。那时尽管我花很多时间树立自己的职业形象,好像时间总能过剩。我会找机会去游览胜地恢复体力,或者放松一天去购物享乐。轻松自如是我那时打造个人公共形象的重要组成部分。

而现在,我唯一要擦拭打造的是家里的各式家具。

为了能在家中卧室的角落从事写作,我已经将位于办公室拐角处的位置与别人交换。现在我正在思考不带孩子们去杂货店是否是一种逃避。我已经很久没有在装潢精美的那些饭店享用工作餐了,我过去到饭店吃饭时常穿的那套海军蓝制服也落伍了。我已经与我的工作和它所带来的实惠快乐彻底脱离。

哦,我不是在抱怨。这里真的是我想待的地方。当我的著作代理人打来电话,告诉我第一部书的出版商给我提供了由他付费进行全国范围内的宣传旅游时,你可以想象我经历的情感拔河赛。

最初,似乎一想到出公差我就很胆怯。我最后一次整夜离家不归是因为生孩子。我已经有10年光景外出时不在包里塞满各种各样的金鱼牌小饼干和神奇画板游戏机了。我必须要跨出舒舒服服做妈妈的行列,去扮演一个——怎么说呢——一个实业家的角色吗? 从南非短角羚的世界进入受人支配的现实? 从洗衣间进入电视演播室? 我会成功吗? 我不知道。他们不会对我纠缠不放,意识不到我只

they catch on and realize I'm just a mom?

But then I pondered the benefits of the trip.I'd be flying alone,dining alone and sleeping in luxury hotels alone.For an entire week,it would be just me.No school lunches to pack.No baseball practice.No four o'clock panic over what to make for dinner.I started to plan all the adult things I'd be able to do.I could visit each city's famous museums and stare as long as I wanted at each masterpiece without having to divert my eyes to keep tabs on my boys.I would browse through shops instead of racing through them,shouting,"Don't touch! "to my guys.And I would "dine" instead of "eat". It was beginning to sound better and better.

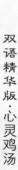

Finally,after making sure the refrigerator was full and the hamper was empty,I was on my way.As the plane took off,it also took my breath away.I was,for the first time in thirteen years,on my own—if only for a week.The curious thing about the trip was this:Instead of feeling like an adult,I actually felt more like a child! I could stare out the window of the plane in awe of the billowy clouds without having to tend to someone else.I could think uninterrupted thoughts.I didn't have to make my bed.I could drop my towel on the floor in the hotel bath and someone else would pick it up.I could order anything I wanted off the menu and not worry if I had enough money to pay the tab.

Even dessert.Twice if I wanted to.

Instead of driving my kids to school and practice and trying to stay on schedule,I had personal author escorts in every city who chauffeured me around.They were being paid to keep me on schedule.While they concentrated on the road I could take in the scenery,the flowers and the people—all things you miss when you're the pilot instead of the passenger.

But San Francisco's cable cars and Seattle's Space Needle left me missing my family.Flying over Mount St.Helen's and seeing New York's skyline on approach to JFK are sights that should be shared.The

是个母亲吧？

　　但是随后我又细细思量这次旅行的收益。我可以一个人乘坐飞机，独自用餐，并且在豪华宾馆里入睡。整整一周，我又可以成为自我。不用给孩子准备学校午餐。不用练习棒球，没有做晚餐的4点钟恐慌。我开始尽可能地计划所有成年人的事情。我可以参观每一座城市著名的博物馆，盯着每一件佳作想看多久就看多久，不用分心去监视我的儿子们。我可以在商店里尽情地浏览，而不是疾速一穿而过，同时还要不停地对着几个儿子大喊，"别动！"。我会好好"用餐"而不是"吃饭"。这件事听起来开始越来越美了。

　　最后，确信冰箱装满了，整理箱腾空了，我出发上路了。在飞机起飞的一刹那我大吃一惊。这是13年来，我第一次独处——尽管将只有一周。这次旅行让我感觉有意思的是：我没有感到自己是个成年人，相反我感到自己其实像个孩子！我可以有些畏惧地盯着飞机窗外如巨浪般翻卷的云层而不必照看什么了。我可以独自思考而没有人来打搅了。我不必整理床铺了。我可以把毛巾掉在宾馆浴室的地板上任由什么人把它捡起来。我可以点菜单上的任何食物而不用操心是否有钱付账。

　　甚至于甜点，如果想要我可以来两份。

　　这回不用开车将孩子们送往学校或者去训练，同时还得尽量卡着钟点。我在每座城市都有私人作家陪同，他们开车送我去各处。他们受人雇佣保证我准点到场。他们聚精会神地赶路时我则能欣赏四周美景、鲜花和人群——这些是你做舵手而不是乘客时缺失的。

　　但是旧金山的缆车和西雅图的太空针塔让我想家了。飞越圣海伦山上空，在慢慢接近肯尼迪国际机场时看到的纽约轮廓真应该是

guy in the seat next to me was snoring.

During a layover in Denver,I watched an exhausted mother chase her toddlers through the terminal.She apologized as they knocked my luggage over."It's okay,"I smiled."I'm a mom,too."

But after days without doing any mom stuff I didn't feel like one.I had morphed into this other person,but the spell was starting to wear off. I knew I'd be turning back soon,and the weird thing was,I was looking forward to it.

It became clear to me that for moms,coming home is what getting away is all about.Whether it's cruising the Caribbean or cruising the aisles of the grocery store alone,I know now how important it is to get away.

When I returned home my children looked angelic.The exploding hamper was a challenge,not a chore.I looked forward to filling up the empty refrigerator.I was refreshed.I was home.

A week later,up to my ears in mom stuff,I decided to write another book.

Kimberly A. Porrazzo

与人共享的美景。但坐在我旁边的一个人却在打鼾。

在丹佛做短暂的中转停留时,我曾看到一个筋疲力尽的母亲紧跟着她的几个年幼的孩子走过终点。孩子们撞翻了我的行李时她向我道歉。"没关系,"我笑着说。"我也是个妈妈。"

但是几天来不做母亲的家务活我倒感觉不自在了。我似乎一下子变形成了另一副模样,而这模样对我的魅力开始消失。我知道我想快快地回去,真是很怪异,我竟然还迫不及待地要变回去。

我这下明白了,对于做母亲的人来说,回家就是逃跑的全部意义。不管是在加勒比海岸还是在杂货店的通道上独自漫游,我现在知道从家里短期逃跑一下有多么重要。

我回家时孩子们像天使一般可爱。满得要爆出来的整理箱成了一个挑战,而不是让我不愉快的杂活。我想赶快把空荡荡的冰箱填满。我恢复了活力,我到家了。

一周后,在耳朵里又灌满了母亲的家务事时,我决心开始写另一本书。

基伯利·A.波拉若

Career Day

It was only 7:45 A.M.,but already I was multitasking.I stood at the kitchen sink,simultaneously slapping together cheese and mustard sandwiches for Max's lunch,while frantically brainstorming ways to put an exciting new spin on the twelve-hundred-word article due later that day. "We'd really like something compelling,"my editor had said.The topic was thrush.Who said my work wasn't challenging?

Then the cry came out. "Mom,I need you! "Max called from his seat in front of the computer."It's a 'mergency! "

Okay,so I know that moms are supposed to be ultraresponsive to their kids' every need,but this was the fourth "emergency"this morning.

"There's a problem with Stuart-Little-dot-com,"he told me. "The Snowball coloring book isn't loading."

"It'll have to wait,Max,"I told him."We have to get going.I have to get to work."

Then I added the kicker."My work is more important than Stuart-Little-dot-com."

Max looked extremely skeptical.He stared at me in silence,but "That's what you think,Mom"flickered in his wide blue eyes.

Still,despite what my son may think,my work is important. Validation of that fact came the very same night,in the form of a phone call from a total stranger.

"Mary Dixon Lebeau?"the voice asked,stumbling over my last name."Hi.This is Linda Goodparent from the Cross County Elementary School.I'm on the Careers Day committee,and some of the committee members said you'd be a good choice to represent the newspaper on

职业介绍日

才刚刚早上7点45分,我就已经忙得不可开交。我站在厨房的洗涤池前,一边快速地给迈克斯的午餐三明治上涂抹奶酪和芥子酱,一边在脑海乱糟糟地构思如何以一个令人振奋的新方式撰写那天要交稿的1200字文章。"我们喜欢能真正引起人们强烈兴趣的东西,"编辑曾经这么说过。这次要写的话题太蹩脚了。谁说我的工作不是充满了挑战性呢?

一声喊叫传出来。"妈,来一下!"迈克斯从电脑前的座位上喊我。"是个突发事件!"

唉,这下我可算是知道了母亲对孩子的每一种需要都得负极端责任,可是这已经是今天早上的第4个突发事件了。

"斯图亚特网站出问题了,那个雪球涂色盒不负载了。"

"那要等一等,迈克斯,"我告诉他。"我们得走了,我得去工作。"

然后我加上了令孩子感到意外的话。"我的工作可比斯图亚特网站重要得多。"

迈克斯看上去非常怀疑我说的话。他不作声地盯着我,但是他大大的蓝眼睛里闪烁的是,"那是你这样想,妈。"

不管我儿子怎么想,我的工作是很重要的。那天晚上,一个陌生人的电话使这个事实得以证明。

"请问是玛丽·迪克森·丽比尤吗?"这个声音结结巴巴地念着我的最后一个名字问着。"你好,我是县小学的琳达·古德帕瑞特。我在职业介绍委员会工作,有些会员说在职业介绍日选你做报人的代表

Career Day."

That was more like it.Here were my people—people who have read and chuckled over my column and wanted me to share the wonder of writing with their children.

Perhaps they knew me from my feature writer days,when I tracked down the best of the "feel good" stories and brought Pee Wee hockey teams,foreign exchange students and anti-drug campaigns into their homes on a weekly basis.

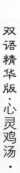

Maybe they had followed me since the beginning of my work at the paper.Maybe they recognized me as a talented reporter,one whose eagle eye and precise writing skills held corruption in our schools and on our planning boards at bay,keeping our county safe for all of its citizentry.

Or maybe Dave Barry was busy.

"Sure,I'd love to.Just send me all the details."

"Great! "Ms.Goodparent sounded really enthusiastic.Then she paused."Now,what is it you do at the newspaper,exactly?"

Hmm,I had a feeling I wasn't dealing with a fan.

So that's how I found myself at this particular Career Day,explaining beats and deadlines and inverted pyramids to the ten-and-under set. The agenda was simple—each of the guests would give a brief,under-five-minute explanation of their work,then answer questions from the crowd.Later,we would take our places at booths in the cafeteria,and the kids could wander around and learn more about the jobs that most interested them.

The line-up that day included a legal secretary,a truck driver,a dentist,a minor-league hockey player,a policeman and me."You'll be speaking last,"the teacher informed me.I thought this was an honor—like the rest of the speakers were the "warm-up acts" and I was the main attraction.

比较合适。"

这还差不多。这里全是我的人——他们读过我的作品,对着我的专栏咯咯直笑,想让我与他们的孩子一起分享写作的乐趣。

也许他们是从对我写作生涯的专题报道中了解我的,那时我极力捕捉那些"感觉尚好"的故事中的佳作,比如,每周给曲棍球队带来理查德·科克兰德,给他们的家庭带来外国交换学生和反毒品运动的报道等。

也许他们是在我刚开始报人的这份工作时就关注我了,也许他们意识到我是个天才的记者,我雄鹰般雪亮锐利的眼睛和措辞准确的写作技巧能阻止我们学校和海湾计划委员会的腐败,保证我们县所有公民的安全。

亦或是大人物戴夫·巴瑞太忙,所以他们来找我。

"当然,我很高兴。把详细的材料送给我好了。"

"太好了!"古德帕瑞特夫人的声音听起来非常热情。然后她停顿了一下问道,"那么你在报纸上究竟做什么工作呢?"

哦,这下我感到我不是在与我的粉丝打交道了。

这就是我为什么发现自己居然在这个特别的职业介绍会上给10岁以下的学生解释新闻题材、截稿日期和"倒金字塔"结构的原因了。日程安排很简单——每位客人都要对个人的工作做一个不超过5分钟的简单介绍,然后回答观众提问。最后我们将轮流去自助餐馆的小隔间,孩子们可以前来对那些更令他们感兴趣的工作做更多的了解。

那天我们这组人里有法律秘书、卡车司机、牙医、一个小冰球队队员、一个警察和我。"你最后一个发言,"这位教师通知我。我想这对我是个荣誉——就像其他人的发言只是"热身表演"一样,而我才是真正的焦点。

Later, however, I learned I was last because the attention span of an average third-grader is approximately twenty minutes. "We want to make sure they're fully awake when the policeman talks," the teacher said.

We each gave our mini-explanation. One by one, the volunteers talked about the importance of their jobs. They did a great job, too. In fact, the minor-league hockey player even had me convinced that skating across fake ice in pursuit of a puck is essential to the American way of life.

Finally, it was my turn. I tried to explain how reporters are the eyes of the people at every meeting, every event and every crime scene. "If you know what's going on, down the street or across the country, it's because a reporter was there," I finished.   Thirty-seven little faces stared back at me as their teacher applauded. (Sure, the policeman had a more enthusiastic response, but he demonstrated the use of handcuffs. No one told me we were allowed to bring visual aids!)

Then it was the question-and-answer time. A little blonde asked the legal secretary how fast she types. A skinny kid with a runny nose inquired about goalie pads. "Did you ever meet O.J.?" An inquisitive tot asked the policeman.

No one asked me anything. I attributed that to the outstanding job I did in the initial presentation. After all, if they already know everything, who needs questions?

"Does anyone have a question for Ms. Lebeau?" the teacher prodded.

"I thought all reporters were superheroes, like Clark Kent," one tike commented. I shook my head. "They should've had a pirate here. Or a cowboy," he said. I could see his point.

Things weren't much better on the homefront. My sons have their future ambitions picked out already—one wants to be a veterinarian, because of his passion for reptiles and rodents. One wants to go to law school after a career with the WWF.

然而,后来我才知道我被安排在最后是因为三年级孩子的注意力一般只有20分钟。这位老师说,"我们想在警察发言的时候,让他们保持完全清醒。"

我们每个人都做了简短发言。一个接着一个,志愿者们谈论着自己工作的重要性,他们也都在从事伟大的工作。事实上,冰球队队员甚至让我相信在人造冰上滑翔、追逐冰球是美国人生活方式的重要组成部分。

终于轮到我了。我想解释说明的是记者如何成为人们在每场会议、每个事件和每次犯罪现场的眼睛。"如果我们知道街上或者全国都在发生什么事,这都是因为有记者在场。"我以此结束了发言。老师鼓掌的时候,37张小脸都在盯着我看。(确实,警察的发言反响热烈,但他是演示了如何使用手铐,没有人和我讲过我们可以带直观教具)。

接下来到了回答提问的时间。一个长着金黄色头发的小孩问法律秘书他打字有多快。一个拖着鼻涕骨瘦如柴的孩子要守门员护垫。"你见没见过影星O.J.呀?"一个好奇的孩子问警察。

没有人向我提问。我把这归结为我在一开始的表演中表现出色。毕竟,如果他们什么都明白,那谁还需要提问呢?

"有谁有问题要问丽比尤夫人的吗?"教师督促道。

"我认为,所有的记者都向克拉克·肯特一样是超级英雄,"一个小淘气这么评论,我摇了摇头。"他们应该找个海盗或牛仔到这里来,"他说。我明白他的意思。

家里小天地的情况也没有好多少。我的儿子们已经选择了自己未来的远大抱负———一个儿子想当兽医,因为他钟情于爬行动物和啮齿目动物。另一个儿子想上法律院校,追寻在世界野生动物基金会里的某个职业。

And Max wanted to be an artist—or at least I thought.(He's already practicing the "starving" part by refusing to eat any meal that doesn't come with a prize in the box.)

But then my youngest son surprised me. "Mom,I think I want to be a writer,just like you,"he told me the other night.I smiled.

And I kept smiling,even as I scrubbed his latest best-seller off the bedroom wall.

I'm sure Dave Barry started the very same way.

Mary Dixon Lebeau

迈克斯想当艺术家——或者至少我这么认为。(他还在练习"饥饿疗法",拒绝吃任何在外包装上没有获奖的食品)。

后来我的小儿子让我大吃一惊。"妈,我想像你一样当作家,"他有一天晚上告诉我。我对他笑一笑。

甚至在用力擦洗他卧室墙上的最新畅销书时,我也在笑。

我坚信戴夫·巴瑞也是这样开始他的职业生涯的。

玛利·狄克逊·利伯

"It says on your résumé that you can type
260 words per minute. No offense,
Mrs. Ballas, but I find that pretty hard to believe."

女性系列／聆听花开的声音

Not Just Another Rat

Our character is what we do when we think no one is looking.

It was still dark outside,and my breath floated like a frosty cloud in the cold air.I was feeling sorry for myself again.There was a reason they called it a rat race.

Day in and day out,the same old thing.Up and out of the house before daylight.An hour and a half commute to the office.Eight to nine hours at work,and then the same commute home,still dark outside.The short winter days made me wonder:Did the sun ever come out during the day?I wasn't sure anymore—if it did,I certainly missed it.

I made my way to the train station on that bleak Monday morning. My week stretched out before me like a deep black hole.The week might be new,but I was feeling old and worn-out. The brief weekend respite hadn't provided much relief,what with the laundry that had piled up,not to mention the supermarket and the dry cleaners and the myriad other errands that ate into what was supposed to be our family time together.We barely had a chance to play a quick game of Scrabble before it was time to set the alarm clock and start the week once more.

The train was late again.Any attempt at relaxing thoughts was quickly replaced by memories of the piles of paper sitting on my desk. So much to do,and the days were never long enough.I tuned out the crowd around me and began to mentally sort through the priorities that would beckon as soon as I arrived at the office.E-mails and faxes,reports and meetings.The day would be full,more so because it was the beginning of the week.I cringed as I remembered how often I had put things

双
语
精
华
版
·
心
灵
鸡
汤

不只是另一个竞争对手

我们的性格就是没人在看时我们的所作所为。

外面仍然很黑，我的呼吸就像一片结了霜的云在寒冷的空中飘着。我又一次为自己难过。人们把它称作田鼠似的无休无止的奔忙是有道理的。

一天又一天，全是老一套。在黎明前起床走出家门，乘一个半小时的火车去办公室。工作八九个小时，然后以同样的路线回家时，外面仍旧阴沉昏暗。短暂的冬天白昼让我感到疑惑不解：太阳难道一整天都没有出来吗？我不再确信——如果太阳出来了，那我肯定是错过了。

在那个阴冷的周一早晨，我走在去火车站的路上。这一周就像一个深深的黑洞在我面前伸展开来。这周也许会不一样，但是我感觉自己在衰老，疲惫不堪。有了堆积成一大堆的衣物要清洗熨烫，短暂的周末休息简直不能给人多少调剂，更别提消耗了我们家庭聚会时间的超市采购，去干洗店和忙活其他数不清的差使。我们几乎还没有机会快快地玩一把拼字游戏，就到了定闹钟又开始下一周的时间。

火车又晚点了。任何要放松一下的念头就都飞快地复位。这么多的事情要做，白天从来时间不够。我根本不在意周围的人群，继而开始在脑海里梳理一到办公室就得优先办理的事情。电子邮件和传真，报告以及会议。这个白天安排得太满了，因为它是这一周的开始。一想起我如何经常把要做的事情推到"下一周"，我就深感惭愧。

off "until next week". Well,"next week"was here.Note to self:thinking about things"tomorrow"may have worked for Scarlett O'Hara,but it only created grief for me.

The shifting crowd brought me back to the moment.The train was pulling in,and the army of commuters was of one mind:Grab an empty seat at any cost.Men and women were equal-opportunity pushers,propelling each other to the edge of the platform.Even as I allowed myself to be swept along,I also resolved to seize the first available seat I could find.With a firm grip on my briefcase I pushed along with the best of them,and landed my prize.Sitting would allow me to get a jump on some paperwork,perhaps a memo or two.Any head start would help.

CHICKEN SOUP

Was this what my life had deteriorated to? The highlight of my day was that I got a seat on the train? Surely my aims were loftier than that. We were working so hard,my husband and I.Our goal was to pay off the mortgage,and set aside savings to prepare for retirement.We were almost there.Just another year or two of my imitation of superwoman,and then I could relax.Just another year or two...

That's when I saw her.The young woman looked vaguely familiar. Had I seen her at the train station before,or did I simply recognize the look on her face? The look that reflected resignation at having missed out on a seat again.The look that said,ever so clearly,"I don't have the energy to do this anymore."I knew just how she felt,but I also knew that I had work to do.Memos to answer,reports to write.I had a seat,and she didn't.Nobody said life was going to be fair.

But there was more than just her face.Even under her bulky winter coat,I could see that she was expecting a baby.Her pregnancy was rather far along,and it was all that she could do to hold on to the metal bar as the train lurched into motion.I felt a pang of guilt,and then argued with myself.Surely there were enough men on the train who could see her condition.Chivalry wasn't dead yet,was it?But no one moved.It seemed

哦，"下一周"就在这儿，给自己留个便条：想想"明天"可能给思嘉莉·奥哈拉带来的后果。但这么做只让我又为自己感到悲哀。

攒动的人群将我带回此时此刻。火车正驶进站来，赶车的大军只有一个念头：不惜一切代价抢夺一个空座位。男人和女人机会均等，彼此推动着来到站台边。尽管也让自己随波逐流，我还是决心要抢到我能找到的第一个空座位。紧紧地提着自己的公文包，我跟着人群当中最棒的人一起朝前涌，于是拿到了自己的奖品。有了座位我就能开始看一些文字材料，比如一个或者两个便函。时间上的领先会对我有所帮助。

我的生活就退化成现在这样子了吗？我一天最重要的事难道就是在火车上抢到一个座位吗？我的目标肯定比那要高尚。我们，我丈夫和我，都工作得这么努力。我们的目标是还清抵押借款，节省一笔钱为退休做准备。我们几乎就要达到目标了。我只要再花一年或两年时间模仿超级女人，然后我就可以松弛下来。再有一年，两年……

这时我看到了她。一个看上去隐约有些面熟的年轻女性。是我以前在火车站见过她，还是我只认出了她脸上的表情？这是一种反映出没有抢到座位又一次认输的表情。这种表情如此清楚地道出了她的心语："我对这事再也无能为力。"我很了解她此刻的感受，可是我也明白我有工作必须完成。必须回复的便函，必须要写的报告。我有座位，她却没有。没人说生活要公平起来。

只是除了她的脸，她还有些别的地方吸引了我的目光。在她笨重的冬装下，我可以看出她怀孕了。她怀了很久了，火车颠簸着突然倾斜时，她所能做的就只有牢牢抓紧那根金属把杆。我内心迸发出一种负罪感，随后又与自己争辩。火车上肯定有男人也能看出她的境况。骑士精神还没有死绝，对吗？但是没有人动。似乎火车上的人

as if everyone on the train was studiously avoiding the view of this young woman as they buried their heads in their newspapers,or pretended to be deeply engrossed in their conversations.

I put the memos and the pad back in my briefcase,stood up,and motioned to get her attention.The work could wait.There certainly was enough of it,and one or two more memos wouldn't make much of a difference in my schedule.If I had any second thoughts,they were wiped away by the look on her face.A new look—one of relief and thanksgiving.Words didn't need to be exchanged,but as she said thank you I realized that this small act of kindness was as much for me as it was for her.A reminder that even though I was part of the rat race,I didn't have to become a rat.

It was still Monday morning,but the emerging sunrise told me it was going to be a beautiful day.

Ava Pennington

都专心埋头读报纸，或者假装对各自的谈话很投入，顾不上看一眼这位年轻女子。

我把便函和拍纸簿放回公文包，站起身来，招手以便引起她的注意。工作可以等等再做。时间肯定还来得及，多上一份两份便函在我的日程安排上不会有多大区别。假使我再一细想，那这些想法会被她脸上的表情一扫而光。我看到了一种新的表情———一种宽慰和感恩的表情。不需要语言交流，不过她说"谢谢你"时，我意识到这个小小的善行对我和她都意味着许多。它提醒我，尽管我是社会激烈竞争的一部分，但我可不一定要变得残酷无情。

依旧是个星期一的早晨，但是慢慢浮现的日出告诉我这将是美好的一天。

艾夫娃·彭妮格通

The Real Lesson

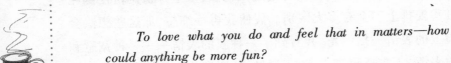

To love what you do and feel that in matters—how could anything be more fun?

Katharine Graham

As a speech-language pathologist,I spent many years teaching students in a classroom setting.These students had such significant speech and language impairments in their native language that they required a smaller class size and instruction in classroom curriculum to be taught by someone with a background in the development of language.

While rewarding,at times this job could be exhausting. Imagine working all day with people who have difficulty getting their point across and understanding your point.These students needed instruction in the language that was to be used in the lesson before the lesson could ever be taught.Many days I was filled with frustration for I never got to the "real"lesson.I never got to the subtraction lesson.I was too busy teaching what the words "more""less""take away"and"equal"meant to students that did not naturally have these words in their everyday vocabulary.The lessons in my lesson plan book,the "real"lessons for the day,never seemed to take form.

On the Wednesday before Thanksgiving break,I got a"real"lesson from one of my students.I was busy trying to teach the"real"meaning behind the holiday of Thanksgiving.This is a holiday about feelings and emotions.Feeling and emotion words are difficult for language-impaired students.These words fall into a gray category.They are abstract.They are not simple to explain. Yet we never really think about having to teach a child what"happy""sad""exhausted"or"thankful"really means.

真正的一课

热爱你的职业,并且在琐事中感觉职业——还有比这更快乐的事吗?

凯瑟琳·格瑞汉姆

身为言语方面的病理学家,我花了多年时间在教室里教导学生。这些学生在母语表达上有一些语言方面的不完善,他们需要有语言发展背景的人在小一些的教室里给他们上一些指导性课程。

回想起来,这项工作有时真是令人疲惫不堪。你可以想象,整天跟一些不能流利表达自己的观点,而理解别人的观点又有困难的人待在一起是什么滋味。这些学生在课前就需要得到课内需使用语言的指导。我沮丧了很久,因为我从来没有接触到真正的教学单元。我从没有上过减法课。我一直忙于给学生们教授"更多""更少""减去"和"等于"这些词是什么意思,这些是他们日常的词汇里所没有的。我教学计划书里的那些教学单元,那些真正的教学单元似乎从来没有实施过。

在感恩节假期前的星期三,我从一个学生那里上到了"真正的"一课。我当时正忙着要教导学生感恩节背后的真正含义。因为这是一个有关感情和情感的节日。而这两个方面的词汇对于有语言损伤的学生来说是很难的。这些词是智慧类语言,很抽象,不能对之简单地加以解释。然而我们确实没有考虑过教孩子"幸福""伤心""筋疲力尽"或者"感激"意味着什么。

CHICKEN SOUP

On this particular day,I was experiencing all of these emotions: happy,that a four-day weekend was coming,sad that my "real"lesson about Thanksgiving was getting lost in a sea of unexplained words, exhausted from the cooking and preparing we had done all week for our big classroom Thanksgiving feast,and thankful it would all be over in thirty minutes when the 2:30 bell rang.

In an attempt to teach the real lesson of this holiday,I read books to the students about the first Thanksgiving.We had to have elaborate discussions at the end of every sentence,sometimes in the middle,to explain vocabulary words such as:cranberries,mashed potatoes,cornucopia,pheasant,and so on.Most confusing were some of the Indian names.How could a full sentence be someone's name?Boy Who Runs with Wolf;Little Laughing Coyote.In an attempt to explain this,I gave each student an Indian name that fit their likes and dislikes.First this required a lesson on the words "like"and "dislike"and once again I was blown off course from the real lesson.I persevered,however,and each person got a name that fit his or her personality.

Now it was time to go to the long table we had set with our feast. With the announcement,"It's time for our Thanksgiving feast,"the students ran to the table.As if they were siblings fighting for parental attention,the seat at the head of the table became the most desired spot in the classroom.To end the arguing,I firmly announced,"My Indian name is 'She Who Sits at the Head of the Table'and I will be sitting at the head of the table."With this announcement,the students took their seats.

In an attempt to teach the real lessons of Thanksgiving,that we should be grateful for what we have for the people that love us and care for us,I called each person by his or her Indian name and asked each to tell what he or she was most thankful for on this Thanks-giving.A surge of emotions,sadness,disappointment,exhaustion,surfaced as the responses were all material items."Boy Who Runs Quickly"was most thankful for

在这个特别的日子，我正经历所有这些情感：幸福，是因为4天工作日的周末就要来到了；难过，是因为我真正的关于感恩节的这一课——正在迷失方向，掉进了一个有许许多多无法解释的词汇的海洋；精疲力竭，是因为烹饪和为我们这个大班的感恩节聚餐所做的各种准备；感激，是因为当2:30的钟声一敲响一切就会在30分钟内结束。

为了上好有关这个节日的真正一课，我给学生们读了有关第一个感恩节方面的书籍。我们在每一个句子结束的时候就要仔细讨论，有时在句子中间就要解释一些词汇，例如：越橘，捣碎的马铃薯，丰饶角，雄鸡等。最令学生困惑的还是印第安人的姓名。像"与狼赛跑的男孩""带笑的小人形精怪"这样一整个句子怎么能做人的名字呢？为了解释这一点，我按照学生们的喜好给他们每人起了个印第安名字。首先，这需要有一节课讲授"喜欢"与"不喜欢"这些词，所以我又一次偏离了真正的教学单元的航线。不过我锲而不舍，于是每人有了一个适合他（她）个性的名字。

现在是去我们摆好了节日盛宴的长桌前的时候了。随着那声宣布，"现在开始我们的感恩节盛宴。"学生们跑到了桌前，就像争夺父母注意力的同胞兄弟姐妹一样。桌子上座的座位成了教室里学生们相争的焦点。为了平息这场战争，我郑重地宣布，"我的印第安名字是'坐在桌子上座的她'，所以我要坐上座。"听了这番话，学生们都纷纷各就各位。

为了教授感恩节的真正教学内容，我们应该对我们拥有的一切充满感激，对爱护和关心我们的人表示感恩，我用印第安姓名称呼每一位同学，并请他们说一说在这个感恩节他们最感激的是什么。当他们的回答是各式各样的物质名称时，我百感交集——伤心、失望、筋疲力尽。"跑得快男孩"最感激的是他的家庭游戏机。"带着微

his Nintendo. "Girl with a Smile"was most thankful for her Barbie Dream House.Nobody got the real lesson.Had I even taught the real lesson or was all my instruction just a bunch of words with no meaning for these students?Had I wasted my time with hands-on activities to help these children know the emotional words associated with Thanksgiving： love,happiness,thankfulness?I knew the answer to this question as each Indian boy and girl said they were most thankful for a meaningless object.No one was thankful for their mother,father,sister,brother,friends,not even a family pet.These were good,sweet kids with no way of expressing emotions I knew they had experienced.I knew they loved their parents.They were thankful for their families,the roof over their heads and the food in their stomachs,but no one had the words or the ability to recall the words and present them in the correct sequence for others to understand how they felt.

My last student,my quietest student,my most language-impaired student, Christopher, responded in a quiet simple voice. He found the words.He put them in the correct order.He connected them to an emotion.He showed me I had taught the real lesson.This quiet Indian boy stated,"I am most thankful for 'She Who Sits at the Head of the Table'".

Ruth Reis Jarvis

笑的女孩"最感激的是她的芭比姐妹梦幻之屋。没有人学到了真正的一课。我教过这一课吗？或者我的教导对这些学生只是一堆毫无意义的词吗？用这些代代相传的活动帮助这些孩子了解与感恩节有关的情感词汇——爱、快乐、感激，难道是在浪费时间吗？在每一个印第安男孩和女孩说他们对没有意义的物体非常感激时，我知道了这个问题的答案。没有人感激母亲、父亲、姐妹、兄弟，或者哪怕是一只家庭宠物。这些非常善良甜蜜的孩子，我知道他们无法表达所经历的各种情感，我知道他们爱父母，他们感谢家庭，感谢头上的屋顶和肚子里的食物。但他们没有人知道这些词汇，或者没有人有回想起这些词汇的能力，并且能在正确的背景场合进行表达，让别人理解他们的感受。

我的最后一个学生，最安静的学生，语言损伤最严重的学生，克里斯托弗，用安静简洁的嗓音做了回答，他发现了这些词，并把它们排出了正确的顺序。他把它们连接成一种情感，他向我表明，我已经教过一个真正的教学单元。这个安静的印第安男孩说：我最感激的是"坐在讲桌旁边的她"。

露丝·里恩·杰威斯

Getting My Priorities Straight

*The great dividing line between success and failure can
be expressed in five words:"I did not have time."*

Robert J.Hastings

One of today's most precious commodities is time.No matter how many gadgets we buy,books we read or classes we take,there is no quick fix to busyness.

As a working mother,I constantly juggle the demands of work,personal interests,household errands and my children's school activities—games,practices,music lessons,rehearsals and performances.These activities are designed to enrich my children's lives and develop their skills, talents and values.

However,mothers can be so busy juggling that they lose sight of the true purposes for the child's participation in these activities.From infancy,children seek parental approval and attention.Parents heap tons of encouragement and praise as the baby learns to crawl,pull up,walk,speak, hit the ball—the list goes on and on.As the child grows older,simple learning tasks are replaced with other activities such as sports,cheerleading or music.Parents are always on the sidelines or in the audience cheering,cajoling,clapping and encouraging.

However,sooner or later,a working mother is faced with a major conflict between some personal or business commitment and her child's game,play,concert or other event.She can't be in two places at once.Her heart is ripped into pieces trying to decide what to do;what is best for her child;what would a good mother do;how to make a bad situation into a win-win for everyone.

I experienced one of those decisive situations when my daughter's

什么最重要

> 成功与失败最大的区别可以用5个字来表示，"我没有时间"。

罗伯特·J.黑斯廷斯

今天最宝贵的商品之一是时间。不管我们买了多少个精巧的小玩意，读了多少本书，上了多少节课，我们仍然不能快速地解决我们忙忙碌碌的问题。

身为职业母亲，我常常要在工作、个人爱好、家庭琐事以及孩子们的各种学校活动——游戏、实践、音乐课、练习和表演等方面维持平衡。这些活动都是为了丰富孩子们的生活，培养他们的技能、才华和价值观。

然而母亲们有可能太忙于维持这种平衡而忽略孩子们参与这些活动的真正目的。从童年时代起，孩子们就寻求父母的认可与关注。在婴儿学会爬行、提东西、走路、说话、击球等不断成长的过程中，父母亲给予孩子大量的鼓励与赞许。随着孩子长大，单纯的学习任务由其他的诸如运动，当拉拉队或者音乐等活动取代。父母总是在运动场的边线或者观众席上欢呼喝彩，哄孩子，为他们鼓掌并且激励他们。

但是有时，职业母亲要面对一些因个人或者公务需要与孩子的游戏、玩耍、音乐会或者其他事情之间产生很大矛盾冲突的情况。她无法有分身术。在决定该做什么的时候，她的心会被撕扯成碎片。她需要考虑什么对孩子最好；好母亲都做些什么；如何才能让困境变成父母与孩子的双赢。

当我女儿学校所在的地区要主办每年一度的"弦乐演奏会"时，

school district hosted its annual "String Fest",where five school orchestras are packed into a gymnasium along with a sea of family and friends.The participants were to arrive about forty-five minutes earlier than the event's start time so that the musicians could tune and warm up their instruments.As often happens,the event occurred during a crunch period for both my husband's and my jobs.We arranged for my teenage son to drop off his sister at the appointed time.

My daughter,who was very much aware of my time-management efforts,attempted to cut me some slack by saying,"Mom,you don't have to come tonight.Just be there on time to take me home."I couldn't have asked for a better solution.I wouldn't have to fight the rush-hour traffic for my thirty-two mile commute.I could work a couple more hours.By then the traffic would be light,and I could make it to the gymnasium in record time. Besides,how many concerts had I already attended?I could afford to miss this one,right?

After pondering my choices,I decided it was not okay with me if I was absent.Even though my daughter had given me her permission to miss the concert,it did not justify my absence.I felt guilty enough for my not taking her to the concert.I left work and arrived just before the concert began.I found a seat in the bleachers several rows directly across from my daughter's orchestra.I had her in my line of sight,but in the ocean of faces,she would never see me.

As I watched,the warm-up session ended and my daughter put her violin aside.I saw my daughter's eyes as they began to scan the audience row by row,looking for a familiar face.When her eyes found me,I was waving my arms in that embarrassing way mothers do,and we exchanged smiles.Her body language said it all.I had "made her night".No promotion,raise,bonus or anything could ever pay for that moment.It was an image that is forever etched in our hearts and memories and could never be recorded with a camera or camcorder.It was just two hearts exchanging love across the gymnasium.

Sybella V. Ferguson Patten

我经历了一次这样的关键时刻。来自5个学校的管弦乐队将聚集在一个体育馆里,那里面会成为家庭与亲友的海洋。参会者们要在比赛开始前45分钟到场,这样这些未来的音乐家们就能调试和温习各自的乐器。像往常一样,这次演奏会时我丈夫和我的工作都处在关键时刻。我们于是安排了十几岁的儿子让他妹妹在约定的时间下车。

我女儿非常清楚我这样安排时间的用意。她想为我减轻些负担,她对我说,"妈,今晚你不用去。只要按时来接我回家就行。"我真是喜出望外。不用在交通高峰时间乘坐长达32英里的公交车往返,我就可以多工作几个小时。那时交通就不拥挤了,我可以准时到达体育馆。而且我已经听了多少场音乐会呀?不听这一场也能承受,是吧?

对我们的抉择深思熟虑之后,我感觉如果这次缺席还是不合适。尽管女儿已经同意我不用来听这场演奏会,那也不能为我的缺席开脱。不送她去参加演奏会我就已经够内疚了。我抛开工作,几乎在演奏会开始前赶到。我在露天看台上找了个座位,距离我女儿的乐队只隔着几排。我一直把她放在我的视线范围之内,但在一片面孔众多的海洋里她永远看不到我。

在观望中,演奏前的准备结束了,我女儿将小提琴放到了一边。我看到女儿的眼睛在观众席上一排一排地扫过,想寻找一张熟悉的面孔。当她的双眼看到我时,我正以母亲特有的复杂方式向她挥动双臂,然后我们彼此笑笑。她的身体语言诉说了一切,我使她非常快乐地度过了一个夜晚。晋升、提拔、奖金或者任何事都换不来那个时刻。这是一个将永远铭记在我们两人心里和记忆里的一幅美景。照相机或者摄录机是无法记录的。这是两颗心通过体育馆交换的挚爱。

西比拉·V.弗格森帕藤

Just a Few More Minutes

The best thing to spend on your children is your time.

Louise Hart

"Just a few more minutes…please,Mommy! "

Although my own children were grown,I found myself turning instinctively in the direction of the little voice.He was trailing after his mother,looking reluctantly over his shoulder at a display of remote-control toys in the large department store.

He couldn't have been more than four years old.With chubby cheeks and wispy blond hair going in several directions,he trotted behind his mother down the main aisle of the department store.His boots caught my eyes.They were green.Really green.Bright,shiny,Kermit-the-Frog green.Obviously new and a little too big,the boots stopped just below his knees,leaving a hint of dimpled legs disappearing into rumpled shorts.Perfect boots for the rainy transition from summer to fall.

He stopped abruptly at a display of full-length mirrors,lifting one foot at a time,grinning and admiring his boots until his mother called for him to catch up to her.Dressed in a suit,heels clicking on the tile floor, she was tossing items into her cart as she and her son made their way to the checkout lanes at the front of the store.

I smiled at the picture he made clumping noisily behind his mother. I found myself wondering if she had just picked him up from daycare after a busy day in an office somewhere.I sighed as I selected an item and put it in my own cart.My days of trying to juggle a full-time job and two small children had been busy,sometimes even hectic,but I missed them.

再多几分钟

花在孩子身上最好的东西是时间。

路易斯·哈特

"就再多几分钟……求你,妈妈!"

虽然我自己的孩子现在都长大了,我发现自己仍然本能地转向有那细小声音的方向。他正跟在母亲身后,不情愿地回头看着巨大的百货大楼里展出的遥控玩具。

他最多不超过4岁。脸蛋胖乎乎的,几小撮金黄色的头发分不同方向翘着,他小跑着跟随母亲走下百货大楼的主通道。他的靴子让我眼睛一亮。它们是绿色的,纯绿色,鲜艳发亮,就和名为Kermit的那只绿青蛙一样的颜色。靴子很明显是新的,有点太大,一直到他的膝盖,隐约露出被皱巴巴的运动短裤盖着的长着肉窝的两条小腿。从夏季到秋季多雨的过渡季节,这双靴子可真是完美无瑕。

他敏捷地停在跟他身体差不多高的一排镜子前,一次抬起一只脚,咧着嘴欣赏他的靴子,直到他母亲喊他跟上。穿着套装,鞋跟咔嚓咔嚓地击打在瓷砖地板上,她和她儿子一边径直走向商场前面的收银台通道,一边正把一些商品甩进购物车。

看着他脚步沉重地在母亲身后发出很大的噪音,我笑了。我发现自己在猜想,她是否是经过某处办公室忙碌的一天之后,刚刚才把他从托儿所接出来。我过去一边上全职班,一边带着两个孩子也是很忙的。有时甚至是忙乱不堪,但是我想念这些日子。

Finishing my own shopping, I forgot about the little boy and his mother until I stepped outside the store. There's a panorama unfolded before me. The rain had slowed to a drizzle, perforating the numerous puddles in the parking lot. Several mothers with their small children were hurrying in and out of the department store. The children were, of course, making beelines to the puddles that dotted their way from the cars to the store's entrance. The mothers were right behind them, scolding.

"Get away from that puddle! "

"You'll ruin your shoes! "

"What's the matter with you? Are you deaf? I said, GET OUT OF THAT PUDDLE! "

And so it continued. The children were being pulled away from the puddles and hurried along. All except for one... the little green-booted boy.

He and his mother were not rushing anywhere. The boy was happily splashing away in the largest puddle in the parking lot, oblivious to the rain and to the people coming and going. His wispy hair was plastered to his head and a huge smile was plastered on his face. And his mother? She put up her umbrella, adjusted her packages and waited. Not scolding, not rushing. Just watching.

As she fished her car keys out of her purse, the boy, hearing the familiar jingling, paused in mid-splash and looked up.

"Just a few more minutes? Please, Mommy?" he begged.

She hesitated, and then she smiled at him.

"Okay! " She responded and adjusted her packages again.

By the time I got to my car, loaded my packages and was ready to ease out of my parking space, the green-booted boy and his mother were walking toward their car, smiling and talking.

How many times had my own children begged for "just a few more minutes"? Had I smiled and waited like the mother of the green-booted boy? Or had I scolded?

双语精华版·心灵鸡汤·

自己买完东西,我暂时忘记了小男孩和他母亲。直到我走出商场,我才发现在我面前展现了一幅怎样的全景图。中雨慢慢地下成了毛毛雨,在停车场上出现了许多的小水坑。有几个母亲匆匆忙忙地带着孩子进出商场。孩子们当然是径直奔向点缀在他们汽车和商场入口中间的水坑。母亲们则紧跟在他们身后,训斥着。

"不要去那个水坑!"

"你把鞋子要搞坏了!"

"你怎么回事?聋了吗?我刚说过了,不-要-去-那-个-水-坑!"

这一幕继续着。孩子们被从水坑边拉开并快快地走了。都走了,只剩下一个——那个穿着绿靴子的小男孩。

他和他母亲不急着赶往任何地方。孩子在停车场最大的水坑里快乐地打着水玩,全然忘却雨和周围来来往往的人们。他的几小撮翘头发贴在了脑门上,他快乐的大笑则贴在了脸上。他母亲呢?她撑着伞,不停地调整购物袋等候着。没有训斥,没有催促,就这么看着。

当她把车钥匙从钱包里摸出来时,正打水玩得起劲的那个孩子听到了熟悉的叮当声,他停下来抬起了头。

"就再多玩几分钟? 行吗,妈妈?"他恳求道。

她迟疑了一下,然后朝他笑了笑。

"好吧!"她答道,然后又一次调整了一下手中的袋子。

等我上了车,放好我的购物袋,正准备悄悄退出泊车位时,那个绿靴子男孩和他母亲正朝着他们的车子走去,边笑边走。

我自己的孩子曾经有多少次恳求"再多几分钟吧"? 我有没有像那个绿靴子男孩的母亲一样微笑着等待呢?或者我只是训斥他们来着?

Just a few more minutes of giggling and splashing in the bathtub.So what if bedtime got pushed back a little?

Just a few more minutes of rocking a sleepy toddler.So what if toys were strewn around the room,littering the floor?

Just a few more minutes of life with them before they were grown and gone.So what if my career goals didn't fit my original timeline?

Just a few more minutes.Everything I have read about time management for working mothers can be summed up in one picture.The picture of that young mother standing under her umbrella,arms full of packages,smiling at a wet,green-booted boy who had asked her the universal time-management question for working mothers everywhere,"Just a few more minutes?"

Sara Henderson

再多几分钟在澡盆里咯咯大笑着玩水,把上床时间往后推迟一点,又能怎么样?

再多几分钟轻摇昏昏欲睡的学走路年龄的孩子,孩子把玩具扔得满房间满地板都是,又能怎么样?

在他们长大从身边走开前,就多花几分钟的时间和他们待在一起吧。就算我眼前的职业目标与我原先的时间计划不符,又当如何?

就再多几分钟。我所读过的关于职业母亲工作安排的每一个方面都可以用一个画面来归纳,这就是那个站在伞下,胳膊上挂满了购物袋,正对着一个浑身湿漉漉,穿着绿靴子的小男孩微笑的年轻母亲,和问她各地的职业母亲都熟知的关于时间安排问题的孩子的画面,"就再多几分钟?"

萨拉·亨德森

女性系列／聆听花开的声音

This Is the Best Day of My Life

The purpose of life,after all,is to live it,to taste experi-ence to the utmost,to reach out eagerly and without fear for newer and richer experiences.

Eleanor Roosevelt

Being a mother of five children who were all born within seven years tells me I am either very crazy or I love being a mother.For me it is the latter.From the moment I felt the first baby moving within my womb I was hooked.I knew my calling in life.I went to college;I did all the things that the modern woman is told to do.But,all I really wanted was to be a full-time domestic goddess(as Roseanne Barr used to say).

For many years I was a full-time mother;however,I did have to supplement my husband's income to make ends meet.So I would tend and fall in love with yet more children.Not children that I gave birth to but working mother's children.I loved those kids like my own.This allowed me to stay home with my own and share my love for others' children.A working mom is a happy mom when her kids are happy. Well,I did my very best to make sure that their kids were happy.

When my last child started school I decided that I would substitute teach at the local schools.I loved it.Again I was allowed to be home with my kids when they were at home.What I didn't realize was that I would be able to go on field trips with my own children.I would have freedom that I hadn't had in a long time.I had never been able to do this when I ran home daycare.I felt that it was a fair trade-off to be home with my kids.

一生中最美好的一天

生活的最终目的是要生活其间，尽情地品味各种经历，热切而毫不畏惧地迎接更为丰富多彩的新经历。

艾丽娜·罗斯福

7年里生了5个孩子的经历告诉我，我要么是发疯，要么是热爱做母亲。对我来说，那当然是后者。从我感到第一个婴儿在子宫里的活动那时起，我就上瘾了。我知道生活对我的感召。我上了大学，做了人们要求现代女性要做的所有的事情。但是，我真正想要的却是做一个全职的爱家天使(就像罗珊娜·巴尔过去常常所说的那样)。

我做了多年的全职母亲，但是我的确必须增加丈夫的收入，平衡家庭开支。因此我照料孩子，后来甚至坠入与更多孩子的爱河。他们不是我生的孩子，而是其他职业母亲的孩子。我像爱自己的孩子一样热爱这些孩子。这使我可以待在自己家里，并且将母爱分给其他人的孩子。孩子们快乐时，职业母亲们就开心。所以，我尽全力使她们的孩子快乐。

等我最小的孩子上学时，我决定在当地的学校找个教书的工作换换口味。我喜欢这个工作。这次我又可以在我的孩子们在家的时间里与他们一起待在家里。让我意想不到的是，这次我可以与自己的孩子一起做校外考察旅行。我可以拥有许久不曾有的自由了。我办家庭托儿所以来从来没有体验到这一点。我这下子感到与孩子们一起待在家里真是个相当不错的选择。

My son,who was eight at the time,brought home a note for a field trip to be signed.For years I had always checked the"No"box where they ask for chaperones.He pleaded with me to go.I already had a substitute job scheduled for that day.I thought about it for a while and I checked the"Yes"box.Jonathan was thrilled to say the least.I quickly notified the teacher that I wouldn't be able to sub on that day,and she would have to find someone else.She wasn't thrilled but she understood.

The field trip day arrived.We were going to ride the "Bell Carol" steamboat down the Cumberland River and then walk to the Spaghetti Factory for lunch.The anticipation was just about to kill my son.He beamed with pride as we walked into the school building together.He introduced me to his class.I was so touched by his tender words and pride in me.

The bus ride from LaVergne,Tennessee,to downtown Nashville is about thirty minutes on a good day.This can be a very long time with ninety-plus kids on a bus.Jonathan wanted me to sit by him.I chose not to be the disciplinarian to the children that I was sitting by that day.I let the teachers and their aides do that. I focused my entire attention on my son,and we talked the entire ride.We talked about many fun and silly things.I listened while he talked.Our eyes met,and he looked deep inside mine and said, "Mama,this is the best day of my life,"My heart was filled with true joy.A soft tear or two rolled down my face and Jonathan asked me,"Mama,don't cry;Mama,why are you crying?"And I answered, "Because you have made this one of the best days of my life."

The true joy of motherhood comes from the simple things that we do for and with our children.

Dian Tune Lopez

我的儿子那时8岁，他带回家一份有待签名的校外旅行通知。多年来，我总是在要求有成人陪护的"不同意"框里打钩。他恳请我一道去。我那天已经约定与别人换班了。但我还是想了一会，随后在"同意"的框中打了钩。乔纳森简直激动得说不出话来。我飞快地通知那位老师我那天不能为她替班，她得另找其他人了。她并不激动，但能理解我的心情。

　　校外旅行的那天来到了。我们将乘坐"贝尔·卡罗"号汽船沿着坎伯兰河而下，之后步行去通心粉厂吃午饭。光是设想一下这些美景我儿子就要乐死了。我们俩一起走进教学大楼时，他自豪的脸上放着光彩。他把我介绍给同学，他亲切的话语和为我而感到的骄傲让我非常感动。

　　汽车在晴天从田纳西州莱弗吉到纳什维尔市中心大约要花30分钟。这对于车上的90多个孩子来说是一段很长的时间。乔纳森想让我坐在他身边，我那天尽量不让自己显得像个说教者。让老师们和他们的助手去说教吧，我把全部精力放在儿子身上。我们交谈了一路，谈了很多有趣而又傻乎乎的事。他说的时候我就认真地倾听。我们四目相对，他的眼睛深深地看进我的双眼，他说道："妈，这是我一生最美好的一天。"我充满了发自内心的快乐，有一两滴眼泪从我脸颊上滚落。乔纳森问我，"妈，别哭；妈，你为什么哭啊？"我回答道，"因为你也让我拥有了一生中最美好的一天。"

　　母亲真正的快乐来自于我们为孩子以及跟孩子一起做的简单琐事。

迪安·特尼·洛普斯

What Goes Around, Comes Around

Sitting at my desk one morning,I was deeply engrossed in an important project—trying to rebutton my shirt so each button lined up with the right hole.One side of my blouse was definitely hanging at an odd angle and I wanted to fix it before most of my coworkers arrived.Making sure I'm dressed properly is something I normally do at home in front of a toothpaste-speckled mirror,but this morning there'd been no time.This morning I had played the home version of army boot camp.

My goal:to leave the house and drive to work.The obstacles:a toddler and a nine-year-old boy.Every time I tried to make a strategic move,like tying my shoes or finding my keys,there was a child at my feet who desperately needed something.My nine-year-old claimed he had to have a sandwich for school because the cafeteria was serving the wrong kind of pizza.He likes "personal pizza",which is round,but this day it was square.　Apparently,the round pizza tastes like it just came from the oven of Italy's finest bistro,while the square pizza is inedible.

"It's too tomatoey,"he explained.

Then my two-year-old sneezed just after I placed a heaping spoonful of oatmeal in his mouth.This necessitated a change of my clothes,but there was no time to be choosy.It was my turn to drive my nine-year-old and his friend to the bus.I grabbed a clean blouse from the dryer,threw it on,and ran out the door with the whole gang.We made the bus,and I dropped my toddler at the sitter's before racing to work.Is it any surprise my shirt was buttoned wrong?I'm just glad it was buttoned.

As I contemplated what I could have done to ease the morning mayhem,several colleagues arrived in the office,including my boss.He

顺其自然

一天早晨坐在办公桌旁,我全神贯注地进行着一件很重要的工程——想要把我衬衫上的纽扣重新钉一下,这样每一粒纽扣就能和扣眼对上了。我的衬衣有一边倾斜得很古怪,我想在大多数同事到来之前把它补好。确保自己穿着得体是我在家中有牙膏斑点的镜子前常常做的事。但是今天早晨时间来不及了。早晨我上演了一场家庭版新兵训练营节目。

我的目标:离家驱车去上班。障碍物:一个牙牙学步的小孩和一个9岁大的男孩。每一次在我想做另外一件事的时候,比如说系鞋子或者找钥匙时,在我脚旁就总有个孩子拼命地要什么东西。我9岁的儿子说他需要一块三明治去上学,因为自助餐厅只供应他不想要的那种比萨饼。他喜欢个人风味的比萨饼,那是圆形的,但是今天的比萨饼都是方形的。很明显,圆形的比萨饼吃起来就像是刚刚从意大利最棒的餐馆烤炉上烤出来的一样,而方形的比萨饼却难以下咽。

"那个番茄味太重了,"他解释说。

接下来,我两岁大的儿子在我就要把一整勺燕麦片放进他嘴里时打了个大喷嚏。这搞得我不得不换衣服,可我却没时间讲究。今天轮到我开车送我9岁的儿子和他的朋友去搭校车,我从烘干机里抓起一件干净的罩衫,快速地套在身上就跑到门口去跟大家汇合。我们赶上了校车。然后我再赶着在上班前把蹒跚学步的孩子丢给了替我们照看孩子的人。如果我衬衣的纽扣扣错了有什么稀奇的吗?纽扣还能扣上我就挺满意了。

我正想着如何减轻早晨的忙乱所带来的破坏,有几个同事就到

had a funny expression on his face,like he was trying to hold in a sneeze.But it wasn't a sneeze,it was a grin.

"I have good news and bad news,"he said.All present opted for the good news first.It turns out he and his wife are expecting a baby this summer—thrilling news.

My colleagues and I,many of whom have children,told him we knew he'd be a great dad.He and his wife,a schoolteacher,have been married several years and have big hearts.Their house is already filled with the playful chaos of five formerly homeless cats.

After a round of congratulations,I remembered his early words. "What's the bad news?"I asked.

"The bad news is the same as the good news,"he said.He'll take a block of time off when the baby's born—good news for him,but bad news,i.e.,a tougher workload,for the rest of us.

I didn't see it as bad news.Like they say,what goes around comes around.When I gave birth to my younger son,I took a four-month maternity leave.My boss covered for me,and I'm more than happy to do the same for him.Besides,when he's a father he'll have a better understanding of what it's like to juggle work and childcare.

The announcement that he'll soon be crib shopping meant we had a new person to initiate into the ranks of parenthood.We began giving him a preview of how his life will change.

"You won't be going to the movies anymore because you'll need to buy diapers—lots and lots of diapers,"one colleague intoned.

"Yeah,and then when the baby is out of diapers you'll be able to go to the movies again,but they'll all be cartoons,"warned another."Your whole life will be rated G."

My boss laughed and said that's why stores rent videos.He pointed out that he and his wife can still enjoy the pleasures of dining out.

"For now,"said a female coworker."But once the baby's older you

了办公室,其中包括我的老板。他脸上有一个非常可笑的表情,就像他正忍着要打一个喷嚏一样。但是不是喷嚏,是咧嘴大笑。

"我这里有好消息也有坏消息,"他说。所有在场的人都选择先听好消息。结果是他和他的太太今年夏天要有一个孩子了——真是振奋人心的好消息。

我的同事们和我,很多人都有孩子,我们告诉他我们知道他会是个了不起的父亲。他和他太太,一个中学老师,已经结婚好几年了,两人都雄心勃勃。他们的房子现在被5只以前无家可归的小猫搞得乱七八糟。

我们都向他表示祝贺之后,我想起了他刚刚说过的话。"那么坏消息是什么呢?"我问道。

"坏消息跟好消息一样,"他说。等孩子出生以后,他就要花大量的时间——这对他是个好消息,但是对我们其他的人是坏消息,那就意味着我们的工作将更加繁重。

我倒不觉得这是坏消息。就像他们所说的,要来的迟早会来。我生小儿子的时候,也请过了4个月的产假。老板帮我打点了一切,我很高兴这次能为他做同样的事。还有,等他当了父亲,他就能更好地理解摆平工作与照看孩子的矛盾是个什么滋味了。

当他宣布他很快就要去买一张儿童床时,我们明白这就意味着在父母的圈子里又增加了一个新人。我们大家都开始帮他预测他的生活会发生怎样的变化。

"你再也不能去看电影了,因为你得去买尿布——很多很多的尿布,"一个同事拖长着嗓音说道。

"是的,当孩子不需要尿布的时候你就又能去看电影了,不过那时就都得是卡通片,"另外一个人提醒他。"你的全部生活就是当个普通观众。"

我的老板大笑着说他这下明白为什么商店都出租录像机了。他指出他和他太太仍然能够享受出去吃饭的乐趣。

"那也只能是现在了,"一个女同事说道。"可是一旦你的孩子长

won't be asking about the soup du jour anymore.You'll be reading the 'Happy Meal'menu and trying to get through a dinner without someone spilling their drink all over you."

"So let me get this straight,"my boss said."I'll spend all my money on diapers,and I won't ever go to the theater or eat out?Well,I can still ride my bicycle this summer."

A male coworker,an experienced father,slowly shook his head. "Nope,you won't be doing any of that.No more bike trips."

My boss gave him a smug look and announced he could always get a buggy that attaches to his bicycle.

"Sure,you could do that,but it'll be a waste of money,"said the dad. "My son didn't sleep through the night for months.His sleep cycles were reversed.When's your baby due?June?Trust me,you'll be too tired to go biking."

At this point a female coworker,the mother of two teenage daughters,walked over to put her two cents in. "Actually,you should go home and go to sleep right now.That way,you might have a chance at getting through this whole fatherhood thing,"she advised.

"And don't worry if you come to work with your shirt buttoned wrong,"I added."We'll understand."

Linda Tuccio-Koonz

大一点,你就不再点特色汤了。你会阅读'快乐食品'菜单,然后想好好地吃上一顿饭,不让任何人把饮料洒在你身上。"

"那就让我现在就有这种生活好了,"老板说道。"我把所有的钱都花来买尿布,我不能再去剧院看戏或者出去吃饭吗?那好,我可以在这个夏天骑自行车旅行。"

一个男同事,一个有经验的父亲慢慢地摇了摇了头。"不可能,你再也做不到了,你再也没有自行车旅行了。"

老板沾沾自喜地看了他一眼,然后宣布他会一直把婴儿车装在他的自行车上。

"当然,你可以做到那一点。但是那得浪费很多钱,"这个父亲说。"我儿子有好几个月夜里不睡觉,他的睡眠颠倒了。你的孩子什么时候出生?6月吗?相信我吧,你会累得骑不动自行车。"

这时一个女同事,两个十来岁女孩的母亲,走过来讲她的小小建议,"真的,你现在就应该回家去,好好睡觉。那样的话,你就有机会从容不迫地把整个为人之父的时光捱过去了,"她劝告道。

我又加了一句,"如果你来上班时衬衣纽扣扣错了,别担心。我们都能理解。"

琳达·图西欧·库尼斯

Household Chores

For the first few years after my marriage ended,I worked part of the time from home and added in a couple of part-time jobs to help make ends meet.Getting the housework done—never one of my favorite things,even when I was at home full time—tended to fall by the way-side.

As my eldest son's twelfth birthday approached,I thought of something that might help.Birthdays are major celebrations in our family.The night before the big day,I rummage through photo albums and boxes to find pictures that illustrate the birthday child's life—from birth to now. These are taped all over the side of the fridge.We have cake and ice cream and candles and many small presents to be opened and enjoyed.

That year,I added something extra. "Now that you are twelve, Matthew,"I told him,"you are old enough for the Laundry Initiation."He laughed as I pinned a towel around his neck like a cape.

"To the laundry room! "I announced.The other three children followed us,but I held up my hand to stop them at the door. "I'm sorry,"I told them, "but you have to be twelve years old for the Laundry Initiation."I closed the door firmly,with them on the other side.

I introduced Matthew politely to the washer and dryer and told him how the Magic Knobs work.Then I produced a basket of his laundry and demonstrated how to sort the clothes,and the settings to use for each type.

"Now,"I told him,"you are a Laundry Master! "

From that day forward,Matthew did his own laundry.And as each of the other children turned twelve,they,too,were initiated and became

双
语
精
华
版
·
心
灵
鸡
汤
·

家务劳动

在我的婚姻结束的头几年里，我曾经离家出去做兼职工作,或者再额外打些临时工以补贴家用。家务活从来就不是我最喜欢的事情,哪怕我整天待在家里——我做家务一般都会半途而废。

随着我大儿子的12岁生日越来越近,我开始想辙了。庆祝生日是我们家的一个重要活动。在那个隆重日子的头一天晚上,我翻出影集和箱子,想找些对过生日的孩子生活有启发的照片——从出生开始到现在的。这些照片现在都被我捆扎起来放在了冰箱顶上。我们还有蛋糕、冰激凌、蜡烛和许多小礼物要打开享受。

那一年,我增加了些新花样。"你既然12岁了,马修,"我告诉他,"你的年龄就大得可以洗衣服了,"我把一块毛巾像个披肩一样别在他脖子上时他大笑。

"到洗衣房去,"我向他郑重宣布。其他三个孩子跟在我们身后,但我却伸出手把他们挡在门口。"我很抱歉,"我告诉他们,"不过你们得等到12岁才能洗衣服。"我把门紧紧地关上,把他们留在了门外边。

我彬彬有礼地向马修介绍洗衣筒和甩干筒的用法,并告诉他那些神奇的按钮是如何工作的。然后我找了一篓他要洗的衣服,给他演示如何将衣服分类,以及每一类衣服用洗衣机里的哪个位置设定好。

"现在,"我告诉他,"你是个洗衣能手了!"

从那以后,马修就自己洗衣服了。等其他的孩子到了12岁,我也

Laundry Masters themselves.

I was amazed at how much it helped me to be relieved of that one responsibility.I helped them master other skills over the next few years: washing dishes,dealing with garbage and recycling,putting away groceries in an organized way.It didn't occur to me at the time that it was benefiting the children as well.Years later,when they went off to university,they regaled me with stories of their inept roommates who couldn't do laundry,wash dishes or prepare meals.They appreciated that I'd helped them learn the skills of everyday life.

Dan,my third child,was especially proud of his ability to prepare meals.That came about because some six years after starting out as a single parent,I finally got my first full-time job.I liked the work,but the office was an hour away and the days were long.

For the first few weeks,I'd arrive home at 6:45 or 7:00 at night and start preparing supper.I was hungry,the kids were hungrier,and by the time we actually sat down to eat everyone was tired.I found that they were snacking on buttered toast and bowls of cereal in the hours after school so often they didn't have room for the more nutritious meal I'd prepared.

So we came up with another plan.Each Sunday I would sit down and plan meals for the following week,based on the food we had in the house.

But who would do the cooking?Matthew had a part-time job after school.Lisa was in rehearsal for the school play.It turned out that fourteen-year-old Dan was usually the first one to arrive home,and so he took the responsibility to prepare the meal for us each night.

We spent a couple of weekend evenings cooking together,and I taught him basic techniques.And for the rest of that year,he made supper for us every night.

Yes,there were a few disasters.We still laugh about the time he

向他们传授洗衣的基本知识,他们也一个个成了洗衣能手。

发现这个办法让我从一项职责中解脱出来,我大吃一惊。在随后的几年里我又帮助他们掌握了别的技能:洗盘子、处理垃圾和可回收物品,井井有条地储存杂货,等等。那时我可没有想到这些还会对孩子们有好处。多年以后,等他们去上大学后,他们回家跟我讲一些自己不会洗衣服、洗盘子、不会做饭的笨拙室友的故事让我高兴。他们感激我帮助他们学会了日常生活的技巧。

丹,我的老三,对他会做饭的本领特别自豪。他会做饭是因为在我成为单亲家长6年以后,我终于有了一份全职的工作。我喜欢那份工作,但是办公室离家有一个小时的路程,而且工作时间很长。

刚开始几周,我晚上6点45分或者7点到家,然后开始准备晚饭。我很饿,孩子们更饿。等最后坐下来吃饭时,我们都疲惫不堪。我发现他们放学后的几个小时里一直在吃奶油吐司和一碗碗的谷类食品,以至于我做的更有营养的饭菜他们都没有肚子装了。

所以我们又做了一个计划。每个星期天我会坐下来,根据家里现有的食物计划下一周的饭菜。

但是谁来进行烹饪呢?马修放学后要打一份临时工。丽莎为学校的表演在彩排。最后我发现14岁的丹通常是第一个到家的,于是他就接过重任,每天晚上为我们大家准备晚餐。

我们两个人花了好几个周末晚上一起做饭,我教他基本的技巧。所以那一年的其他时间,每晚都是他帮我们做晚饭。

当然,有过好几次灾难。我们至今对他在通心粉沙司里加的那

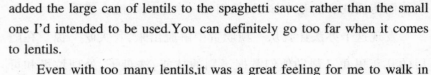

added the large can of lentils to the spaghetti sauce rather than the small one I'd intended to be used.You can definitely go too far when it comes to lentils.

Even with too many lentils,it was a great feeling for me to walk in the door and smell dinner cooking in the oven or simmering on the burner.We were able to start our evening around the table together,enjoying a simple but nutritious meal and sharing the events of the day.

A couple of years later,when I was no longer working full-time but doing freelance work and some part-time contracts again,I read an article about things that make us feel loved.The author commented that some people need to hear the words"I love you",others feel loved when they receive gifts and others need physical affection to really feel cared for.Intrigued,I asked my children what made them feel loved.

Dan's answer surprised me the most."I felt loved when I made dinner every night when you were working fulltime,"he said.

"That made you feel loved?"I was incredulous.I'd often had moments of guilt over asking so much of my children,worrying that as a single parent I was overburdening them with chores.

"Yeah,it did,"he said."I liked learning to cook with you.And I felt that you trusted me to make the meals for the whole family.That was a big responsibility,and that made me feel loved."

I look at our household chores differently now.They are not painful and annoying tasks to be parceled out;they are part of what it means to be a family together.They are opportunities for each of us to demonstrate love for each other and to feel loved in return.

Teresa Pitman

一大罐,而不是我通常放的一小罐扁豆大笑不止。等沙司里满是扁豆时,你肯定是做过了头。

就算是有太多的扁豆,当我们跨进家门,闻到烤箱里烤制的或者炉膛里正在炖的饭菜香味,我们都感到非常开心。我们大家围着桌子开晚饭,享受简单却有营养的饭菜,分享一天来的大小事件。

几年后,当我不再做全职工作,而是又做自由职业者以及一些兼职的承包工作时,我读到了一篇关于让我们感受到有关爱的文章。这篇文章的作者认为一些人需要听到诸如"我爱你"之类的话语,有些人收到礼物时感受到爱,有些人需要身体的情感表达才能真正地感受到别人对他们的关心。受到这篇文章的启发,我问我的孩子们是什么让他们感受到了爱。

丹的回答最让我吃惊。"在您做全职工作,而我每晚做饭时我感受到了爱,"他说。

"那让你感受到爱吗?"我怀疑。想起来让孩子们做了那么多事情我常常深感内疚,担心自己作为单亲家长给孩子们带来了过于繁重的家务琐事。

"是的,是真的,"他说,"我喜欢跟您一起学做饭。我感到您让我给全家做饭是对我的信任。那可是一个重大的责任,那让我感受到您的爱。"

我现在对家务琐事看法不同了。它们不是让人痛苦、烦恼、理应被束之高阁的义务;它们是家庭组成的一部分。它们是我们向别人表白爱意,并感受到爱的回报的大好机会。

特丽萨·皮特曼

First in Her Heart

A mother is she who can take the place of all others but whose place no one else can take.

Cardinal Mermillod

My daughter,Ariel,was two months old when I returned to my more-than-full-time job as a psychiatry resident.I'll always remember how anxious I felt the first time I put her in our nanny's arms.Before long,friends and relatives started barraging me with "working-mother conflict"questions:How was I balancing things?What time did I get home at night?Did I worry about the nanny horror stories I'd heard?

But the question that continued to haunt me for more than a year was the one I heard from women who had decided to stay home with their children:"Your baby still knows who her mommy is,right?"Remembering those words could turn my feelings of relief and gratitude that we'd found a great sitter to feelings of jealousy and insecurity as I let myself wonder:Did Ariel know who her mommy was?Would she consider the woman with whom she spent eight waking hours a day—when I was only home for two or three—her mommy?Would she and I be able to bond?

I should have known better.The child of a working mother myself,I was raised in a family where everyone had a career,and I've always heard stories about how my brother and I would rush from our nanny to our mother at the end of every day.My mother and I have always been close,speaking on the phone almost daily,sharing confidences,support

女儿心中第一人

> 母亲能扮演其他所有人的角色,而她的位置则无人能替代。

卡迪诺·莫密罗德

在我重返精神病高级住院实习医生的繁忙工作岗位时,我女儿阿瑞尔才刚刚两个月大。我永远忘不掉第一次把她放在保姆怀里时我深切体验到的那种焦虑感。没多久,朋友和亲戚们就开始拿"上班族母亲"的问题接二连三地向我发问:我如何摆平所有的事情?我晚上什么时候到家?我过去听到的有关保姆的恐怖故事是否让我担心?

不过一年多来,最一直不断地困扰我的却是我从那些决定留在家里与孩子待在一起的女士们那里听到的问题:"你的小宝贝还知道母亲是谁,对吗?"听了这些话,我本来以为我们找到了一个了不起的保姆的放松感和感激顷刻间转化为不停地思考、嫉妒和不安。阿瑞尔知道母亲是谁吗?在她白天8个小时清醒的时间里,我每天只能在家里待两三个小时,她会把这段时间里与她待在一起的那个女人当成妈妈吗?她能和我紧紧地联系在一起吗?

我应该对此有更多的了解。我自己就曾经是上班族母亲的孩子,我在一个人人都有工作的家庭里长大,我经常听人讲我哥哥和我如何在每天傍晚从保姆身旁冲向母亲怀里的故事。我母亲和我一直都很亲近,我们两个人几乎每天都通电话,分享彼此的信任、支持

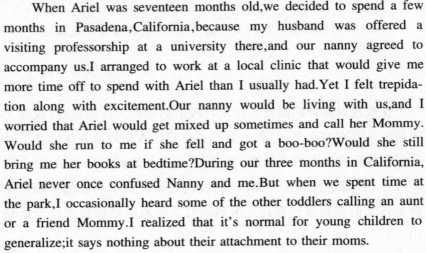

and advice.But still,I worried.My mother,a nurse,had always worked fewer hours than I do,and she was never away overnight on call.My brother and I also spent lots of time with other relatives,who never let us forget who our mother really was.

When Ariel was seventeen months old,we decided to spend a few months in Pasadena,California,because my husband was offered a visiting professorship at a university there,and our nanny agreed to accompany us.I arranged to work at a local clinic that would give me more time off to spend with Ariel than I usually had.Yet I felt trepidation along with excitement.Our nanny would be living with us,and I worried that Ariel would get mixed up sometimes and call her Mommy. Would she run to me if she fell and got a boo-boo?Would she still bring me her books at bedtime?During our three months in California, Ariel never once confused Nanny and me.But when we spent time at the park,I occasionally heard some of the other toddlers calling an aunt or a friend Mommy.I realized that it's normal for young children to generalize;it says nothing about their attachment to their moms.

Ariel made it obvious that she loved her nanny—asking for her in the morning,giving her hugs and greeting her with a big smile when we returned from an outing—but she also knew that their relationship was different from hers and mine.

When I was at home,Ariel always wanted me to be the one to read to her or give her lunch.And although she'd wave bye-bye happily when I told her I was going to work,she'd protest loudly if I left for any other reason.One morning she cried when I said I was going for a run,but cheered up when I amended to it,"Mommy's going to work out."Ariel had come to think of work as an ordinary and expected event that separates us only temporarily,and apparently the only acceptable reason for my absence.I always try my best to convey to her that even when we are apart she remains my top priority.A working mom is still a full-time mom.

双
语
精
华
版
·
心
灵
鸡
汤
·

与建议。但是，我仍然担心。因为我母亲以前是个护士，她每天工作的时间总是比我现在少好几个小时，并且她从来也没有接到过通知整夜不回家过。我哥哥和我过去跟她的亲戚也在一起待过很多时间，他们从来没有让我们忘记谁是我们真正的母亲。

阿瑞尔17个月大的时候，我们决定到加州的帕萨迪纳过几个月，因为我丈夫要去那里的一所大学做访问教授。我们的保姆同意陪着我们一起去。我安排自己到当地的一家诊所工作，以便我比平时有更多的时间和阿瑞尔待在一块儿。然而兴奋之余，我有些惊恐不安。保姆将和我们住在一起，我担心阿瑞尔有时会糊涂，管保姆叫妈妈。如果摔倒碰伤了她会跑向我吗？就寝时间她还会把她的书拿给我吗？幸运的是在我们住在加州的3个月里，阿瑞尔从来没有把保姆和我搞混淆。但是在公园里玩的时候，我偶尔听到过其他一些蹒跚学步的幼儿喊一个姨妈或者朋友妈妈。我意识到小孩子把母亲的概念广义化其实很正常；它并不能说明他们与母亲依恋与否。

很明显，阿瑞尔喜欢她的保姆——早晨要她，拥抱她，当我们从外面回来的时候她用灿烂的微笑问候她——但是她也知道她和保姆的关系与我的关系不同。

我在家时，阿瑞尔总是想要我给她读书或者喂饭。虽然我告诉她我要去上班时她快乐地摆手跟我再见，但是我要是因为其他原因离开她就会大声地抗议。有一天早晨我说我要去跑步她哭了起来，但是当我补充说"妈妈要到外面工作"，她开心起来。阿瑞尔逐渐地认为工作是件普通而又预料得到的事情，它只是暂时地把我们分开，很明显对她来说，这是我不在家的唯一可以接受的理由。我总是尽一切可能向她传达即使我们分开，她也是我最重要的生命组成部分的信息。上班族母亲也可以是全职妈妈。

It's clear to me now that the women who had asked me whether Ariel knew I was her mommy weren't purposely trying to make me feel guilty;they were trying to reassure themselves that their decision to stay home was the best thing for their babies. Most of us want to do a superlative job,and there are no easy definitions of what that is.Unfortunately,at-home mothers and working mothers continue to throw darts at each other,and I'm convinced that it's out of insecurity.We all want to know that the choice we have made is the right one—and both choices involve sacrifices.All parents need to feel that the sacrifices are indeed worth it.

During these first two years of Ariel's life,I've come to a better understanding about what it means to be a mother.It's not the number of hours you devote to your child,nor the specific activities you share.It's more the way your child gets inside your very being and remains there twenty-four hours a day.

As creative,caring and responsible as our caregiver was,her relationship with Ariel was still defined by the fact that it was a job.She eventually left us to get married and start a family of her own.Our new babysitter used to work for friends who moved out of state.Sitters come and go in families,just as children come and go for sitters.But a mother is there forever:physically,for the first eighteen years or so,and spiritually,for the rest of a child's life.

Doris Zarovici

我现在明白了,那些曾经问我阿瑞尔是否知道我是她妈妈的妇女并不是有意地要我感到内疚;她们是想要向自己证实她们和自己的宝宝一起留在家里是最好的选择。我们大多数人都想做一份最了不起的工作,但是却很难说清楚那究竟是什么。不幸的是,留在家里的母亲和上班族母亲不断地相互攻击。我想那可能是出于不安全感。我们都想知道自己的抉择是否正确——而且双方的决定都需要做出自我牺牲。所有的父母都需要感到自己的牺牲奉献确实有价值。

在阿瑞尔生命的头两年里,我越发理解做母亲意味着什么。它不是你奉献给孩子多少小时这个数字,也不是你分担的抚养孩子的具体行动,它是孩子成为你身体里重要的一个组成部分,并一天24个小时跟你在一起的方式。

不管我们的保姆多么有创造力,多么有爱心,多么负责任,她与阿瑞尔的关系事实上也只是工作关系。后来,她离开我们结了婚,开始了自己的家庭生活。我们的新保姆过去常常为我们那些不在家的朋友们打打临活。保姆在家庭中来了又走,就像孩子们出生又需要人护理一样反复循环。但是母亲永远是母亲:在孩子生命的大约前18年母亲是孩子的物质依赖;而在其余时间,母亲是孩子的精神靠山。

多丽丝·艾恩维斯

A Hug for Your Thoughts

"Mom,you're always on the computer! "Laura grumbled.

"No,I'm not,"I defended.

"Every day I come home from school you're working on the computer."

"Well,at least I'm here for you! "

My daughter,Laura,at twelve years old,was right.Day after day,in my home office,I would stare into space as my hands typed out the thoughts of a presentation or of research completed for an article.It seemed that my work as a writer and speaker cemented my fingers to the keyboard and my mind to valuable ideas.What Laura did not realize was that during her day away,I'd also be doing a load of laundry,answering incoming phone calls,cleaning up dirty dishes,crunching an editor's deadline,sorting the family mail,networking and marketing my speaking service.It was only around three in the afternoon that I'd finally collapse at my desk for a few precious moments of deep thought. Then she'd come in from school.

I prided myself on being available to my children.After all,I am a speaker on child behavior and parenting.But Laura's observation stung my conscience.Her perception of me must have been of a mom who was available but unapproachable.Hardly the image I wanted to project.My relationship with my children is more important than any other career.

"Laura,"I called,"come here a minute."

Out of her bedroom,Laura strolled down the hall to my doorway.I had decided to have her alert me when I was obsessed with work.I wanted her to have the power to let me know when she thought I was being aloof.

拥抱你的思想

"妈妈,你老是在玩电脑!"劳拉向我发牢骚。

"哪里,我没有,"我辩解道。

"每天我从学校回来你都在电脑上工作。"

"哎,我至少是专门为你才在这里的。"

我12岁的女儿劳拉说得对。一天又一天,我在家庭办公室里总是两眼盯着某块空白处,双手不停地忙着把发言稿或者调查研究中的思想观点整理成文章。我身为作家和演说家的工作似乎把我的手指牢牢地固定在键盘上,而我的思维则被拴在了有价值的想法上。劳拉没有注意到的是在她白天不在家的时候,我也洗衣服,接听打进来的电话,把脏盘子洗干净,为了保证按时完成编辑交给的活拼命地工作,把家庭邮件分类,上网销售我的演讲服务,等等。只有到了下午3点钟左右,我才终于能够疲惫地来到工作桌前,花一些宝贵的时间陷入深深的思考。然后,她就放学回来走进家门了。

我为自己能跟孩子们在家亲近而感到自豪。毕竟,我是研究儿童行为和如何做父母这两方面的演说家。但是劳拉的细心观察刺痛了我的内心。她一定感到我是个虽然待在家里,但是却不能亲近的妈妈。这根本也就不是我想要打造的形象。我与孩子们的联系比其他任何事情都重要。

"劳拉,"我喊道,"到这里来一下。"

劳拉慢腾腾地从她的卧室走过客厅,来到我的门口。我下定决心要劳拉在我痴迷于工作的时候提醒我。我想给她权利,以便我能了解我显得疏远她时她的感受。

"So you think I'm preoccupied?"I asked.

"Most of the time,"came her honest reply.

After I explained my full schedule and the fact that I chose to office from home to be accessible to her and her sister,I offered Laura this compromise.

"Whenever you feel I'm ignoring you or you need my attention,I want you to hug me,"I said."Just come up and give me a little hug,and that'll be our signal that you need me."

Years later we still have that unspoken sign.I've become much more sensitive to my daughters' comings and goings.And on the days I'm not,Laura gives me a little squeeze to remind me of the real reason I work from home.

Brenda Nixon

"那你觉得我忙吗?"我问她。

"大多数时间忙,"她很诚实地回答。

在我给她解释了我的全部日程安排,以及我目前在家办公的目的就是为了跟她和她妹妹亲近之后,我向劳拉做出了这个承诺:

"不管什么时候,要是你觉得我忽略了你,或者你需要我关注你的时候,我希望你能来拥抱我,"我说,"只需要走过来,轻轻地抱我一下就行,那就是我们两个约定好你需要我的暗号。"

几年以后,我们仍然用那个不用表白的暗号。我对女儿们的走来走去也变得更为敏感。要是我做不到,劳拉就会过来,稍稍抱紧我一下,提醒我我在家里工作的真正原因。

布伦达·尼克松

CLOSE TO HOME   JOHN McPHERSON

HAPPY TIME DAY-CARE CENTER

5-29   © 1996 John McPherson/Dist. by Universal Press Syndicate

"His parents want to make sure
they don't miss seeing him take his first steps."

女性系列／聆听花开的声音

The Gift of Understanding

For many years,I have been a nurse.I have tended to the needs of my community members,friends,neighbors,relatives and strangers.I have loved and hated my job,sometimes within the same shift.Nursing can be exhilarating and uplifting.It can also be stressful and exhausting.Most of all,it can be lonely.The shift work,the work on holidays,the need for confidentiality,all of these can contribute to a sense of isolation,especially for a single person.

Holidays are the hardest time.I don't think that I could count,nor would I want to,the number of times that a coworker or supervisor has asked me to work a holiday for another,because, "You don't have a family."So I work Thanksgivings so that families can serve the holiday dinner in their home.I work Christmas Eves so that mothers can see their children in the Christmas pageant at church.I work the nights before Christmas so that fathers can assemble toys.I work Christmas Days so that parents can see the wonder in their children's eyes on Christmas morning.

These are difficult shifts to work.Many of the patients hospitalized during this time will not see another holiday.They are there because they are too ill to go home.There are not many elective procedures scheduled during these times,and anyone who is able will hastily be discharged in time for the festivities.So nurses are usually left with the sickest and the saddest of patients. It is a time to minister to both the physical and emotional needs of your fellow man;it can be a time of great communion. After the shift is over,it can also be a time of great loneliness.

Going home to an empty house on Christmas morning can be a

理解的礼物

　　我做了许多年的护士。我护理过我所在社区里的人们、朋友、邻居、亲戚和陌生人。有时就在同一个班上，我会既热爱又憎恨自己的工作。护理工作可以让人振奋精神，情绪高涨；也能让人压抑郁闷，筋疲力尽；而最多的，可能是孤独。倒班，节假日上班，所需要的信任，所有这些都可能导致一种孤独隔离感，对于个人尤其是如此。

　　节假日是最难过的时间。我想我数不清，也不想数清楚同事或者上司有多少次让我在节假日代班，因为，"你没有家庭"。所以我在感恩节上班，这样有家的人就可以在家里享用节日大餐。我在圣诞节前上班，这样母亲们就可以在教堂露天演出中看到自己的孩子。我上圣诞节前的夜班，这样父亲们可以去收集玩具。我上圣诞节期间的白班，这样父母在圣诞节早晨可以看到他们孩子眼睛里的奇迹。

　　这些都是工作当中艰难的换班时刻。很多在这个时间被送进医院的病人看不到下一个节日。他们之所以留在医院里是因为他们病情太严重，回不了家。在这些时间里，没有多少可做或者可不做的程序安排让人们去随意选择，任何可以自由选择的人早早地就被打发回家过节去了。因此这时护士们往往要与病得很重、很难过的病人在一起。这是个关照你的亲人物质与精神需要的时间；它可以是沟通思想情感的好时机。等这一个班次过去了，就又将是孤独的日子。

　　圣诞节的早晨回到家里，进入一个空荡荡的房子是一件让人倍

desolate thing.

This is what I faced the year that I received my most beloved Christmas gift.I was scheduled to work night shift on Christmas Eve, from 7:00 P.M. to 7:00 A.M.. My family of origin lived several hours away and would be going to church,opening their gifts,having Christmas dinner.I would be working during most of these events and sleeping during the remainder.Eventually.When the celebration was nearly over,and I had attained some much-needed sleep,I would make the trip home.

It was a bitterly cold winter night when I arrived for work. The wind bit through my uniform and whipped at my face.The parking lot was nearly empty,as the hospital was down to a skeleton crew.I made my way through the lot,the corridors and to the elevator that would deliver me to my floor.Cursory glances at those around me revealed a subdued mood.But when the elevator doors opened on my floor,I could sense excitement.I thought maybe there were carolers on the unit,or that a favorite patient was going home to be with his family for one final Christmas.All of the nurses,coming on shift and going off shift,were milling around the desk at the nurses' station.This was rather unusual, because change of shift tends to be a very busy event,with not much time for idleness.After I clocked in,I made my way to the nurses' station to find out what was going on.When I rounded the corner,all of my coworkers were waiting for me with big smiles.Anticipation was hanging in the air,as heavy as the big red garland hanging from the pillars of the station.I knew something big was up,and that they were waiting for me to be a part of it.Just then,one of my coworkers stepped forward,and I realized that I was not just a part of it...I was it.

This kind and gentle person,whom I had not felt especially close to before that moment, had done a most amazing thing. She had celebrated an early Christmas Eve with her daughter so that I could have the shift off,and go home to be with my family. Another coworker had taken her

感凄凉的事情。

这是收到我最喜欢的圣诞礼物那年我所面临的境况。圣诞节除夕我被排上夜班，从晚上7点一直到次日早晨7点。我的亲戚住在距离我几个小时路程之外的地方，他们要去教堂，拆开礼物，吃圣诞大餐。而我则肯定是在他们进行大多数这些活动时正在上班，其余时间是睡觉。最后，当庆祝活动接近尾声，我也补充了一些急需的睡眠之后，就打道回府。

这是一个非常寒冷的冬夜。我来接班时，寒风吹透了我的制服，抽打在我的脸上。驾车向医院主楼方向开去时，我发现停车场上几乎空旷如野。我穿过停车场、过道，来到能将我送到我值班所在的那一层电梯旁。匆匆地看看我身旁的这些景物就让人感到极其抑郁。但是当电梯门在我要到的那一层打开时，我感到兴奋起来。我以为也许是唱颂歌的人来到了病区，或者是深受家人爱戴的某个病人就要回家，去跟家人欢度最后一个圣诞节。所有的护士，来来往往地进行着交接班，正忙乱地围在护士工作台前。这异样反常，因为换班是件非常忙乱的事情，一般没有时间闲逛。等打了考勤卡之后，我朝着护士工作台走去想看看出了什么事。来到近旁，我才发现所有的同事都满脸堆笑地在等着我。我有些预感悬在半空，沉重得就像工作台柱子上悬挂下来的巨大花饰一样。我知道有什么大事在酝酿，而他们都在等我加入其中。就在那时，一个同事向前走来，我此时才意识到我不仅仅是其中的一部分……这件事就与我有关。

这是个善良和气的人，在这之前我并没有感到与她关系密切，但她却做出了一个很让人吃惊的事情。她宣布已经与女儿提前过了圣诞除夕，为的是换我的班，让我回家与家人团聚。另一个同事顶了

shift,and two more had split that person's shift.My coworkers,my friends,my family;the line of demarcation was shifting irrevocably and the definitions were melding together at that moment.Happy tears filled my eyes as I was escorted back to the elevator and offered best wishes. By the time I reached the parking lot,I was crying in earnest.The tears froze to my cheeks as I reached the car.

There was hardly any traffic as I sped along the deserted roads toward home that night.Most anyone who was going somewhere was already there.The stars twinkled in the black sky,and I sang along in hearty voice to the Christmas carols playing on the radio.The air was frigid,and I was alone on long stretches of highway.But I was not alone in my heart,for it was filled with gratitude and wonder.My coworkers had given me the greatest Christmas gift I had ever received—their gift of friendship,understanding and insight into my world.Because of that gift,and the sweet memories of that night,I would never be alone on Christmas again.

Susan Stava

她的班，又有两个人分担了那个人的班。我的同事、朋友、家人，在那一瞬间，分界线无可挽回地发生了变化，这些概念统统混为一体。当我被大家簇拥着回到电梯旁，人人都向我表达祝福时，幸福的泪水充满了我的双眼。等走到了停车场，我已经情不自禁地哭起来。走到自己的车前，眼泪凝结在了我的面颊上。

那个夜晚，我快速驶过无人的街道时，路上几乎没有车辆行人。大多数要到某个地方的人们都已经到了那儿。星星在漆黑的夜空里一闪一闪，我跟着收音机里播放的圣诞颂歌开心地唱着。空气寒冷，我独自一个人行驶在漫漫公路上。但是我的内心可一点都不孤独，因为它充满了感激和惊奇。我的同事们给了迄今为止我所收到的最好的礼物——他们的友谊、理解和对我的世界的洞察力。因为那个礼物和那个夜晚甜蜜的记忆，我在圣诞节再也不会感到孤独。

苏珊·斯塔瓦

Respect and Pride

I do not come from a military family,nor was there anyone in my family who had ever been a United States Marine and there definitely were not any females in my family who went into the service,let alone the marines.But somehow,in my upbringing,I developed this great sense of pride in my country,and the Marines were the only choice.

As a Marine,I was accustomed to many traditions and rituals,one of those being the daily ritual of "Morning Colors and Evening Colors". This is the raising and lowering of our National Colors,or the American flag.There is a set procedure for this.At 8:00 A.M.each morning,colors are sounded and the flag is raised.At sunset each night,the flag is retired. During the raising and lowering of the flag,all activity ceases.If you are outside,you stop what you are doing,face the direction of the flag,stand at attention,and if in uniform,salute,until the last note of the music is played.If you are in a car,you pull over to the side of the road and wait for the end of the music.

Fifteen minutes before the color guard is to raise or lower the flag,a warning will sound.This will allow you to get inside,get to your destina-tion,or prepare yourself for the raising or lowering of the flag.During my ten years in the Marines,I saw many Marines run to get inside so that they would not "get caught in Colors".I always felt this was a sense of disrespect to the flag;however,I too,was guilty of rushing to get inside so as to not"get caught in Colors".

One particular drizzly day at Naval Air Station Whidbey Island, Washington,where I was stationed as an active-duty Marine sergeant, training the reserve marines in the United States Marine Corps,I was

双语精华版·心灵鸡汤·

向国旗自豪地致敬

我没有出生在军人家庭里,我家里也没有任何人曾经当过美国海军陆战队队员,并且没有一个女性在部队里服过役,更别说海军陆战队了。然而,在成长的过程中,我逐渐产生了对伟大祖国的自豪感,尤其是对海军陆战队。

作为一个海军陆战队队员,我习惯了许多的传统和仪式,其中之一就是日常的"早晚升降旗"仪式,即升起和降下我们国家的旗帜也就是美国国旗。这个仪式有一整套程序。在每天清晨8点钟,升旗仪式的警报响起,随后国旗升起。每天傍晚日落时分,国旗被降下来。在升降旗的过程中,一切活动都要停止。如果你在室外,你要停下手头正在做的事情,面向国旗方向,立正站立。如果身着军服,要敬礼,直到音乐的最后一个音符奏完。如果你在汽车里,你必须驶向路边等待音乐结束。

在升降旗卫兵升起或者降下国旗前15分钟,预备警报会响起。你可以有时间进入室内,到达目的地,或者为升降旗做准备。在海军陆战队服役的10年期间,我看到许许多多的陆战队员跑进室内,这样他们就不会在"升降国旗中被困"。我一直感到这是对国旗的不尊重;然而,我却也内疚地随波逐流,随大家一道冲进室内以免"被困"。

一个细雨蒙蒙的一天,在华盛顿州惠德贝海岛的海空军基地,我作为现役海军陆战队中士在该岛驻防,训练美国海军陆战队的预

taking my two-year-old daughter to the doctor's office for a check-up.It was shortly before 8:00 A.M.and the warning was sounded for colors. We were in the parking lot walking towards the Naval Hospital.I heard the warning and said to my daughter,"Come on,Honey,we must hurry to get inside."After realizing what I said and what this would teach my daughter,I stopped and then asked her "Sweetie,would you like to watch them raise the flag?" "Yes,Mommy,"she replied.So we walked to a bench close by and waited.While we waited,I taught her how to stand tall and proud and showed her how to put her hand over her heart,and not to remove it until the music stopped.I told her the importance of re-spect for the flag and the meaning of the flag.We waited.Just then the first note sounded. We both stood and faced the flag.She placed her hand over her heart and I saluted.We stood there,Marine,mother,and daughter and gave our flag the respect it so greatly deserved.We watched our comrades in arms raise the flag and then salute it himself. At the last note of music,we all cut our salute and proceeded on with our business.

The pride I felt that day was immeasurable.Still to this day,I burst with pride when I tell that story.I am proud to be an American and proud to have served my country and the only thing better than being a Marine is being a mom.After ten years in the Marines,I had to make a choice,full-time mom or full-time Marine.I still am raising my daughter with the pride of Country and Corps.I can only hope that as she grows and matures,that a little of my"Esprit de Corps"and love for our country will rub off.And what they say is true, "Once a Marine,always a Ma-rine."

Semper fi.

Dianna C. Bradley

备役人员。我当时正带着两岁的女儿前往医生办公室做检查。快8点钟的时候，升旗的预备警报响起。我们刚巧从停车场里正往海军医院走去。听到警报我对女儿说，"来，宝贝儿，我们必须快快地到房子里去。"意识到自己正在说什么，并考虑了一下这会给女儿教导些什么，我停下脚步来问女儿："甜心，你想看看他们怎么升旗吗？"女儿答道，"是的，妈妈。"于是我们走向邻近的海滩等待着。在等的时候，我教导她如何挺拔自豪地站立，并向她演示如何把手高举过头顶，一直要等到音乐停止再把手拿开。我告诉她尊重国旗的重要性以及国旗的意义。我们等待着。后来第一声音乐响起。我们双双站立着，面向着国旗。她把手放在胸口，我敬着礼。我们站在那里，海军陆战队队员、母亲和女儿向着国旗致敬，它非常值得我们向它致敬。我们看着全副武装的护旗兵升起国旗然后向它敬礼。在音乐的最后一个音符奏完时，我们都收回敬礼，继续进行各自的事情。

那一天我所感受到的自豪是无以衡量的。直到今天，讲起这个故事的时候，我还是深感自豪兴奋。我为自己是个美国人而自豪，为服务祖国而骄傲。只有一件事能让我比作海军陆战队员更自豪，那就是做母亲。在陆战队服役10年后，我必须做出抉择，是做个全职母亲还是全职海军陆战队员。我依然在教导我女儿为国家和军队深感自豪。我只希望等她长大成熟以后，我的一点点"集体精神"和对祖国的爱能够慢慢减弱。看来他们说得对，"一旦当上了海军陆战队员，一辈子就是海军陆战队的人。"

永远忠诚。

黛安娜·C.布拉德利

Performance under the Stars

To fully enjoy life,to derive its greatest meaning and beauty,one needs to enter into it with not only the look of involvement and happiness,but the spirit of involvement,as well.

Luci Swindoll

They slouched in folding chairs in a semicircle,eyeing me suspiciously.Their ages ranged from fourteen to sixteen,and they were there because they loved drama.I was a new teacher,and I had absolutely no experience in directing drama.My background was in teaching,writing and literature.

No problem,I thought.

That was how I found myself in chaos late that fall,staging the musical *Godspell*.I spent countless nights at rehearsals coaxing my Jesus to sing louder and my Mary to tone down her body language.

My three-year-old,Breana,was the least of my worries.She was a sweet child,undemanding and easy to please.Usually I left her at home with my husband.But when he couldn't watch her,I'd throw her in the car and take her to rehearsals.She wandered about the stage,bottle in hand.

When I was wrapped up with responsibilities,I would pass Breana off to students. Her word for bottle was "baboo", and it was common to hear the pitiful cry of "Baboo! " from some corner of the drama room. The student nearest to her would then hunt it down.

As rehearsals for the play progressed,the integration of the acting

群星璀璨

要想好好地享受并追寻最有意义的生活和其中的美，一个人不但需要带着介入其中的态度和愉悦感，还要有走进其中的精神。

露西·斯温道尔

他们懒懒散散地在折叠椅里围坐成一个半圆，不信任地看着我。他们的年龄从14岁到16岁不等，他们在那里是因为他们热爱戏剧。我是个新老师，对指导戏剧完全没有经验。我的背景是教书、写作和文学。

应该没有问题，我想。

在那个秋季，我就是这样在要把音乐剧《圣咒》搬上舞台时发现自己陷入一团糟的。我花了无数个夜晚指导他们进行排练，哄扮演耶稣的演员唱腔声音更洪亮些，让扮演玛丽的演员把身体语言再放柔和些。

我3岁的女儿布瑞娜是最不让我操心的。她是个小甜心，要求不高，逗她开心很容易。我往往把她留在家里和我丈夫待在一起。但是当他看不了她时，我就把她扔进车里带她去排练。她手里拿着奶瓶，对舞台很好奇。

重任缠身的时候，我就把布瑞娜交给学生临时照看。她把奶瓶说成"巴布"，听到她从排练室的某个角落里可怜地呼叫"巴布"是很平常的事情，离她最近的学生自动会给她找回她的"巴布"。

随着剧本排练的进行，表演和舞蹈动作以及音乐的合成变得越

with the choreography and the music became extremely time-consuming and intense.Breana seemed to accept my hectic schedule with character-istic charm.Once the play was over,I reasoned,I would give her back the time I was taking from her.

On the way home from one particularly good rehearsal,I asked lightheartedly,"Do you love Mommy?"She turned to me and said sim-ply,"No."Wounded,I drove on in silence.

Opening night.We played to a sold-out crowd.My Jesus sang like a dove.The crucifixion scene had the audience in tears.At the last song, people were on their feet,wildly cheering for more.

The next night an even bigger crowd appeared,and we had to bring in more bleachers.Those who couldn't find a seat crowded shoulder to shoulder in the back.Breana came both nights.The first night,she sat on her dad's lap—dutiful but fidgeting.As everyone complimented me on a job well done,she fell asleep.

The second night,she was bored.I sat her in a corner where she played quietly.Then she came over and pulled on my arm.

"Go outside,"she whispered.

I looked in vain for her dad.

"Go outside,"she whispered again.

I glanced down.Breana was looking especially pretty in a red dress with petticoats.Loose hair from her pigtails trailed softly down her neck in tendrils.I relented.My cast could be without me for a few minutes.

There was a slight chill in the air.I let her pull me wherever she wished.We ended up outside the cafeteria,where there was a small am-phitheater.

Breana pushed at my waist."Sit,Mommy! "I did.She looked at me with sparking eyes."Watch me! "

Marching up on the stage,she put her arms straight out to her sides and began to twirl.Her red dress lifted up,revealing white tights that

来越耗时间，而且令人紧张。带着独特的兴趣，布瑞娜似乎接受了我忙碌不停的日程安排。我想等演出一结束，就把欠她的时间补回来。

在一次特别精彩的排练结束后我们回家的路上，我漫不经心地问道，"你爱妈妈吗？"她把头扭向我简单地答道，"不爱。"我大受伤害，一路开车再没有说过一句话。

开幕的那个晚上，我们的票已经全部预售一空。我们向提前买了票的观众表演。像只鸽子一般，我的耶稣把歌儿唱得清脆洪亮。耶稣钉上十字架的那一幕让全场观众落泪了。当最后一首歌响起时，人们纷纷站了起来，热烈地欢呼喝彩。

第二天晚上来的观众更多，我们不得不开辟出更多的露天座位。那些找不到座位的人肩挨肩地挤在后面。布瑞娜两个晚上都来了。第一晚，她坐在她爸爸的腿上——很乖但是烦躁不安。当人人赞扬我做了件了不起的工作时，她睡着了。

第二天晚上，她感到厌烦了。我把她安顿在一个角落里，让她静静地在那里玩。后来她过来拽我的胳膊。

"到外边去，"她小声地说。

我用目光寻找她的父亲，但没有找着。

"到外边去，"她小声地又说了一遍。

我低下了头。布瑞娜穿着带衬裙的红色长裙显得特别漂亮。从她的辫子里散落出来的碎卷发柔软地顺着脖子垂下。我不禁怜悯起她来。我不在场几分钟对我的演员们来说没有什么关系。

空气里有点凉意。我让她随意地拽着我走。我们停在了一家自助餐厅门外，那里有一个小小的梯形楼座。

布瑞娜推着我的腰。"坐，妈妈！"我坐下来。她看着我，眼睛闪闪发光。"看着我！"

她费劲地登上舞台，把双臂向身体两旁伸展开来，开始了旋转。她的红裙子飘了起来，露出了有点松的白色紧身裤。我忍不住身体

were bagging a little.I leaned forward and chuckled.She threw her head back and laughed gleefully as she spun.

Around and around she twirled like a plane out of control.I could hear the noise from the auditorium,but it began to subside as I focused on my daughter.

I remembered my countless hours at rehearsals.I remembered handing Breana off to others because I didn't have the time.

A rousing cheer came from the theater,but that was only background noise now.I was at the best performance—sitting under the stars, watching my three-year-old revel in her delight.   She spun.She skipped. She finally bowed.And straight-backed on a wooden bench,I sat alone and clapped and clapped.

Rayleen Downes

前倾咯咯发笑。她朝后甩甩头,也一边旋转一边高兴地大笑。

一圈儿又一圈儿,她像个失控的飞机一样地转着。我可以听到剧院观众席那边传来的声音。但是当我只专心致志地看着我女儿时,那声音渐渐地减弱了。

我记得排练中数不清的一个又一个小时。我记得因为我没有时间所以把布瑞娜转交给其他人照看。

剧院那边传来振奋人心的欢呼声,但是那些现在都只是背景声音了。我眼下在观看一场最棒的表演——坐在星光下,看着我3岁的女儿快乐地展示才艺。她转着,跳跃着。最后,她鞠躬谢幕。我直直地坐在一张木制长凳上,独自坐着,不停地鼓掌,鼓掌。

雷琳·道尼斯

To help employees feel more in touch with their children, the company day-care center incorporated a creative new design concept.

女性系列／聆听花开的声音

Running for Office, Running for Life

Keep away from people who try to belittle your ambitions. Small people always do that, but the really great make you feel that you, too, can become great.

Mark Twain

November 7, 2000: At the Holiday Inn in Bismarck, North Dakota, Heidi Heitkamp, the Democratic candidate for governor, charges to the podium, her trademark mane of red hair moussed into submission. Heitkamp, forty-five, is big, beautiful and lit up from the inside. The election results aren't all in, but she appears jubilant.

"Isn't this a wild ride?" she shouts to the cheering crowd. As she speaks, she pummels the air with her right fist—the one sign that something about this campaign is different.

The fist is grotesquely swollen, each finger is a sausage, with no break between wrist and forearm. It's the telltale sign of lymphedema, the fluid retention that may occur after losing lymph nodes. And it is the only evidence that six weeks earlier, Heitkamp had her right breast and eighteen cancerous nodes removed—the only hint that she is fighting not just for her career, but for her life.

All that summer Heitkamp, the state's popular attorney general, and Republican John Hoeven had been in statistical dead heat in the race for governor. Then Heitkamp saw her doctor about a lump under her arm. On September 15 she and her husband, family practitioner Darwin Lange, learned it was malignant.

竞选职位,抗争生命

远离那些试图小看你的雄心壮志的那些人。小人往往
那么做,但是真正的伟人却让你感到你也能够成为伟人。

马克·吐温

2000年11月7日:在北达科他州的俾斯麦市假日酒店里,海蒂·海特坎姆普,民主党竞选州长的候选人,兴致勃勃地来到了讲坛前。她长而密的红色头发用摩丝做得很柔顺,宛如她本人的标记一般。海特坎姆普,45岁,是个高个子,美丽动人,从里到外都容光焕发。虽然竞选结果还没有全部出来,但是她显得喜气洋洋。

"这难道不是疯狂的竞赛吗?"她对着欢呼的人群喊道。她一边说,一边伸出右拳向空中击打着——这是一个使这个竞选与众不同的标志。

这个拳头很奇特地鼓起,每根手指都像一支香肠,在手腕和前臂之间没有突然变粗的过渡。这是淋巴组织发生突变的迹象,即丧失淋巴结以后出现的体液潴留物。这也是6周以前,海特坎姆普通过手术摘除了右乳和18个癌变肿瘤的唯一迹象——唯一的表明她不仅是在为事业奋斗,也是在为生命抗争的唯一迹象。

整整一个夏天,海特坎姆普,全州广受民众爱戴的首席检察官和共和党候选人约翰·侯文的统计得票率一直很高。就在那时,海特坎姆普因为胳膊下的一个肿块去看医生。9月15日,她和她丈夫,家庭开业医生达尔文·兰奇得知这个肿块是恶性肿瘤。

95

Heitkamp didn't dwell on the negative. "I know this sounds corny, but when you come from a big family,you always worry about how something that happens to you will affect them,"says Heitkamp,who has six siblings and two children (ages fifteen and eleven)."I felt this would be rougher for them to hear than it was for me.My personality type is, okay,you get three minutes to feel sorry for yourself,then you start dealing with it.

CHICKEN SOUP

"Well,"Heitkamp adds with a laugh,"maybe I would give myself a few more minutes."

But Heitkamp had something else to contemplate:474,000 voters. She never considered keeping her cancer a secret."People have a right to know about the health of elected officials,"she says.But she wanted to wait—first,to find out the kind of cancer and second,to tell her family.

She didn't have that luxury:Someone leaked the news. Heitkamp gathered her family,who took it hard—"very hard",says her sister Holly. Then on September 20 at a press conference,she didn't hold back. "I mean,this is as much a surprise to me as it is to you guys,"she said,her eyes filling up.

About a week later,after Heitkamp's surgery,she learned the cancer was Stage ⅢA—it was advanced and had spread to her lymph nodes. Yes,she would need chemotherapy and radiation,but she could stick with the campaign.Besides,her family wouldn't let her do it otherwise.Her fifteen-year-old daughter,a swimmer,was direct. "Well,you're not going to get out now,are you?It's like quitting in the last leg of the 100 meter."

The press focused on her health.A candidate with breast cancer is news;one with advanced cancer—stop the presses!

North Dakota's Forum and *Tribune* ran stories putting the five-year survival rate for a Stage ⅢA at fifty-six percent. Although they quoted experts saying Heitkamp's prospects were better,word was out:The

海特坎姆普没有因为人们对她参加竞选的否定意见而止步不前。"我知道这消息听了让人伤心,但是当你来自一个大家庭,你总是会担心发生在自己身上的什么事情会影响到他们。"有6个同胞兄弟姐妹和两个孩子(一个15岁,一个11岁)的海特坎姆普说,"我感到他们听到这个消息会比我更难过。我这个人的性格是,哦,你有3分钟的时间为自己难过,然后你就要着手解决这件事情。"

"唉,"海特坎姆普接下来大笑一声,"也许我会多给自己几分钟。"

但是,海特坎姆普还有别的事儿要好好地考虑一下:474,000张选票。她从来没有想到过要对她患了癌症这事儿保密。"人们有权利了解被选举官员的健康状况,"她说。然而,她想要等一等——首先,查出所患的是哪一种癌症;其次,告知她的家人。

但她却没能享有那种奢侈:有人走漏了风声。海特坎姆普把全家召集起来,家里人很难接受——"非常难,"她姐姐豪丽说。后来在9月20日的一次记者招待会上,她没有隐瞒真情。"我的意思是说,我和你们一样感到这个消息令人震惊,"她说这话时双眼溢满了泪水。

一周后,大约在海特坎姆普做过外科手术之后,她得知自己患的是第三期A级癌症,并且它已经发展并扩散到了淋巴结。是的,她需要化学和放射疗法,但是她会坚持竞选。还有,她的家人也不会让她去做别的事。她15岁的女儿,一个游泳健将说得很直截了当。"好,你现在不准备出门了,是吗?那就像100米的速泳中你放弃最后一腿的动作吧。"

记者们瞄准了她的健康。一个患乳腺癌的候选人是条新闻;癌症在继续恶化的候选人——停止这些报道吧!

《北达科他州论坛》和《论坛报》刊登了56%的第三期A级癌症患者存活期是5年的一些报道。尽管他们都引用专家的话,说海特坎姆

woman who would be governor could have as little as a fifty-six percent chance of being alive a second term.

After reading what she took to be her death sentence,Heitkamp rushed to reassure her family."My daughter's at a swim meet—how can I control what she's listening to?And I'm worried about my mother."

Her mother's reaction surprised her."She said,'How are you?'—not all grim and serious,but like,'Hi!How the heck are ya?'And I said,'Not bad for someone who's halfdead! 'We couldn't stop laughing."

As it turned out,the outlook was not so grim."I've received some good news,"she told the public."Doctors expect me to make a full recovery."

At any point,Heitkamp could have shaken fewer hands,cuddled fewer babies,stopped those 200-mile treks between Bismarck and Fargo. After her first chemo treatment,she needed her white-blood-cell count checked.If low,it meant she was susceptible to infection.Retreating into a back room of a Fargo clinic to have blood drawn,she looked pale and forlorn.

But when the results came,Heitkamp waved the paper at a campaign worker."Look! "she said."A normal count is about 4.5 to 11;I'm 4.9.The doctor told us if the count went to one,I'd have to avoid crowds and take precautions.But my white blood cells are reading favorably. We're ready to fight the rest of the campaign! "

Fight, as it turned out, was the operative word. During a radio show,outgoing Republican Governor Ed Schafer described his initial eighteen-hour days,then added,"I hope Heidi isn't going to get herself in a situation where physically it would be to her detriment to continue on in this job."

Then things got weird.A Bismarck man contacted the Heitkamp campaign to tell this story:A man identifying himself as a pollster had asked whom he was voting for.When he said Heitkamp,the pollster

普的前景要更好一些,然而,有消息透露:将要当上州长的这个女人可能只有最多不超过56%的机会活到第二届任期。

在读了那些对她来说简直是死亡判决的报道之后,海特坎姆普赶忙安慰家人。"我女儿正在参加一个游泳比赛——我怎样才可能不让她听到这个消息呢?我也为我母亲担心。"

她母亲的反应倒是让她吃了一惊。"她说,'你好吗?'听起来一点也没有被吓倒,而且她尽是说这样一些让人不感到紧张的话,比如,'哎,你到底感觉如何?'我就对她说,'对一个半死的人来说还不坏!'接着,我们两个人就都忍不住哈哈大笑起来。"

后来发现,检查结果并非如此令人恐怖。"我收到了一些好消息,"她告诉公众,"医生期待我完全康复。"

从任何一方面来说,海特坎姆普都可以少跟人握手,少搂抱一些婴儿,停止在俾斯麦市和法戈市之间200英里的那些艰难跋涉。在她的第一次化疗之后,她需要进行血液中白细胞数量的检查。如果白细胞偏低了,就说明她有可能受到感染。在法戈的一家诊所偏僻的房间里抽血时,她看上去面色苍白,孤独而凄凉。

但当结果出来时,海特坎姆普向一个竞选工作者挥舞着化验单说,"看哪!正常的数量大约是4.5到11,我是4.9。医生告诉我们如果数量到1的话,我就得避免与公众再见面,并要采取一些预防措施了。但是我的白细胞的读数非常鼓舞人心。我们准备继续为剩下的竞选活动拼搏。"

结果,"拼搏"成了一个产生重大影响的词。在一个广播电台的节目里,即将离职的共和党州长爱德华·夏法描述了自己最初每天工作18个小时的日子,最后他加了一句,"我真希望海蒂不要让自己陷入这样的困境,继续进行这样的工作会对她的身体很不利。"

后来,事情就变得很诡异。俾斯麦市的一位男士联系海蒂竞选工作组,讲了这样一个故事:一个自称是民意调查者的男子询问他投谁的票。当他说海蒂时,这名男子紧接着又问他,"你知道她病得

pressed on, "You know she's very sick,right?"Then the pollster cited possible side effects of cancer treatment—"hair falling out,lack of strength and so forth"—and concluded, "And you're still going to support Heidi Heitkamp?"

Hoeven's campaign denied involvement.Still,said his campaign manager,Carol Olson,there was no way to control thousands of supporters.And by November,Hoeven was leading by three percentage points,according to a poll.Even more significant,Heitkamp had dropped among women.

Election night,11:00 P.M.Heitkamp can't ignore Hoeven's ten-point lead.Tearfully,the woman who would have been North Dakota's first female governor concedes,saying, "This is the proudest moment of my life."

Now spending time with her kids and volunteering,Heitkamp has a message for anyone who has a loved one with cancer:"I hope everyone gives her the ability to do her job and live her life.Because if the message is 'Go home,quit and if you can prove you're cancer-free, we'll let you back in the land of the living',well,you start to believe it yourself."

Pausing,Heitkamp beams. "Every day is a contest,"she says simply. "Gotta keep your eye on the prize."

Judith Newman

很厉害,对吧?"然后这名民意调查者列举了癌症治疗中可能出现的一些副作用——"掉头发,体力匮乏,等等,"——最后,他又问道,"你还要支持海特坎姆普吗?"

侯文的竞选工作组否认参与了此事。他的竞选总管卡罗·奥尔森说,尽管如此,他们还是无法控制成千上万的支持者。到了11月,根据一项民意调查,侯文领先了3个百分点。但此时更至关重要的是,海特坎姆普在女性选举者心目中的地位下降了。

选举那天晚上11:00,海特坎姆普已经不能再忽略侯文10个百分点的领先了。这个满脸泪水,本应成为北达科他州的第一位女州长的人退出了。她说,"这是我一生里最荣耀的时刻。"

海特坎姆普现在将时间花在与孩子们相处和一些志愿事情上。她给任何有亲人患了癌症的人传递这样的信息:"我希望每个人都能够给她力量做她自己的工作,以及让她过自己的生活。因为如果我们得到的信息是'回家去吧,别干了,等你能证明自己的癌症好了,我们就让你回到生活的空间来',那么,你自己就会开始相信它。"

停顿了一会儿,海特坎姆普又放出光彩。"每一天都是一场竞争,"她简短地说,"我们应该用眼睛盯着奖品。"

朱迪思·纽曼

注释:
　　海特坎姆普(1955年10月30日—),美国北达科他州律师和政治家。1980—1981年在州环保局工作;1981—1986年在州税务专员办公室工作;1986—1992年任州税务专员;1993—2000年任州律政司检察总长;2003年至今,任州气化公司董事。

女性系列／聆听花开的声音

Pennies and Prayers

The three of us were gathered around our breakfast table.It was 7：00 A.M.on a Monday.

Our three-year-old son was perched on his booster chair,wearing cowboy pajamas,bunny-rabbit slippers and a corduroy robe.He looked up at us intently through oversized,sparkling blue eyes with long,fluttering lashes.Chewing his Cheerios,he started asking his usual questions.

"Is today a go-to-work day?"

"Yes,sweetheart,it is."

"Can I go,too?"

"No,honey,"

"Does Daddy have to go to work?"

"Yes,he does."

"Why does Daddy have to go to work?"

"Daddy has to go to work to make money.We need money to live in this apartment and buy food and milk and juice and cereal at the grocery store.We need money to buy other things,like our TV,these dishes and hamburgers and ice cream at McDonald's.We need money for all that.If Daddy doesn't go to work,we won't have any money."

This Monday morning was going to be very different from all the others,though.Today,I was going to have to leave for work,too.My husband,Alex,had just changed careers,and his compensation was now based solely on the promise of future commissions.We decided that I would begin working outside the home to help supplement our income until he got established.New questions from our son were sure to follow.

"But why do you have to go to work,Mommy?"

小钱币大心愿

我们3人围坐在早餐桌旁。那是一个星期一早晨7点。

我们3岁大的儿子坐在他的可升降的椅子里，身穿牛仔面料的宽松裤和灯芯绒的罩衣，脚上是兔宝宝拖鞋。他那双超大的、一闪一闪的眼睛专心致志地看着我们，长长的睫毛快速地移动着。他一边嚼着他的谷物小食品，一边开始问他常问的问题。

"今天是要上班吗？"

"是的，宝贝，要上班。"

"我也能去吗？"

"不能，亲爱的。"

"爸爸要上班吗？"

"是的，要上。"

"为什么爸爸要上班呢？"

"爸爸得上班挣钱。我们需要有钱才能住在这套房子里，才能在杂货店里买食品、牛奶、果汁和麦片。我们需要钱买别的东西，比如我们的电视机，这些盘子，麦当劳的汉堡包和冰淇淋。我们需要钱买所有的东西。如果爸爸不去工作，我们就什么钱也没有了。"

不过，这个星期一早晨与往日大不相同。今天，我也要离家去工作了。我的丈夫阿列克斯刚刚换了工作，他现在的赔偿金只能指望他以后的工作了。我们俩已经决定我开始出去工作以便增加我们的收入，一直到他发展稳定为止。我们的儿子对此肯定会问新的问题。

"但是为什么你要去工作，妈妈？"

"Well,Vince,Mommy is going to work because we need ... just a little extra money."

All of sudden,those big blue eyes of his lit up—as if finally he actually understood what we were trying to tell him.He jumped from his chair and took off running down the hall for his bedroom.We heard him open a drawer of his dresser,and then a clinking sound filled the air.The chink-chink-chink noise kept getting louder.It matched the cadence of running feet.Vince appeared,clutching his piggy bank to his chest.

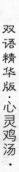

Each time that grandmas,grandpas,aunts and uncles or friends came over,they gave Vince money.He gripped every coin with his elfin fingers and carefully positioned each one to drop through the narrow slot.One at a time,they clinked into the top of his chubby,yellow,plastic pig.We thought this was a valuable tool to teach our son the concept of saving money.We explained to him that after there were many coins inside,it could be used for something very special.He counted the contents often and always referred to it as "my money".

He proudly raised his plump little piggy toward us.Still panting, with excitement in his voice and a big smile on his face,he said, "I'll give you all my money so you can stay home and we can all be together."

We couldn't speak.The lumps in our throats brought tears to our eyes.A sharp,cruel,arrow of guilt penetrated deep into my spirit.Could it ever be successfully removed?It felt like my heart had been wounded beyond repair.Could I ever forget the words my child just spoke?Would that look of anticipation in his eyes ever leave the camera of my mind? Had we made a mistake?Was the decision we made a bad one?Our desire was only to do what we thought best for our family.

That incident took place thirty-two years ago.In the years between then and now,we have learned how to seek God's guidance in our decisions and our finances.If at times,we felt we had made a mistake,we

双语精华版·心灵鸡汤·

"哎,温斯,妈妈去工作是因为我们需要……再多一点点钱。"

忽然之间,他那两只大大的蓝眼睛熠熠闪光——仿佛他终于真正明白了我们想告诉他什么。他从椅子里跳了起来,飞快地跑过客厅,奔进他自己的卧室。我们听到他打开了衣柜的一个抽屉,然后空中就充满了叮叮当当的响声。叮当声越来越大,伴随着跑动的脚步节奏。温斯出现在我们眼前,紧紧地把他的猪型储蓄罐抱在胸前。

奶奶爷爷,姥姥姥爷,姑姑叔叔或者朋友们来我们家时,他们每次都给温斯钱。他用他那小巧的手指捏起每一个硬币,小心翼翼地把它们都塞进储蓄罐上那一道窄窄的缝隙。一次塞一个,硬币叮叮当当地掉进他那只圆滚滚的黄色塑料猪里。我们认为这是教会儿子节约用钱的一个很有价值的方法。我们以前向他解释过,等里面有很多硬币后,就可以用来买一个特别的东西。他经常清点里面的硬币,总是把这叫做"我的钱"。

他自豪地朝我们举起他的小胖猪。他还在气喘吁吁,童音里充满了兴奋,脸上是开心的微笑,他说道,"我把所有的钱都给你们,这样你们就能留在家里,我们就能在一起了。"

我们俩都说不出话来。嗓子里的硬块让我们的眼睛里充满了泪水。一支锐利无情的负罪之箭深深地刺入我的心灵。这种负罪感还能成功地被清除掉吗?我的心仿佛被刺伤得无以修复。我还能忘记孩子刚刚说过的话吗?他眼睛里那种期望的眼神还能够离开我心灵的摄影机吗?我们犯了一个错误吗?我们做的决定不明智吗?我们的愿望只是要做对我们的家庭最合适的事情。

这件事发生在32年以前。从那时到现在的岁月里,我们已经学会了如何在我们的决定和家庭收入之间追寻上帝的指引。如果偶尔

entrusted the outcome to God in faith.

That blue-eyed boy now flies 757 and 767 jet aircraft all over the world for a major airline.His profession has located him in a different state from where we live.Just recently we enjoyed a memorable seven-day visit at our son's home.A major topic of conversation during our stay was the possibility of our buying a condo as a second home in the area where he lives.

The three of us were sitting around his breakfast table. Sipping his coffee,Vince looked up at us with his sparkling eyes and said,"Listen Mom and Dad,don't worry about the money part of it.I've saved a lot over the years and I can pay your taxes and fees and whatever expenses you need help with.Just do it and we can all be together in the same place."

Some things never change.We have contacted a real estate agent and will fly back to look at property.Piggy banks are profitable partners. God's protective,loving hand can help overcome obstacles and mend a mother's heart until it is filled with overflowing gratitude,not guilt.

Peggy L. Bert

我们感到犯了错,我们就忠诚地把结果交给上帝裁决。

那个蓝眼睛的小男孩现在已经在一家大航空公司驾驶着757和767喷气式飞机穿梭于世界各地。他的职业使他的居住地与我们的居住地不在同的一个州里。最近,我们刚刚在儿子家享受了一次难忘的7天短期做客。在那儿逗留的7天里,我们谈话的一个重要主题就是我们可否在他居住的地区买一套住房。

我们3个人围坐在他的早餐桌旁。他一边小口地喝着咖啡,一边抬起头用他亮闪闪的双眼看着我们说,"听着,妈妈爸爸,别担心钱的事。这些年来我已经存了很多钱,我可以给你们付税和各项费用,以及你们需要帮助的任何开支。尽管去买吧,这样我们就可以住在同一个地方了。"

有些东西是永远不会改变的。我们已经联系了一个房地产代理商,就要飞回去查看房子的所有权了。小猪储蓄罐是孩子成长中非常有益的伙伴,上帝庇护众生的博爱之手能够帮助我们克服障碍,修补一颗母亲的心,直到它充满了孩子的感激之情而不是父母的内疚。

佩吉·L.伯特

What Do You Want to Do with the Rest of Your Life?

So many of our dreams at first seem impossible,then they seem improbable,and then,when we summon the will, they soon become inevitable.

Christopher Reeve

I will never forget my college guidance counselor,Cathy Martin.I met her when I transferred to Northwestern University as a sophomore.

Cathy invited me into her office and asked, "What do you want to do?"

I thought I was ready to respond boldly to the question.Proudly I announced, "I want to be in broadcasting."

Cathy seemed unimpressed by my declaration.She asked, "What, specifically,do you want to do in broadcasting?"

"I'll do anything."

"So will a lot of other people,"she said sharply. "Broadcasting is a very competitive field.You need to know exactly what you want to do in order to succeed.You need to decide right here and now what it is you want to do."

I looked Cathy squarely in the eyes and stated with conviction, "I want to be a television news anchor and reporter."

She smiled. "Good! Now you know what you want to do.   When you leave here,you tell everyone who you know what you want to do with your life—that you want to be a TV anchor and reporter.And on

双语精华版·心灵鸡汤·

接下来的人生你怎样安排？

> 很多梦想一开始似乎完全没有可能，后来他们变成了不太可能，再后来，当我们坚定意志的时候，梦想就变成了在所难免的事。

克里斯托弗·里夫

我永远不会忘记我大学时代的指导顾问，凯茜·马丁。认识她是在我转到西北大学读大二的时候。

凯茜请我到她的办公室，问我："你想做什么？"

我认为我是有备而来，可以很有底气地回答这个问题，于是骄傲地答道："我想从事播音工作。"

可是对于我的豪言壮语，凯茜的反应似乎很冷淡。她问我："具体地说，在播音行当里你想做什么？"

"做什么都行。"

"那你不比别人高明，"她犀利地说。"播音是一个竞争性很强的领域。要想取得成功，你必须明确地知道自己的目标。此时此地，你就要决定好要做的是什么。"

我直视着凯茜的眼睛，斩钉截铁地说："我想成为电视新闻的主持人、记者。"

她露出笑容。"不错！现在你知道自己要做什么了。你离开这儿以后，告诉所有你认识的人，你的人生想这样安排——你想成为电

109

those days when you're feeling uncertain,you share that uncertainty with your family,with your friends,with me.But as to the rest of the world, you address them with certainty in all that you do."

I walked out of Cathy Martin's office.I had direction.I had a mission—to become a broadcast journalist extraordinaire.In December 1973, I graduated half a year early,to get a jump on the June graduates.Within several months,after countless rejections,I got that first job as a TV reporter.In fact,I was almost the first,as well as the youngest,female co-anchor in the United States at the time.I went on to become a coast-to-coast TV news reporter,anchor and talk show host.

When it came time for me to move on in my career,I thought back to how Cathy Martin motivated me to set a goal,to become all that I can be,to achieve my dream.I decided to take my broadcasting background and become a trainer and motivational speaker,sharing my secrets on how to make better presentations and enhance one's image,thus helping people to get the results they want by winning every audience.In essence,I became a coach.Once again,Cathy Martin's wisdom allowed me to achieve what I wanted to do.It all happened to me! Pushing through our fears and self-doubt can be a prolonged process or a simple decision.Cathy Martin taught me to decide—and to go for it.

Not long ago,a woman named Carol came to see me,seeking advice about the direction of her career.As I searched my mind for what would be most helpful to her at this important time in her life,Cathy Martin's words came flooding back.

"What do you want to do?"I asked her.Carol was ready to respond to the question.Proudly she told me,"I want to give talks to groups."

Acting unimpressed by her declaration,I asked,"What,specifically,do you want to speak about?"

"I'll speak on most anything uplifting."

"So will a lot of other people,"I said sharply."Speaking is a very

双语精华版·心灵鸡汤·

视节目主持人和记者。当你的想法游移不定的时候,把疑惑告诉你的家人,你的朋友,还有我。但是对于除此之外其他的人,无论你做什么,同他们说话的时候你都要信心十足。"

我走出凯茜·马丁的办公室。我有了方向,有了使命——要成为一个功夫过硬的播音记者。1973年12月,我大学毕业。为了比次年6月份毕业的同届学生多些优势,我的毕业提前了半年。几个月后,在经历无数次失败的应聘之后,我终于得到了第一份电视记者的工作。在当时的美国,我几乎是首位和男播音员一起主持节目的女播音员,也是最年轻的一个。后来我又陆续成了全国新闻记者、主持人和脱口秀节目主持人。

等我筹划让事业再上一个台阶的时候,我又想起凯茜·马丁,想起了她当年怎样促进我制定目标,发挥潜能,以及实现梦想的。我决心利用我的播音背景,转行当教练员和演讲动员家,公开成功演讲以及提升个人形象方面的秘诀,从而帮助人们征服听众,实现理想。我果然当了教练员。凯茜·马丁的智慧再次让我获得了想要的东西。它在我身上一一应验了!抛开所有的恐惧、不自信,你也许需要一个漫长的过程,也许只需要做一个简单的决定。凯茜·马丁教会我的是确定目标——然后朝着目标去努力。

不久前,一位叫卡罗尔的女子来见我,希望我能给她一些建议,帮助她明确事业的发展方向。在她人生中如此重要的时刻,怎样做才能对她最有帮助?我绞尽脑汁地思考这个问题的时候,凯茜·马丁的话在我的耳畔响起。

"你想做什么?"我问。卡罗尔有备而来。她骄傲地回答:"我想做面向大众的演说。"

听了她的豪言壮语,我故意表现得很冷淡,问道:"具体地说,你想演讲什么主题?"

"大半能够激励人的主题都可以。"

"那你不比别人高明,"我犀利地说。"演讲是个竞争性很强的领

competitive field.You need to know exactly what you want to speak about in order to succeed.You need to decide right here and now what it is you want to do."

Carol looked squarely in my eyes and stated with conviction, "I want to validate people's pain and make them feel better.I want people to love themselves and go for their dreams.I want to be a professional speaker giving talks on self-esteem."

I smiled."Good,"I said."Now you know what you want to do.When you leave here,you tell everyone who you know what you want to do with your life—that you want to be a professional speaker who gives talks on self-esteem.And on those days when you're feeling uncertain, you share that uncertainty with your family,with your friends,with me. But as to the rest of the world,you address them with certainty in all that you do."

Carol left our meeting full of determination and confidence.Four years later,I learned she had become a sought-after professional speaker on self-esteem.

I can't help but wonder when she will pass on the invaluable advice my guidance counselor so generously shared with me so many years ago.

Linda Blackman,C.S.P.

域。要想成功，你必须清楚地知道你想选择什么主题。此时此地，你就要决定好你想做的是什么。"

卡罗尔直视我的眼睛，斩钉截铁地说："我希望证明人们是痛苦的，希望减轻他们的痛苦。我希望人们能够爱自己，为自己的梦想奋斗。我想成为职业演说家，我选择自尊作为主题。"

我微笑着说："好，现在你知道自己想要做什么了。你离开这儿以后，告诉所有你认识的人，你的人生想这样安排——你想成为专业演说家，演讲的主题是自尊。当你的想法游移不定的时候，把疑惑告诉你的家人，你的朋友，还有我。但是对于除此之外其他的人，无论你做什么，同他们说话的时候你都要信心十足。"

会见结束。卡罗尔离开的时候，充满干劲，信心十足。4年之后，我得知她已经成了一位吃香的职业演讲家，她的演讲主题是自尊。

我禁不住想：多少年前，我的指导顾问毫无保留地与我分享了这条宝贵的建议，不知道多久之后，卡罗尔会把这条建议传授给别人。

琳达·布莱克曼

One Hour a Week

What we love to do we find time to do.

John L.Spalding

William waits for me in front of Room 210,hands holding something behind his back,head tilted away as I approach. "I don't feel like reading today,"he announces,avoiding eye contact.He is almost ten, handsome and polite,with dark brown eyes as big as pennies.And he's on to me.As the year has passed,he's figured out that I'm a pushover.

"How about one book?"I suggest, "In our favorite spot?Then we can play your game."Negotiations complete,he pulls the board game front and center,and we walk down five steps to a white window seat to begin reading *Frog and Toad Together.* Suddenly,he stops.

"Too many pages.I can't read that many pages."

"How about if you read one,then I read one.I'll start."

"No,"says William. "I'll start."

And so it goes.Once a week for one hour,going on three years, William and I meet with the assigned task of improving his literacy. Mostly we goof around.On his high-energy days,we whip through Easy Readers.I celebrate every new word he masters with a cheerleader-like frenzy. "Wonderful! Great! You are a reader,William! "He fires back with enthusiasm of his own: "How many books can we read today?Ten? Twelve?Let's read eighteen! "

Sometimes we just play games—Trouble or Mancala.He plays to win,and does.Sometimes,we sneak into the school cafeteria,scouring it

每周一小时

喜欢做的事情,找时间去做。

约翰·L.斯波尔丁

威廉在210房间外面等我。我朝着他走过去的时候,他双手放在背后,好像藏着什么东西,侧着头。"我今天不想读书,"他说着,不敢看我的眼睛。他快10岁了,相貌英俊,彬彬有礼,棕黑色的眼睛大得像硬币。他太了解我了。经过这一年的相处,他已经看出我是个好说话的人。

"就读一本怎么样?"我建议道,"到我们最喜欢的地方去读?读完了,就玩你爱玩的游戏。"谈判结束,他把棋盘拿到身体前面来。我们一起往下走了5个台阶,坐在窗边的白色座位上,拿出《青蛙与蟾蜍——好伙伴》读了起来。突然,他停住了。

"页数太多了。我读不了这么多。"

"那你读一页,我再读一页,怎么样?我先来。"

"不,"威廉说,"我先开始。"

于是,他读一页我读一页。3年来,每周一小时,我和威廉一起努力,帮他完成提高识字能力的任务。大多数时间我们进度很慢。碰到他状态好的时候,简易读物不在话下。他每多掌握一个词汇,我都会像拉拉队长一样,欣喜若狂地报之以赞美。"太棒了!好极了!你能阅读了,威廉!"他也会激动地跟着喊:"我们今天能读多少本书?10本?20本?我们读18本吧!"

有时候,我们只是做做游戏——玩Trouble或者是Mancala游戏。他玩的目的就是赢我,他也确实能赢。有时候,我们溜到学校餐厅,

for a Popsicle or a bag of salty chips.Other days are a chore.He's distracted,annoyed even,watching his buddies swat each other's heads as they march down the hall to the Media Center while he's stuck with me. "William," I tease,"where are you?"On those days,I feel defeated.But I'm never sorry I came.

Once William came to school with a family crisis embedded in his face.As we sat together on the white bench,he shed his bravado and tucked wet eyes into my shoulder and I would have held him there forever.But he is,after all,nine years old.The storm passed quickly.He sat up,wiped his eyes and asked,"Can we play Trouble?"

A teacher I know stopped me in the hall one day to ask if I would be returning the following year."Of course,"I told her. "Well,good,"she said. "William needs you."I wanted to correct her:Actually,I need William.

I am forty-three years old,with a full-time job I like and three neat kids who,so far,still like me.But sometimes I catch myself letting work problems distract me from them at home,when I open the mail instead of focusing on a detail of their day,or rush through their bedtime rituals so I can crawl into bed with a book.

Sixteen years into marriage,I'm a decent spouse.But the most romantic getaway we have these days is to the wholesale club to buy in bulk.At work,where I manage nine creative people,most days go well. But last week I missed a deadline and screwed up an administrative detail and got some facts wrong in a meeting and wondered why they ever hired me.

I have friends I adore who complete my world.But we can never seem to find time for lunch anymore,and one is battling depression and my words,meant to comfort,come out trite and patronizing. "Hang in there,"I tell her."It will get better."Dear God.

My world is safe and solid and good,except when the wheels come

为的是买根冰棍或者弄一包咸薯条吃。其余的就是些恼人的日子了。看到一群孩子相互拍打着头,穿过大厅,去多媒体中心,他还得和我待在一起,威廉就会变得心不在焉,甚至有点气急败坏。"威廉,"我逗他玩,"你在哪儿呢?"每逢这样的日子,我觉得自己很失败。但是我从不后悔到这儿来。

有一次,威廉来上学的时候,我看到家庭危机明明白白地写在他的脸上。我们一起坐在那白色的座位上的时候,他不再假装坚强,满眼泪水,伏在我肩头哭泣。我很愿意坐在那儿,永远地搂住他。不过,他毕竟已经9岁了。暴风雨很快过去了。他坐直了,擦干眼泪,接着问我:"我们玩Trouble游戏好吗?"

一位我认识的教师有一天在大厅里拦住我,问我,第2年还来不来。"肯定来。"我告诉她。"那就好,"她说,"威廉需要你。"我想纠正她的说法:实际上,是我需要威廉。

我已经43岁了,有一份我喜爱的全职工作,有3个至今爱我的好孩子。可是,有时候,我发现工作问题会把我的注意力从家里、从他们身上带走。那时,我会去看邮件,而不是去留意他们当天生活的某个细节,或者会急急忙忙安置他们上床睡觉,给自己留出空闲,爬到床上看点书。

结婚16年了,我是个体面的配偶。但是,这些年,对我们来说,最浪漫的休闲就是到批发俱乐部去大量购物。在单位,我管理9位有创意的手下,大多数日子里,工作上不会出什么差错。可是就在上个星期,我的工作没有遵守最后期限,我弄错了一个管理细节,还在开会的时候讲错了一些事实。我不明白单位怎么会聘用我。

我还有一些我珍爱的朋友,他们使我的世界变得完整。可是我们似乎连共进午餐的时间都再也找不着。其中有一位朋友正在经受着抑郁症的煎熬。我本想说一些安慰的话,结果说出来的却是:"挺住,事情会好起来的。"这话没有新意不说,反倒还有点摆臭架子的味道。天哪。

我的世界总体上是安全、稳固和美好的。只是一些意外事件发

女性系列／聆听花开的声音

off unexpectedly and I feel as though I will drown in self-doubt.When I say something stupid,or feel envy,or bark at my kids because I'm tired, or forget to call my mother,or call my mother and feel ten years old again,or go to work with graham crackers ground into my shoulder and my sweater buttoned wrong.

But I have one hour.

One hour a week when I have no self-doubt.When I walk down a noisy elementary school hallway covered with children's art and my respite awaits me.

"When will you come back?"William asks.

"Next Wednesday,silly.I always come on Wednesday."

"I wish you could come on Mondays instead,"he says. "Then I wouldn't have to wait so long for you."

One hour a week I am granted the greatest reward possible：The comfort of knowing that I am absolutely in the right place,doing the right thing.

My life will catch up to me soon enough.But for the moment,it will just have to wait.

Gail Rosenblum

生的时候，我会觉得不自信要把我淹没。比如，我说了些蠢话，妒忌别人，累了的时候冲着孩子们吼，忘记给母亲打电话，或者打了电话觉得自己又变成了10岁的孩子，或者去上班的时候，发现肩膀上还挂着葛拉翰饼干的碎屑，毛衣的扣子扣错了位置，等等。

可是我有一小时。

每周有一次这样的一小时，我可以甩开不自信。在那所喧闹的小学里，穿过那条满眼都是学生绘画作品的走廊，我的心灵就得到了释放。

"你什么时候再来？"威廉问我。

"下个星期三，小傻瓜。我都是周三来。"

"我希望你改到周一来，"他说，"这样我就不用等那么久了。"

每周这样的一小时里，我得到了世界上最大的回报：即自信在正确的地方做着正确的事情时体会到的宽慰。

我的生活会有所改进，需要的时间不会太久，但是此时，能做的事就是等待。

盖尔·罗森布洛姆

To Return Tomorrow

We deceive ourselves when we fancy that only weakness needs support.Strength needs it far more.

Madame Swetchine

The phone rang on a dateless Friday night.John's family requested a visit from the hospice nurse.They said he wasn't able to make it to the bathroom,his weakness had increased.I assured them I would visit in about forty-five minutes,the time I needed to drive to their home.I was not John's primary nurse,but I had made a few visits.This sounded pretty routine.They needed support and an assessment.I would be home in a couple of hours.

John was in the room they had made for him on the first floor next to the kitchen.It was the hub of activity because he could see everywhere yet had privacy in his recliner,his bed for several months now.John was thirty-two years old in the final stages of testicular cancer.

"Hello,John,"I greeted,making a visual assessment.I listened to his mother,and then proceeded toward the blue recliner with the footrest up. Gently I took his cool hand in mine.Dull eyes and a different lusterless voice greeted me back.Ashen skin with a fine transparency sat me down quickly to take vital signs.They concurred.John was near death,just as my years of experience told me when I entered the room.

Standing directly behind me was John's mother. "What is wrong, Susie?"

召唤明天

认为我们只有虚弱时才需要帮助，那是自欺欺人，坚强更需要支持。

斯维琴夫人

一个没有约会的周五的晚上，我的电话铃响了。约翰家要请一位临终关怀护士。他们说约翰已经不能走到卫生间去了。他的身体越来越弱。我向他们保证我会在45分钟以后赶到，因为开车到他们家需要那么长的时间。我不是约翰的责任护士，但是我去看过他几次。一切与往常相比没什么太大的不同。他们需要支持和病情诊断，而我待上几个小时后就回家。

他们把约翰安排在一楼厨房旁边的一个房间里。那儿是个枢纽位置，既可以看到全家的活动，又可以保持隐私。一张躺椅是约翰现在的床。他在那儿躺了几个月了。现年32岁的约翰，是肠癌晚期患者。

"你好，约翰。"我和他打招呼，通过肉眼观察来判断他的病情。听过他母亲的介绍之后，我走到蓝色的躺椅边。他的脚凳支得高高的。我把他的手放到我的手上。他手很凉，双眼无神，嗓音不再润泽，但是依然回应了我的问候。他皮肤发灰，有一点透明。看到这儿我赶快坐下来，检查一些重要的征兆。这些征兆都对上号了。约翰是快要死了。其实凭借多年的经验，我进屋时就看出来了。

约翰的母亲就站在我后面。"是怎么回事，苏西？"

John was drifting,and I took her to the next room.Making eye contact,I said,"He is dying."

"You are wrong! He is not! "She screamed,then pivoted and leaped onto the day bed next to his chair.Leaning to his ear she said,"John,you can't leave me.I need you,John.Don't leave me."Tears streamed down her face as she stroked his head,"John."

I watched as John came back from the shadow of death's door unable to even lift his hand to hers.Their eyes met and he started in a garbled voice to recite Robert Frost's poem—"Whose woods these are…"

With each word he had a little bit more clarity as his spirit rose to the moment.When he completed the poem he looked into her eyes and told her it was time to leave,he was tired."Mom,I love you,and I know we will meet again.I have fought very hard,but it is time for me to go. You will be okay."

"But I will miss our time together reciting poetry and scripture. John…"

"Mom,I love you."He drifted and never spoke again,although death didn't come for two more hours.Tears cascaded over both our cheeks. This was a moment I had never experienced in my long hospice career.

John's mother and I were the only ones to experience this resurrection of spirit to help a loved one come to grips with the final departure of her son.

Three days later a memorial service was held in an old huge Presbyterian church close to the hospice office.The wooden pews were full from front to back with mourners.I sat alone.It was normal to attend funeral services,but this was unequaled.John's brother stood at the pulpit and read the entire poem *Stopping by Woods on a Snowy Evening"* by Frost.

The tears that could not be repressed wet my clothes and embarrassed me.I was sobbing and I was the hospice nurse. Finally the service was over,

约翰在弥留之际。我带她来到隔壁的房间，望着她的眼睛说："他不行了。"

"你弄错了！他不会的！"她大声喊着，转身就跑，蹦上放在约翰躺椅边上的沙发床。她伏在约翰的耳边说："约翰，你不能离开我。我需要你，约翰。不要撇下我。"她的眼泪哗哗地流淌下来。摸着约翰的头，她喊着："约翰。"

我观察着约翰从死亡的阴影里又转了回来。他向她抬手，可是手举不起来。他们的视线相交了，约翰用模糊的声音背起了罗伯特·弗罗斯特的诗——"我知道林子的主人是谁……"

他念得兴奋起来，一个字比一个字念得清楚。念完后，他看着她的眼睛，告诉她他该走了，他很累。"妈妈，我爱你，我知道我们会再见面的。我已经尽了努力，可是是时候了，我该走了。你会没事的。"

"可是我会怀念我们一起背诵诗歌和经文的时候。约翰……"

"妈妈，我爱你。"他又开始迷糊，从此，再也没有开口，死神降临是在两个多小时以后。我们的眼泪像小河一样哗哗直淌。我在临终关怀医院工作了这么久，这还是头一回。

约翰回光返照，帮助他深爱的人战胜别离的苦痛。见证这个场景的只有约翰的母亲和我。

3天后，在临终关怀医院办公地点附近的一个巨大的古老的长老会教堂里举行了一个追悼仪式。从前到后的木椅上全都坐满了前来哀悼的人。我独坐在一个椅子上。参加葬礼是寻常的事情，不过这不是寻常的葬礼。约翰的兄弟站在讲坛上，完整地诵读了弗罗斯特的《雪夜林边小驻》。

止不住的眼泪打湿了衣襟，让我难堪。我在抽泣，而我却是临终关怀医院的护士。终于葬礼结束了，我回到办公室，坐到我的上司卡

and I returned to the office and sat in front of my boss,Carole.

"I am done in this career,Carole.I can't do it any more. There are no more tears.Today I cried for John,the experience I shared with John and his family,and all the other patients and families.I couldn't stop the tears."

Carole came around her desk and took my hands in hers."You are grieving for many today.I think you will be okay but today you need to take care of yourself.Take the rest of the day off."

She gave me a solid hug and sent me home.I left the hospice office questioning if I could ever return to my present position.I found Carole's warmth and wisdom my healing salve. Rarely do employers see your needs and try so desperately to meet them.

Hospice has support groups for their staff,but it was giving me the time to heal that mattered most.In a few years I became a hospice director.This hospice experience was shared many times in telling the public what a difference hospice can make.John had given me a memory,and Carole had given me her wisdom.

Susan Burkholder

罗尔的跟前。

"卡罗尔,这份职业我干不了,我做不下去。我不能再哭下去了。今天我为约翰流了眼泪,为我与他的家人共同的经历流了眼泪,也是为其他所有病人和家庭的经历。我忍不住要哭啊。"

卡罗尔绕过办公桌,抓住我的手。"你今天是在为很多人的命运伤心。我想你会恢复的,但是今天,你要照顾好的是自己。今天的工作放一放吧。"

她给了我一个紧紧的拥抱,然后把我送回了家。我离开了临终关怀医院的办公室,问自己是否可以回到现在的岗位。我发现卡罗尔的热情与智慧是一剂愈合伤口的良药。很少有老板考虑员工的需要并且如此努力去满足员工需要的。

临终关怀医院有员工互助小组,但是最重要的是给我时间,让我自己恢复。几年之后,我成了医院的主任。我在告诉人们临终关怀医院的重要作用时,和人们多次分享过这段经历。约翰给了我回忆,而卡罗尔给了我智慧。

苏珊·伯克侯德尔

Princess of the City

It had been a long day and the call that had just come in to our visiting nurse agency—a report on two abandoned children—would make it even longer.I had looked forward to getting off on time for once,but now that was out of the question.I hurried out into the darkening winter afternoon.It was bitterly cold.All day news reports had predicted snow.

When I arrived at the address,an apartment in a decaying tenement, I found two little girls huddled together to keep warm.A cold wind was blowing in through a window that was stuck open. As I struggled to close it,the shivering children clung to me.They looked about three and four years old.Both had dark curly hair and huge brown eyes that now were filled with tears.They were shabbily dressed in stained,ill-fitting jumpers.I wondered when they had last eaten a decent meal.When I checked the refrigerator,it was empty except for a half-empty can of beer.On the kitchen floor lay a dead mouse.Even a rodent couldn't survive in this place,I thought.

Carefully I checked the children for bruises or any sign of injury. They were hungry and frightened,but unharmed,at least physically.I tried to console them as they cried pitifully for their mother.

"Where's Mommy?"they kept crying.Hurriedly I got them dressed and into some old jackets I had found in a jumbled heap at the bottom of a closet.They were a pathetic sight indeed,with their tear-stained faces,tangled hair and ragged clothing.

By the time I got the girls fed and placed in an emergency foster home,the lights were going on all over the city.The snow was starting to

城市公主

　　这一天很漫长,刚刚打进探访护士处的电话使漫长的一天更加漫长了(有人打电话报告有两个儿童遭到遗弃)。我原本还盼望着今天能够破天荒地准时下班,现在看来是根本无望了。我急忙冲出去。这是一个晦暗的冬天的下午,寒气逼人。全天的新闻都预报说有雪。

　　我的目的地是破烂的廉价公寓楼里的一套住房。到了那儿,我发现有两个小姑娘挤在一起,相互取暖。窗户支开着,冷风往里灌。我费力地想把窗子关起来,这时,两个瑟瑟发抖的孩子紧紧地抱住我。她们看上去大约三四岁,都长着黑色的卷发,棕色的大眼睛里噙着泪水,衣衫褴褛,套头衫脏兮兮的,且不合身。不知道她们最后一次好好吃一顿是在什么时候了。我打开冰箱看看,里面空空如也,只剩下半罐子啤酒。厨房的地面上有一只死老鼠。这儿可是个老鼠都养不活的地方,我暗自想。

　　我仔仔细细地检查了孩子的身体,看看有没有青紫的地方,或者其他受伤的痕迹。她们虽然饥肠辘辘,又受了惊吓,可是都没有受伤,至少肉体上没有受到伤害。她们伤心地哭着要妈妈,我尽力地安慰她们。

　　"妈妈在哪儿啊?"她们一个劲儿地哭。我从一个衣橱的底下一堆乱衣服中翻出几件旧夹克,匆忙给她们穿上。小姑娘被泪水弄脏的小脸,缠结的头发,破烂的衣服,看着直叫你心疼。

　　等我让小姑娘们吃饱,在一个紧急寄养家庭里安顿好,城市里

fall,and a harsh wind had risen.I hurried along the deserted streets feeling exhausted as I headed for home.

My apartment,hardly lavish,seemed like Shangri La after the grim tenement that was home to the little girls.Too tired to read or even watch TV,I thought about my job and how tiring and frustrating it was. Our office was always short-staffed;it was hard to get people to work among the poor in the inner-city.All day long,I walked the forbidding streets of blighted neighborhoods,then climbed dark staircases or braved ancient creaking elevators to visit my patients.Often the family problems seemed overwhelming—teenage pregnancies,drug addiction and chronic illnesses.All the problems were made worse by poverty.

As I sat alone in my apartment,I was haunted by the thought of the two children I had found today.What could the future hold for them?I felt overcome by sadness.I found myself thinking with envy of several of my friends who were married to successful businessmen and spent their days shopping,or amused themselves playing golf and tennis.At last I went to bed,only to toss and turn,troubled by dreams of crying children.

When I returned to work the next day,my assignment was even heavier than usual.How would I ever manage to see all the patients on my list?I took a deep breath to organize my thoughts. First,I had to visit the foster home where I had placed the children the night before.I worried that they would still be traumatized,unable to recover.I felt overwhelmed as I climbed the long flight of stairs to the foster mother's apartment.

But my weariness vanished when I saw the girls.Comfortably settled in the back bedroom of the cheerfully furnished apartment,they were playing "dress up"in the foster mother's old clothes.The four-year-old was resplendent in a flowing faded satin bathrobe she'd adorned with dime store jewelry.But her crowning glory was a blonde wig,

双语精华版·心灵鸡汤·

已是万家灯火了。雪开始下起来，狂风大作，街上空无一人。我已经精疲力竭，急急忙忙往家赶。

我的寓所虽然不豪华，可是，从小姑娘们住的破屋子回来之后，这里简直就是香格里拉。实在太累了，我不想看书，甚至连电视都不想看。我想想我从事的工作，它怎么就这么累人，这么令人沮丧。我们办公室总是缺少人手，因为很少有人愿意在城中心的穷人堆里工作。为了去看望病人，我整天都穿梭在令人望而却步的破败的街区的大街小巷上，爬上黑漆漆的楼梯，或者鼓起勇气乘上嘎吱作响的老掉牙电梯。经常有让你心情无比沉重的这样一些家庭问题——少女怀孕、吸毒成瘾和慢性疾病。而贫困使这些问题愈发严重。

我一个人待在寓所里的时候，今天找到的两个孩子总是在我的脑海里转来转去。等待她们的将是什么样的命运？悲伤的情绪主宰了我，我想起几位嫁给了富商的朋友。她们的生活就是逛街购物，打打高尔夫、网球来娱乐身心，我发现我现在真是羡慕她们。后来我虽然是去睡觉了，可是辗转难眠，梦里哭泣的孩子让我心神不宁。

第二天我去上班，发现工作量比往常还要重。名单上的这么多病人，我怎么能够一一探访到？我深呼吸了一口，理清了思路。首先，我要到昨天收留两个小孩的寄养家庭去看一看。我担心她们的创伤不能够平复。我的心里沉甸甸的。通往寄养母亲家的楼梯竟是那么长。

可是见到她们之后，我的疲倦顿时消失得无影无踪。后卧室布置得很热闹，孩子们舒服地住在那儿。她们正穿着寄养母亲的旧衣服，做"化装"游戏。那个4岁的小女孩看起来散发着美丽。她穿着缎子睡袍，虽然褪了色，可是看起来很飘逸。她还给衣服配上了一些从

perched atop her coal black hair.

"I'm a movie star,"she told me,preening in front of the mirror.

"I'm calling her 'Princess',"the foster mother said,laughing,as she hugged the three-year-old.

The snow outside had melted and sunlight poured in through the window.Brightly colored toys were scattered throughout the room.A teddy bear sat in a rocking chair and seemed to be regarding "Princess" with admiring eyes.

I could see that the foster mother was enchanted with the children.I felt my heart lift with hope.Who knew?Maybe a better future beckoned for the girls.

As I left,Princess waved good-bye to me,her bracelets jingling.She looked beautiful,hardly resembling the weeping,disheveled child of the night before.

I carried that image in my mind for the rest of the day.Such are the rewards that come to a working woman,never to be found on a golf course,or a tennis court,or in the most magnificent shopping mall.

Eileen Valinoti

廉价商品店买来的珠宝。不过最给她添光加彩的是戴在炭黑色头发外面的金黄色的假发。

"我是电影明星,"她一边告诉我,一边对着镜子精心打扮。

"我叫她'公主'呢,"寄养母亲笑着说,怀里搂着另外一个3岁的孩子。

外面的积雪融化了,阳光透过窗户倾泻进来。房间里到处都是色彩鲜艳的玩具。一只玩具熊坐在摇椅上,用仰慕的眼神注视着"公主"。

能看出来,寄养母亲非常喜欢这两个孩子。我心里又燃起了希望。谁说得清?也许美好的未来在向孩子们招手呢。

我离开的时候,公主与我挥手道别,手镯摇得叮叮当当地响。她那么漂亮,与头一天晚上哭泣的邋遢小孩判若两人。

在这一天接下来的时间里,这个美丽的印象占据着我的脑海。这种乐趣只有工作的女性享受得到。而在高尔夫球场、在网球场、在最高档的购物中心你是找不到它的。

伊琳·瓦里诺提

United We Stand

When we quit thinking primarily about ourselves and our own self-preservation, we undergo a truly heroic transformation of consciousness.

Joseph Campbell

She stood staring at a television set with tears streaming down her face as we walked into the room. As we entered, she shut off the television and then we immediately became quiet. We had never seen our teacher so quiet or sullen. When the last person was in the door, we waited for her to speak.

"There's been a terrible tragedy in New York City this morning. Two planes have bombed the World Trade Center. It is suspected that terrorists have struck on our own United States' soil." Then she walked over to the television and turned the set on. As we watched in horror, we saw the first plane strike, and then the second. We saw people screaming and running from the site with blood and ash all over them. "Mrs. Skop" flipped through the channels to show us that the tragedy had preempted everything else on television. Then, she shut off the set and we began to discuss what this could mean for our country.

Mrs. Skophammer is one of the most positive teachers I know. She always has a smile on her face and a good joke or story to tell us. In her classroom we learn about the world from real-life situations, and she treats us as if we are older than we really are. On that particular day, we learned more from her than anyone could possibly imagine.

团结就是力量

当我们主要记挂的不再是自己,不再是自我保护的时候,我们的意识就经历了一次真正的英雄式的转变。

乔瑟夫·康贝尔

我们走进教室的时候,她站在那儿,眼睛盯着电视,泪流满面。我们进门之后,她随即关掉电视,大家立即安静下来。老师这样一声不吭、闷闷不乐,我们还是头一回见到。等最后一名学生都进门了,我们期待着老师开讲。

"今天早上纽约市发生了一场重大悲剧。两架飞机炸掉了世贸中心。有人怀疑是恐怖分子袭击了美国本土。"然后,她走到电视机前,打开开关。我们胆战心惊地看着第一架飞机撞上去,紧接着第二架。人们尖叫着,从事故的发生地点跑出来,浑身上下都是鲜血和尘土。"斯科普老师"不停地切换频道,我们发现所有电视台全部都在播放这一幕,而其他节目一律停播了。然后,老师关掉了电视,我们开始讨论这场悲剧对于美国的未来意味着什么。

斯科普哈默尔老师是我所认识的老师中最积极乐观的。她总是面带微笑,总是有有趣的玩笑和故事与我们分享。在课堂上,她总是用实际生活中的情形作例子,帮助我们了解世界,而且总是把我们当大孩子对待。就在事故当天,我们从她那儿学到的东西比任何人想象的都要多。

133

Mrs. Skop explained to us that her father had fought in World War Ⅱ.He had seen unspeakable horrors in Europe.He'd been in on the liberation of a concentration camp and had photos of piles of dead people.In the weeks to come she would explain the parallels between the war he had fought in and the one we were engaged in right now.

After her initial crying, Mrs. Skop took action. She took the World Trade Center bombing and used it to teach about history,democracy, freedom,rights,the flag,patriotism and compassion for others.She vowed she would not let terrorists control what she did and where she went.She was going to live her life to the fullest.And because she was so positive, we were no longer as afraid.We understood that people have causes and you can't live your life being afraid to experience it.

Mrs. Skop had one group of students create linoleum printed note cards.She purchased envelopes,and the students packaged the cards and sold them. Then, six weeks after the bombings, Mrs. Skop hopped on a plane and took the relief money to New York City.

Mrs. Skop went directly to Ground Zero.She took lots of photos and brought them back to share with her classes.She explained the site in such vivid detail that we could smell the death in the air.But,along with the death,she helped us feel the hope that was all over New York City. Memorials,people helping people,young children's cards of well wishing, and a country that now seemed to be uniting and caring about something other than material things and themselves were felt.Flags were flying all around and we could feel the United States pull together.United We Stand.Yes,Mrs. Skop was teaching all of us by example to take charge of our lives and know what we stand for.

Before the bombings, Mrs. Skop had always told us that it bothered her that at ballgames people didn't sing the national anthem or put their hands over their hearts.She said that it seemed that only she and a few other older people would sing.It also bothered her that during a parade,

她向我们解释说，她的父亲参加过二战，亲眼目睹了欧洲经历的巨大的恐怖，参与了集中营的解放，拍了很多张尸骨累累的照片。在接下来的几周，她将解释她父亲经历过的战争与目前的这场悲剧之间的可比性。

　　斯科普老师虽然一开始流过眼泪，但是她很快采取行动。她以世贸中心被炸事件作为契机，给我们讲历史、讲民主、讲权利、讲国旗、讲爱国主义、讲对他人的慈悲心。她发誓，她想做什么就做什么，想去哪儿就去哪儿，绝不会受到恐怖分子的牵制。她让生命最大限度地充实起来。因为她这么乐观，我们也变得不那么恐惧了。我们明白人们有各种各样的事业，害怕体验，就无法生活。

　　斯科普老师组织了一组学生制作印上了麻胶版画的信笺。她买来信封，学生们把卡片装入信封，负责销售。在轰炸事件6个星期之后，她跳上飞机，把救济金送到纽约市。

　　她径直赶往世贸大厦遗址，还拍了很多张照片，带回来与学生分享。她对轰炸地点的描述栩栩如生，让我们似乎在空气中嗅到了死亡的味道。但是除了感受死亡之外，她也使我们体会到纽约市上空到处飞扬的都是希望。我们看到了众多的悼念活动，相濡以沫的群众，把良好的祝愿写在卡片上的孩子们，感受到了这个国家正在团结起来，人们在乎的不再是物质的东西，不再只有自己。国旗到处飘扬，我们能感受到美国凝聚力增强了。团结起来，我们就能屹立不倒。不错，斯科普老师以身作则，教育我们，管理自己的人生，清楚自己的立场。

　　在轰炸发生以前，斯科普老师总是告诉我们，每当看到球赛上人们不唱国歌，不把手放在胸前，她都很难过。在她的印象里，只有她和少数几位年龄大一些的人愿意开口唱。在游行的时候，沿途的

people along the route did not stand up to honor our flag or the veterans that carried it.Then during the first football game after the bombings,the national anthem was played.People were singing,hats were removed and hands were placed over hearts.As I looked in her direction,even though she had vowed she was done crying,I saw a few tears slide down Mrs. Skop's face.And,in those tears I could see pride,patriotism,self-respect, democracy,freedom and history glistening.If teachers lead by example, this teacher sets a gleaming example for all.

As a teacher, Mrs. Skophammer, creates culture. She leads by example.She actively involves and challenges students and continuously expects winners.

Jenna Skophammer

人并不站起来向国旗致敬,也不向扛着国旗的老兵致敬,这也一样让她感伤。轰炸之后的第一场美式足球赛上,球场上奏起了美国国歌。人们一起歌唱,一起脱帽,一起把双手放在胸前。我朝着她所在的方向望去,尽管她发誓不再流泪,我还是看见几行泪水从她的脸颊上滑落下来。泪光中折射出了骄傲、爱国心、自尊、民主、自由和历史的光芒。如果说教师的任务是以身作则的话,斯科普老师为所有的人树立了一个光辉的典范。

作为一名教师,斯科普哈默尔创造了一种文化。她总是身先士卒,主动带领学生参与,激发学生,永远对学生寄予厚望。

吉恩纳·斯科普哈默尔

"She'll like it, but she'll count off for spelling."

Reprinted by permission of Martha Campbell.

Never Too Late

One of the most courageous things you can do is identify yourself,know who you are,what you believe in,and where you want to go.

Sheila Murray Bethel

It was an unusually busy day for the hospital staff on the sixth floor.Ten new patients were admitted and Nurse Susan spent the morning and afternoon checking them in.Her friend Sharron,an aide,prepared ten rooms for the patients and made sure they were comfortable.After they were finished she grabbed Sharron and said,"We deserve a break. Let's go eat."

Sitting across from each other in the noisy cafeteria,Susan noticed Sharron absently wiping the moisture off the outside of her glass with her thumbs.Her face reflected a weariness that came from more than just a busy day.

"You're pretty quiet.Are you tired,or is something wrong?"Susan asked.

Sharron hesitated.However,seeing the sincere concern in her friend's face,she confessed,"I can't do this the rest of my life,Susan.I have to find a higher-paying job to provide for my family.We barely get by.If it weren't for my parents keeping my kids,well,we wouldn't make it."

Susan noticed the bruises on Sharron's wrists peeking out from under her jacket.

"What about your husband?"

永远不迟

你能够做的最勇敢的事情就是给自己定位,清楚自己
是谁,知道自己的信仰,明白自己想到哪里去。

希拉·默里·贝希尔

对于6楼医院员工来说,这是个异常忙碌的日子。他们新来了
10位病人。护士苏珊早上和下午都在忙着给病人登记入院。她的朋
友,助理莎伦给病人准备了10个房间,确保他们住得舒服。两人忙完
后,苏珊拉住莎伦,对她说:"我们该休息休息了,一起去用餐吧。"

在喧闹的咖啡厅里,她们面对面坐下。苏珊注意到,莎伦在发
呆,拇指下意识地擦着玻璃杯外面的水汽,而且异常疲倦。一天紧张
的工作不至于会把她累成这样。

"你很安静啊。你累了吗?还是有什么事?"

莎伦迟疑了一下。可是看到苏珊真心关切的表情,她说出了心
底的话:"我不能一辈子干这份工作,苏珊。我得找一份报酬更高的
工作才能养家。我们几乎入不敷出了。要不是父母替我照看着孩子,
唉,我们真的过不下去了。"

苏珊看到莎伦的手腕处原本被夹克遮住的几块淤血的地方露
了出来。

"你的丈夫呢?"

139

"We can't count on him.He can't seem to hold a job.He's got...problems."

"Sharron,you're so good with patients,and you love working here. Why don't you go to school and become a nurse?There's financial help available,and I'm sure your parents would agree to keep the kids while you are in class."

"It's too late for me,Susan;I'm too old for school.I've always wanted to be a nurse,that's why I took this job as an aide;at least I get to care for patients."

"How old are you?"Susan asked.

"Let's just say I'm thirty-something."

Susan pointed at the bruises on Sharron's wrists."I'm familiar with 'problems'like these.Honey,it's never too late to become what you've dreamed of.Let me tell you how I know."

Susan began sharing a part of her life few knew about.It was something she normally didn't talk about,only when it helped someone else.

"I first married when I was thirteen years old and in the eighth grade."

Sharron gasped.

"My husband was twenty-two.I had no idea he was violently abusive.We were married six years and I had three sons.One night my husband beat me so savagely he knocked out all my front teeth.I grabbed the boys and left.

"At the divorce settlement,the judge gave our sons to my husband because I was only nineteen and he felt I couldn't provide for them.The shock of him taking my babies left me gasping for air.To make things worse,my ex took the boys and moved,cutting all contact I had with them.

"Just like the judge predicted,I struggled to make ends meet.I found work as a waitress,working for tips only.Many days my meals consisted

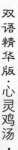

"不能指望他。他连饭碗都保不住。他有些……问题。"

"莎伦,你对病人那么好,又热爱这里的工作。为什么不去读书,然后找份护士的工作呢?你可以申请经济资助的。而且我相信,你读书的时候,你的父母会同意帮你照看孩子的。"

"这对我来说太迟了,苏珊。我早超过读书的年龄了。我一直想当护士,这正是我选择助理工作的原因。至少我有机会照顾病人。"

"你多大?"苏珊问。

"我可以告诉你,我30多岁了。"

苏珊指着莎伦手腕处淤血的地方说:"这种'问题'我熟悉。亲爱的,实现梦想永远不晚。我告诉你,我是怎样领悟到的。"

苏珊说起了她的一段不为人知的故事。通常,她不会说起这些事,除非说出来会对别人有所帮助。

"我第一次结婚是在13岁的时候,那时我还在读八年级。"

莎伦吸了一口冷气。

"我丈夫那时22岁。我压根儿不知道他有严重的暴力倾向。我们婚姻维持了6年,生了3个儿子。有一天晚上,他野蛮地殴打我,把我所有的门牙都打掉了。我拉住孩子们,跑掉了。

"宣判离婚的时候,法官把我们的儿子判给了我的丈夫,因为我那时候才19岁,法官觉得我没有抚养能力。把孩子判给他已经让我惊得目瞪口呆了。更糟糕的是,前夫带着我的儿子搬走了,切断了我和他们的所有联系。"

"就像法官预言的,我辛勤地工作,日子却过得很艰辛。我找到服务员的工作,只能挣到些小费。很多天我的主餐就是牛奶加饼干。

of milk and crackers.The most difficult thing was the emptiness in my soul.I lived in a tiny one-room apartment and the loneliness would overwhelm me.I longed to play with my babies and hear them laugh."

She paused.Even after four decades,the memory was still painful. Sharron's eyes filled with tears as she reached out to comfort Susan. Now it didn't matter if the bruises showed.

Susan continued,"I soon discovered that waitresses with grim faces didn't get tips,so I hid behind a smiling mask and pressed on.I remarried and had a daughter.She became my reason for living,until she went to college.Then I was back where I started,not knowing what to do with myself—until the day my mother had surgery.I watched the nurses care for her and thought:I can do that.The problem was,I only had an eighth-grade education.Going back to high school seemed like a huge mountain to conquer.I decided to take small steps toward my goal.The first step was to get my GED.My daughter used to laugh at how our roles reversed.Now I was burning the midnight oil and asking her questions."

Susan paused and looked directly in Sharron's eyes."I received my diploma when I was forty-six years old."

Tears streamed down Sharron's cheeks.Here was someone offering the key that might unlock the door in her dark life.

"The next step was to enroll in nursing school.For two long years I studied,cried and tried to quit.But my family wouldn't let me.I remember calling my daughter and yelling,'Do you realize how many bones are in the human body,and I have to know them all! I can't do this,I'm forty-six years old! 'But I did.Sharron,I can't tell you how wonderful it felt when I received my cap and pin."

Sharron's lunch was cold,and the ice had melted in her tea by the time Susan finished talking.Reaching across the table and taking Sharron's hands,Susan said,"You don't have to put up with abuse.Don't be a victim—take charge.You will be an excellent nurse.We will climb this

最难以对付的就是心灵上的空虚。我住在一套只有一间居室的小公寓里。有时候孤独的感觉真是让人受不了。我好想与孩子们一起玩耍，好想听到他们的笑声。"

她停住了。虽然已经是40年前的往事了，回忆起来还是令人痛苦。莎伦噙着满眼的泪，伸出手去安慰苏珊。她不在乎淤血的地方是否会被人看到了。

苏珊接着说："我很快发现，哭丧着脸的服务员得不到小费。所以我都是笑脸相迎，奋力工作。我又结婚了，生了个女儿。女儿成了我活下去的理由。可是，她上了大学之后，我的生活又回到了原来的地方，不知道自己该干什么——直到我母亲做手术那一天。我看着护士们照顾她，心里想：我可以干这份工作。可是问题是，我只读过八年级。重新读中学似乎是一座难以翻越的大山。于是我决定一步一步地实现我的目标。第一步是通过GED考试。女儿常常笑我们的角色颠倒过来了。熬夜学习的变成了我，我有问题就向她请教。"

苏珊又停了一下，望着莎伦的眼睛说："我46岁的时候拿到了毕业证书。"

莎伦的眼泪顺着脸颊往下流。她的生活像是囚禁在暗无天日的屋子里，而苏珊给她送来了开门的钥匙。

"第二个步骤就是报名上护士学校。在两年漫长的读书时光里，我流过眼泪，想过退学。可是我的家人不同意。我还记得，我给女儿打电话，冲着她大喊大叫：'你知道人体到底有多少块骨头吗？这些我都得记住！我学不下去了，我46岁了！'但是我坚持了下来。你不知道，拿到护士帽和别针的时候，那种感觉说不出来的美妙啊。"

莎伦的午餐是冷食。等苏珊的话说完，她茶里的冰都融化了。苏珊的手伸过来，抓住了对面莎伦的手，对她说："你不需要忍受虐待。不要做受害者——掌握命运。你会成为优秀的护士。我们一起翻越

mountain together."

Sharron wiped her mascara-stained face with her napkin. "I had no idea you suffered so much pain. You seem like someone who has always had it together."

"I guess I've developed an appreciation for the hardships of my life," Susan answered. "If I use them to help others, then I really haven't lost a thing. Sharron, promise me that you will go to school and become a nurse. Then help others by sharing your experiences."

Sharron promised. In a few years she became a registered nurse and worked alongside her friend until Susan retired. Sharron never forgot her colleague or the rest of her promise.

Now Sharron sits across the table taking the hands of those who are bruised in body and soul, telling them, "It's never too late. We will climb this mountain together."

Linda Apple

高山。"

　　莎伦用餐巾擦了擦脸。她的眼影已经脱妆了,弄到了脸上。"我不知道你承受了这么多痛苦。你看上去似乎是个事事顺心的人。"

　　"我想我已经学会了欣赏生命中的苦难,"苏珊回答说。"如果我用我的经历去帮助别人,我就什么都没有失去。莎伦,答应我,去上学,然后当护士。再把你的经历告诉别人,去帮助别人。"

　　莎伦答应了。几年之后,她成了注册护士,成了苏珊的同事,一直到苏珊退休。莎伦从来没有忘记过苏珊,没有忘记过她的另一半承诺。

　　此刻,莎伦正坐在桌边,在她对面是肉体、心灵上受了伤害的人。她拉着她们的手,对她们说:"永远不迟。我们一起翻越高山吧。"

　　　　　　　　　　　　　　　　　　琳达·艾普尔

From under the Boot Heel

There is nothing like a dream to create the future.

Victor Hugo

In my twenty years as a paramedic,I have been charged with performing duties that require enormous amounts of bravery.I was about to learn a new kind.

Several years ago,I sat in a dilapidated office housed in a condemned hospital building in the center of a nondescript town in south Texas.I lit a cigarette (this was back in the days when one could smoke in a building)and watched a large cockroach climb up the wall in front of my desk.

Tim,an EMT coworker,strolled in and flicked the ugly bug onto the floor,slamming down on it with the heavy heel of a patrol boot.Even with that pounding,the bug wouldn't die.Sort of like me,I thought. Stomped on unmercifully,and I keep coming back for more.

In the year since my divorce,there had been few happy days.My entire existence seemed to depend solely on my life-saving duties. Responding to an emergency was the only time I knew my heart was beating.My thoughts turned once more to the core of my problem.If only I could find a nice man...

I suddenly felt ill.What was I thinking?Am I to waste my entire life waiting for Prince Charming?He certainly had not been around during the first thirty-seven years.

I stood up and walked past Tim and out to the street.   Standing on

双语精华版·心灵鸡汤·

夹缝中逃生

最能创造未来的莫过于梦想。

维克多·雨果

我已经做了20年急救医助的工作，一直以来我负责的都是些没有过人的勇气无法执行的任务。而此时又有一项新任务等待着我。

几年前，我坐在一间破烂的办公室里。那是得克萨斯州南部一个平淡无奇的小城，我们的办公地点就在一幢已经被宣布是危房的医院大楼内。我点了一支烟（那时候在大楼里是可以吸烟的），看着办公桌前面的一只大蟑螂顺着墙壁往上爬。

急救技士蒂姆是我的同事。他溜达进来，一下子把那只丑陋的小虫子摔到地上，抓起一只重重的执勤靴，脚跟对准它狠狠地砸过去。经历了这样的重创之后，虫子还没死。它有点像我呢，我想。我被毫不留情地"踩踏"之后，反倒愈战愈勇。

离婚后的一年里，我过着郁郁寡欢的日子。我的全部存在似乎完全依赖于急救工作。只有在紧急抢救时，我才能感受到自己的心跳。我的思想又一次转回到问题的核心上来：要是我能找到一个好男人多好……

我突然觉得恶心。我在想什么？还要浪费我的一生等待白马王子吗？前37年里我可是没有等到。

我站起来，绕过蒂姆，出了街道。站在路边，审视四周。哦，天哪！

the curb,I surveyed my surroundings.Oh my God! I said to myself while continuing my slow turn.There is nothing to see here,no view,no green trees or water,no spiky mountains.Not even a hill.Why am I here?The question was the internal combustion I needed.I smiled and felt hope welling up within me.   Standing there on the curb of Center Street, dressed in my uniform,I laughed until tears streaked my face.

That night I pulled out a yellow legal pad.On it I wrote:"WHAT I WANT".Under the heading,I listed eight items:1.To live in a beautiful place with a 360-degree view;2.To make a good salary;3.To once again own a red sports car;4.to never see a cockroach again;5.to have a wonderful job teaching EMTs and paramedics;6.To be proud of myself;7.To never,ever need a man again,except for plumbing repairs;8.To spend my next forty years in peace and happiness.I worked until the wee hours of the morning,polishing my resume,and then I sent copies to Emergency Medical Services offices in four northwestern states.

Over fifty people attended my going-away party,and each of them asked the same question."Wendy,how can you just pack up and go to Alaska without knowing anyone there?"Some of the women said, "I could never go off to the wilderness all alone."One man informed me that there were seven men to one woman in Alaska."You're going to get a husband,right?"

Yeah,right.

The truth is,I had chosen to enjoy my own company for a while. Something I had never really done.

In one week,I would become the Emergency Medical Services Co-ordinator for Southeast Alaska.The job required travel by boat and float plane to outlying areas—the frontier of Alaska.I was to spend time in these isolated communities teaching classes on emergency services.I never knew such a career existed,and it was as if I had designed the position myself.

双语精华版·心灵鸡汤·

我一边缓缓地转身,一边想。这里什么都看不到,没有景致,没有绿色的树木,水流,没有笔立的山峰,连个小山坡都没有。我为什么待在这儿?这个问题是我重新启动起来所必需的内燃。我露出微笑,觉得希望在我的心中升腾起来。穿着制服,站在中心街的路旁,我放声大笑,直笑到泪珠顺着脸颊滚下来。

那天晚上我拿出一本黄色底色的横线格本。我在上面抬头处写道"我想要的",然后列了8项内容:1.拥有360°全视野的优美住所;2.有一份高薪的工作;3.再次拥有一辆红色跑车;4.再也不要见到蟑螂;5.找一份急救医助和急救技士的教学工作;6.为自己骄傲;7.永远永远不再需要男人,除非喊他们来修水管;8.平静、幸福地度过后40年。我润色个人简历,一直忙到午夜以后。我把这些简历分别投寄到西北部4个州的急救医疗服务体系办公室。

有50多人参加了我的饯行派对。所有的人问的都是相同的问题:"温迪,在阿拉斯加你连一个熟人都没有,怎么敢收拾包裹就走人呢?"有些女士说:"那样的蛮荒之地我一个人是绝对不会去的。"一位男士告诉我阿拉斯加的男女比例是7:1。"你去那儿找丈夫,是吧?"

对,说得对。

实际情况是,我去享受一下不要人陪的感觉。这是我从来没有真正体验过的事情。

一个星期之后,我就要成为阿拉斯加东南地区急救医疗服务体系的协调员了。这份工作需要我坐船或者是水上飞机到偏远地区——阿拉斯加的边境去。我将到那些人迹罕至的社区给人们上急救课程。没想到世上真有这样的职业存在,感觉好像是我自己设计出来的。

As I looked around at all the doubting faces that day,I felt absolutely no fear—just joy.Two suitcases and four boxes of training materials were all I had packed.I purged myself of all belongings.

As I said my good-byes,I realized it took no bravery to pack up and move to Alaska.The bravery had occurred when I made my list and resolved to fulfill it.I recognized that I could control my own destiny. The weakness was in waiting for change instead of creating it.

Who do I need?Me.Who do I depend on?Me.Who do I love?Me. Who makes me happy?Me.Selfish,you say?Darned right.And there are no cockroaches in Alaska.

Wendy Natkong

那一天，所有的人脸上都写着疑惑二字。我看着他们，没有感觉到恐惧——只有喜悦。收拾完毕，我的行李总共只有两个行李箱和4盒子的培训材料。除此之外的东西，一概不带。

告别的时候，我发现收拾行李和移居阿拉斯加并不需要多少勇气。而写下那份梦想清单和立志实现它们倒是需要勇气。我认识到我可以掌握自己的命运。弱者总是等待命运的改变，而不是创造机会改变命运。

现在我需要谁？我自己。我依靠谁？我自己。我爱谁？我自己。谁能让我高兴？我自己。以自我为中心，你说我？完全正确。阿拉斯加没有蟑螂。

温迪·拉特岗

Life—It's All Good

I have always viewed employment as more than just work to earn money.My belief is that you should work to live,not live to work.Your job should not completely define the person you are,but since it will be the activity you spend most of your time at,you should find meaning and enjoyment in your work.

I lost sight of my perspective in exchange for respectability,prestige and the lure of a good paycheck.Having joined the workforce with a degree in sociology and a background in physical education,I initially jumped into a position as a recreation counselor with "at risk" adolescents in a resi-dential facility.It was hard,draining work,but rewarding and meaningful.I felt similarly about my next position as the Teen Talk/Crisis Line direc-tor at a suicide prevention and crisis center.I enjoyed making a connec-tion and "being there"for the teenagers,but the emotional involvement and constant availability wore me out physically at an early age.My de-cision to return to school to pursue a graduate degree in journalism was based on my dream to write and perform communications work for a nonprofit organization whose mission I could support wholeheartedly.

Instead,I found myself at IBM,first as an intern,then five years later as a Web site manager and corporate communications writer/editor. While my position at IBM afforded me the realization of dreams such as travel to exotic destinations and a large home on acreage in the Rocky Mountains,it did nothing to inspire me or feed my soul that I felt was in the process of slowly shriveling.So,on the verge of the breakup in my ten-year marriage and the recovery from a major mental meltdown and depression,I opted to take a severance package and "find myself".

完美生活

　　我一直认为就业的意义不仅在于为挣钱而工作。我的信念是，工作是为了生活，而生活不是为了工作。虽然工作不能完全决定工作的人是什么样子，但是既然你的大多数时间都放在工作上，工作就必须有意义，能给你带来享受。

　　可是在尊重、威望的面前，在面对高薪诱惑的时候，我却一度偏离了这个原则。最初的时候，我借助社会学学士学位和体育方面的背景，加入了劳动大军的行列，在一家寄宿治疗中心为"危险"少年担任娱乐顾问。这份工作让人心力交瘁，但是同时也让你体会到回报和工作的意义。第二份工作是在一家自杀预防和危机中心担任青少年谈话/危机热线的主任。感觉和第一份工作差不多。我喜欢连线，喜欢为少年人"守候在那里"。可是，尽管年纪轻轻，大量的情感和时间投入一样让我精疲力竭。后来回到学校，攻读新闻学硕士学位，则是为了实现为一家非营利性机构担任写作和交际工作的梦想。我当时愿意全心全意地支持它完成使命。

　　可是，我却一改初衷地去了IBM公司，先是实习，5年后，成了网站经理、公司通讯撰稿人/编辑。在IBM公司的职位使我实现了一些梦想，比如去异域旅行，在落基山脉有一栋占地以英亩来计算的大房子等；可是，这样不能给灵魂带来动力和滋养。我觉得灵魂在逐渐萎缩。于是，就在维持了10年的婚姻行将结束，我从精神崩溃和消沉中恢复过来的时候，我选择了领取遣散费，离开公司，去"找寻真我"。

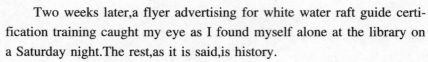

Two weeks later,a flyer advertising for white water raft guide certification training caught my eye as I found myself alone at the library on a Saturday night.The rest,as it is said,is history.

At age thirty-four,I discovered a new calling.I became the one female raft and rockclimbing guide for a company known as "Rock-N-Row".My cushy corporate life with a secure paycheck became a distant memory as I spent my days outside in the sun,wind,heat,cold and snow.I learned to row,to read the water,to steer the paddle boat and call commands with authority,to rescue "swimmers",to tie appropriate knots, to belay safely and entertain the adventurous folk who came to play.

My sense of self,severely undermined in the years preceding the divorce,became stronger,and my self-esteem grew as each day passed with new experiences—successes and disappointments.I learned not to take life so seriously,and to be able to laugh at myself.My physical self benefited from the outdoor challenges and I liked the person I was freeing myself to be.The new man in my life—my best friend—appreciated my inner and outer qualities,and we enjoy skiing,rock climbing,hiking,and even skydiving on occasion.

To emerge from the soft,safe,corporate computer world into the sometimes brutal realities of outdoor life was a wake-up call. Two near-death experiences—one as a result from a flip in a Class IV rapid at high water and the other from a rock shelf breaking loose above me as I belayed a climber—taught me that if I planned to take risks,they should be calculated.I carried my motto of "No Fear"into my professional and personal life and learned to trust in me—my decisions,my emotions,the person I am.The winter before my dramatic life changes was one of discontent,yet the time since has been affirming life and reawakening my soul.I can honestly say,no matter the situation,"It's all good."For what is the alternative?

Patty Lataille

两个星期之后，一个周六的晚上，我独自坐在图书馆里，一张关于水上皮筏漂流导游证培训的宣传单吸引了我。其他，正如人们所说的，化作了历史。

34岁的时候，我发现了一个新的职业，在一家叫"Rock-N-Row"的公司作唯一的漂流、攀岩女性导游。拿着稳定收入的轻松的公司生活已经一去不复返了。现在我的工作在户外，有时在烈日下，有时在大风里，还有严寒、酷暑和雪花纷飞的日子。我学会划船，看懂水流，驾驶脚踏船，威严地指挥，去救援"游泳"的人，正确地打结，给前来游玩的愿意冒险的客人们系牢绳索，给他们送去快乐。

在离婚的前几年里遭到严重破坏的自我意识正在复苏，而自尊也在伴随着每一天的新体验——成功、失望苦壮成长。我学会了对待生活不要过于严肃，学会了自嘲。我的体力也从户外的诸多挑战中受益。我喜欢现在这个内心得到释放的我。新闯入我生命中的男人——也是我最好的朋友——懂得欣赏我内在和外在的品质。我们一起享受滑雪、攀岩、登山，有时甚至是高空跳伞。

从轻松安全的电脑公司的生活里退出，进入这种有时近乎野蛮的户外生活，这次改变让我格外清醒。两次与死亡擦肩而过——一次是在水位很高的4级疾速水面上翻船的经历；另一次，是在我给一名客人系绳索的时候，上方的一块岩石松动了——这两次经历告诉我，如果我打算冒险，这些因素都必须考虑到。我把我的座右铭"无所畏惧"带入了我的事业和个人生活中，开始学会相信自己——自己的决断、自己的感情和自己的为人。在我的生活中的戏剧性变化开幕之前的那个冬天，生活是没有满足感的，但是这之后的日子里我拥有的却是肯定的人生，它唤醒了我的灵魂。我可以很诚实地说，无论处境如何，"一切都好"。因为还有别的答案吗？

帕蒂·拉太里

Take Two Lemons and Make Lemonade

All men who have achieved great things have been great dreamers.

Orison Swett Marden

Our house invariably had an aroma of "home".Scents like the mouthwatering zest of frying onions at dinner-time,and crisp vanilla spice that wafted through the rooms during the day.But after six months wading through the loneliness of widowhood,I realized I didn't like the whiff of sad staleness now permeating the house.

I'd drifted through those last months as though half of me was missing.Not strange,I suppose,after forty years of marriage to the same man.But a day arrived when I realized I had to decide what the rest of my life would be like.Did I want to wander the empty rooms being half a person,or did I want to get out and see if I couldn't become whole a-gain?And if I did want to repair my psyche,how would I go about achieving this metamorphosis?

My children and grandchildren helped me decide.

"You love to write,Mom,"they chorused."Write a book."

Write a book?I thought.At my age?

But how many times had I told my children to live their dream?It was strange,however,to realize I might be able to live my old dream;a vision swallowed up for so many years with housework,husband and children. Not that I would change a minute of it;that was my life and I loved it.

夏日柠檬茶

凡是能取得伟大成就的人都是伟大的梦想家。

奥里森·斯维特·马登

我们的房子里以前总是飘着"家"的香味。晚餐时是令人直流口水的浓烈的炸洋葱的味道,白天屋子里飘荡的是清爽的香草调料的气味。可是现在,家里弥漫的却是阵阵陈腐的伤感。熬过了6个月的孤寂的孀居日子,我明白了我不喜欢这种感受。

迷迷糊糊地度过了这几个月,仿佛身体中有一半已经离我而去。我想,这不奇怪,毕竟他是那个与我共度了40年婚姻的人。但是有一天,我醒悟到该是决定后半生生活的时候了。是该留着这一半的身体,待在空空荡荡的家里无所事事?还是该走出去,看看能不能找回另一半生命?假如我选择了修复心理状态,又要怎样做才能完成这样伟大的蜕变呢?

儿孙们帮助我做出了决定。

"你喜欢写作,妈妈,"他们一起喊,"写本书吧。"

写本书?我思考着。在我这个年纪写书?

有多少回我鼓励过孩子们去追逐他们的梦想?可是,让我自己去圆一个旧梦,这种想法还是很陌生。这么多年操持家务,相夫教子,忙碌的生活早就把我的梦想挤得无影无踪。我并非后悔以前的日子;那是我的生活,是我挚爱的生活。

But it wasn't my destiny anymore,and,as the homily goes,the sooner I realized it the better.Time has a way of slip-sliding through your life and before you know it,your children are married and have children of their own.

Let's face it,if life is made up of seasons I've got autumn challenging me,I thought.

Did I want to find out what else life could possibly contain for me, or wind up a shriveled,bitter old person?That question made me shudder. I'd always been an active optimist.Over the years when my children jumped from sports to dance and back again,I'd volunteered for everything from Girl Scouts,through mentoring youngsters,to vice president or secretary of the many clubs and organizations I'd joined. Then,for eighteen years I'd run my own business,a candy and gift shop. Later I'd handled events and promotions for a local bookstore.

I had what is now referred to as "life experiences".So,did I want to start another business?Volunteer somewhere?When my husband was alive,I'd published a few articles in various magazines.However,my children were correct;I'd always wanted to write a book.

Before I had a chance to dwell in other areas,a new world opened up.An editor,hearing about my desire to link my love of children with my love of Houston,approached me through a mutual friend.Would I write about Houston and what children could see and do in my city? Interesting—I'd tossed a desire into the universe and an answer had drifted down.Without any warning,I had my chance to write that book. From then on,my life took off in another direction.

I spoke with a good friend and we tossed around ideas.Before I knew it,we were on our way,we'd write a special book. Forget the lists, we'd base our book on the core curriculum here in Houston.We researched,interviewed and photographed our way though museums,parks, science exhibits and the many hidden treasures to be found in our city.

不过,我的命运改变了。套用一句说教的话,明白得越早越好。时光如同白驹过隙。在你还没反应过来的时候,你的孩子就成了家,就又添了孩子。

让我们面对现实吧,如果生命如同四季,我现在面对的就是萧瑟的秋季。我寻思着。

是去探究生命还能赐予我什么,还是任凭自己变成干瘪的不快乐的老人呢?这个问题让我不寒而栗。我一直是个积极的乐观主义者。这么多年来,当我的孩子们一会学运动,一会学舞蹈,一会又学运动的时候,我辗转在各种志愿活动当中,从女童子军,到给年轻人做职业辅导,再到所参加的很多俱乐部、组织担任副总负责人或者秘书职务等。后来的18年,我经营着自己的糖果礼品店。再后来,我帮一家书店打点一些事务和促销事宜。

我现在拥有的是人们说的"生活阅历"。那么,我是想再做做别的生意,还是再找个地方当志愿者?丈夫在世的时候,我在几家不同的杂志发表过数篇文章。可是,孩子们说的没错,我一直想要做的事是写本书。

我还没来得及投身到任何领域当中去,一个新世界就打开了。有位编辑听说我想把对孩子们的热爱与对休斯敦市的热爱联系到一起,就通过一个共同的朋友联系上了我。问我愿不愿意就休斯敦市和孩子们在这个城里可以看到什么、做些什么写一些东西。有意思——我刚刚对着宇宙许了个愿,答复就从天而降。没有人告诉我会有这个写书的机会,机会就来了。从此之后,我的生活朝着另一个方向起飞。

我找了一位要好的朋友商量,讨论了各种构思。不知不觉中我们就行动了起来。我们要写的是本特别的书。这本书放弃了罗列的做法,而是以这里的"主干课程"作为主线。我们去了博物馆、公园、科学展,做了调研、采访、摄像,还发掘了这个城市里众多不为人知的珍宝。

When the book was published,I glowed with pride and my children stifled "I-told-you-so".But I was even more thrilled when a national bookstore chain named us "Authors of the Month"in our area,and a major literary group asked us to be featured authors for their annual literacy event.Before we knew it,we had a second contract,and my world and work continued to expand.

At the same time,trying for a social life and further development of my "right brain", I went to Sedona, Arizona, for an Elderhostel art sampler.While watercolor wasn't my thing,I loved working with colored pencils.Back in town,I joined an Artist's Way group facilitated by my coauthor and began colored pencil painting.Once again the universe sent help in the form of a supportive and synergistic group of people who are not only talented,but share their love of art and joy of living.At the urging of one of the artists in the group,I agreed to enter a local art show.To my great surprise,I won three ribbons and sold a painting.

I could have stayed at home and felt sorry for myself.Thank goodness I didn't.Oh,don't get me wrong;I did stay at home,but it wasn't to moan about my loss,but rather to work at fulfilling my life's dream. While doing so,I was also filling my life with something meaningful.

I've always known we have many choices in this world.The trick is to select correctly;don't opt to drain life,choose to fulfill life.

As I write this,I'm pursuing both my writing and art careers.And loving every minute of it.

Yes,the fall season of life is a challenge.But I realize that when those lemons start falling from the trees in summer,it's wise to collect them.Autumn,especially here in Houston,is still hot.What better than to mix some lemonade with ice tea and sip while working on the latest project?

Action,the joy of living life,throws winter far into the future.

Elaine L.Galit

书出版的时候,我非常自豪,容光焕发,而孩子们也硬是没说"是我叫你这么做的"。还有更让人心潮澎湃的事:一家全国连锁书店评选我们为该地区的"本月作家",还有一家重要的文学社团邀请我们以"作家新秀"的身份参加他们每年一度的文化普及活动。同样是在没有思想准备的情况下,我们又得到了第二份合同,我的世界、工作的疆界在延伸。

与此同时,为了增加社交生活和继续开发右脑,我去了亚利桑那州的赛多那体会一下老人游学营的美术课程。因为我在水彩方面不具天分,我喜欢用彩色铅笔绘画。回到家乡,我参加了由我的合著者发起的"艺术家之路"小组,开始了彩色铅笔画创作。老天再次给我送来了帮助。它给我送来了一个相互支持、相得益彰的团队。他们不仅才华横溢,而且分享着对艺术的热爱,以及在生活中体会到的欢欣。应小组中一位画家的催促,我同意参加当地美术展。令我喜出望外的是,我竟然得到了3条绶带,还卖掉了一幅作品。

我本来有可能待在家里,自怨自艾。感谢老天,我没有这么做。哦,别听错了我的意思;我还是待在家里,不过,不是在家里哀叹失去的东西,而是在工作中实现生命的梦想。同时,这些有意义的事情也充实了我的生命。

我一直明白我们在这个世界上有很多种选择。诀窍是做出正确的选择。不要选择让生活流失掉,要选择让生活充实起来。

我写这些文字的时候,也是在同时追求着我的写作和艺术生涯。每一分钟的生活我都热爱。

是啊,秋季对生命来说是一个挑战。但是我明白当夏天柠檬从树上落下来的时候,聪明的做法是把它们收集起来。秋天依然是炎热的,在休斯敦尤其如此。放一些柠檬汁在冰茶里,一边做着手头的工作,一边品茶,如何?

积极行动是生命的乐趣。它把冬天留在了遥远的未来。

伊琳·L.盖立特

Not So Dumb

*Your vision will become clear only when you look into
your heart.*

Who looks outside,dreams.

Who looks inside,awakens.

Carl G.Jung

Lisa Kudrow has created one of television's most memorable"dumb
blondes."But the thirty-eight-year-old actress,who plays Phoebe on the
NBC comedy *Friends*,earned a bachelor's degree at Vassar College and
is known to be logical,analytical and intuitive.

Although she had acted in grade and middle school,Kudrow didn't
consider show business as a career. "I thought all actors were idiots
whose lives didn't work,"she says. "If I became an actor,I was afraid
people wouldn't take me seriously."

What Kudrow was also afraid of was making a mistake.But the pull
towards acting was strong,and by 1990 she had joined an improve
group.Still,she avoided taking risks.Auditions were infrequent.And her
social life was even bleaker than her career. "It was the fear of being
wrong that held me back,"she says. "I finally learned that you can make
a mistake,and the world doesn't come to an end."Kudrow won her role
on *Friends* in 1994 and went on to star in such films as 1997's *Romy
and Michele's High School Reunion*.She got married in '95 and had a
baby in '98,playing a pregnant Phoebe on her show.

"People ask if I'm worried that I'll only play Phoebes and
Micheles,"she says. "What if that's all that happens?Do I care if people
think I'm an idiot?I cared too much about that when I was younger.Now
I listen to myself."

Gail Buchalter

162

大智若愚

> 只有当人能够察看自己的内心深处时,他的视野才会变得清晰起来。
>
> 向外看的人是在梦中的人。
>
> 向内看的人是梦醒的人。
>
> 卡尔·G.荣格

莉莎·库德罗在电视屏幕上创造了一个最让人难忘的"没头脑的金发女郎"形象。在NBC电视台的喜剧片《老友记》中出演菲比的她,现年38岁,拥有瓦萨学院的学士学位,是个人们公认的逻辑能力强、善于分析和直觉灵敏的人。

库德罗在小学和中学时就参加过演出,但是当时她并没有考虑把演艺作为职业。"我当时认为,所有的演员都是白痴,像他们那样的生活是不行的,"她说,"我担心当了演员,人们会不把我放在眼里。"

她还害怕犯错误。但是表演的诱惑力实在很大。到1990年,她加入了一个提高小组。尽管如此,她还是害怕冒险,很少参加试镜。与事业相比,她的社交生活更加黯淡。"正是害怕犯错的心理,使我裹足不前。"她说,"后来我终于明白,人可以犯错,世界并不会因此终止。"1994年,库德罗获得了《老友记》中菲比的角色,后来又继续出演了《罗米和米歇尔的高中聚会》等电影。1995年,库德罗结婚,1998年怀孕,和电视《老友记》里的菲比一样当上了准妈妈。

"人们问,我是否担心自己只能演好菲比和米歇尔这两个角色,"她说,"如果情况真是这样怎么办?如果人们把我想成白痴,我会不会计较?以前的我是过于计较这些了。现在的我听自己的。"

盖尔·波查尔特

A Long Hot Summer

CHICKEN SOUP

There are numerous reasons why a middle-aged woman who has been away from the workforce rearing her children decides to go back to work.The obvious might be for money,but that was not my reason.

After my children departed for college,perhaps I was just bored,or possibly I was suffering from the empty-nest syndrome,but in actuality I think I decided to return to work because I was just plain,hot.Colorado was experiencing an extremely hot,dry summer and my home lacked air-conditioning.It was hot,and I was hot.I determined a cool air-conditioned office was where I belonged! Years ago my first job was that of a book-keeper—it was then that I worked for money.While my children were growing up I worked part time in the school system as a teacher's aide.

This time around I wanted to do something different,something new and exciting,and the money wasn't too important,as my husband made a very comfortable living for us.But what should I do?What sort of job should I look for?I knew I needed to be cautious as to what I became involved with.I am not a "quitter"and therefore I hoped to avoid be-coming obligated to an employer in a job that might turn out to be a mistake for me.

While I agonized over what to do,I was reminded of a past incident where I needed to replace my original engagement ring as the gold was wearing thin.My husband and I shopped and shopped for one,every-where we went,even when we were on vacation.Finally this nonstop searching prompted my poor husband to ask,"Just what kind of ring do you want,what exactly are we looking for?"

My reply was, "I honestly don't know,but when I see the correct

我的夏天

　　曾经为了养育子女离开工作大军的女人在中年时又重返工作岗位,这里面的原因可能有很多种。最容易想到的可能是赚钱,不过这不是我的理由。

　　孩子们上了大学离开家之后,也许是感到无聊,也许是患上了空巢综合征,我决定重返工作。不过真正的原因,在我看来是热。科罗拉多州正经历着一个炙热、干燥的夏天。家里没有空调。天热,我也热。我确定装了空调的办公室是个好去处!多年前我的第一份工作是簿记员——那时候工作确实是为了赚钱。孩子们渐渐长大之后,我又在学校系统作兼职教师助理。

　　这一次,我想换换口味,工作要有新意,要精彩。钱不是特别重要,因为丈夫已经给我们创造了非常优越的生活。可是,我应该做什么呢?找什么样的工作呢?我知道在投入身心地工作之前,一定要谨慎地选择。因为我不是个"半途而废"的人,我要避免选择了不当的工作之后,因为觉得亏欠老板而不得不干下去的情况发生。

　　正在为做什么而苦思冥想的时候,我联想到了过去的一次经历。那时我想换掉原来的订婚戒指,因为金子已经磨得越来越薄了。为了找到一枚戒指,我和丈夫一家商店一家商店地跑。所到之处都找遍了,就连出去度假的机会也没放过。在这番马不停蹄的搜索之后,终于,我可怜的丈夫开口问道:"你到底要什么样的戒指?我们到底在找什么啊?"

　　我是这样回答的:"老实说,我不清楚。但是只要看到了想要的,

setting,I will know it."That was the way I felt about the new career I wished to pursue;I didn't have a clue as to what I wanted to do,but knew there was a perfect fit for me,if I would just be patient.

Fortunately,that summer while attending my twenty-fifth high school class reunion,I overheard a former classmate describing what she did for a living.She was a travel agent,and she and her husband had just returned from a trip to Hawaii where they acted as chaperones for a group of travelers.WOW,that sounded like fun,considerably more fun and exciting than being a bookkeeper.Apparently this profession also had some great travel benefits.I innocently pondered the idea of becoming a travel agent.After all,how difficult could it be to write airline tickets and plan vacations?I reasoned if my friend could do it,I probably could,too,and after all, "I love to travel".I later learned uttering the phrase, "I love to travel",is a surefire way to prevent you from being hired when applying for a job in the travel industry.That phrase is definitely a no-no!

BINGO! It was as if fireworks lit up the night sky! Right then and there I knew without a doubt,I had found the perfect fit;I wanted to be a travel agent.Little did I realize travel agents are a specialized group of individuals whose work is both stressful and demanding.Theirs is a profession requiring special education,training and experience to become proficient.There is definitely more to it than meets the eye.There is unquestionably more to it than just generating airline tickets.

I began scanning the "help wanted"ads in my local newspaper and quickly discovered agencies were interested in hiring "experienced only travel agents,or airline personnel".I was neither.However,one agency located near my home (how lucky can you get)had an entry-level position available that involved answering the phone,typing itineraries and packaging tickets.The owner made it very clear this position would never lead to an agent position or agent training,but offered me an interview if

我就明白了。"对希望从事的新事业,我也抱有相同的感受;想要做什么,我还没有丝毫的想法,但是我知道只要耐心寻找,就一定有一个特别适合我的。

幸运的是,那年夏天参加第25届中学同学聚会的时候,我无意之中听到一位老同学描述她的工作。她是旅行代理人,和丈夫给一群游客做监护人,刚刚从夏威夷回来。哇噻,听起来好有意思,这比簿记员的工作有趣精彩得多。而且很明显,这项职业极大程度上方便了我们自己旅游。我就是这么天真地考虑旅行代理人的工作的。毕竟,写机票、安排度假计划会困难到哪里去呢?我的推理是,只要我的朋友能做到的,我恐怕也能做到,而且嘛,"我喜欢旅游"。我后来才知道,在旅游行业应聘时,想要应聘成功,"我喜欢旅游"这话是万万不能说的,是个绝对的禁忌语!

太好了!那一瞬间似乎有焰火点亮了天空!就在当时当地,我明白无误地知道,我找到了最适合我的;我要当旅行代理人。可是我并不知道旅行代理人都是专业人员,他们压力很大,工作要求很高,需要经过专门的教育、培训和经验才能很好地胜任。这项工作比外表看上去的要复杂,毫无疑问,比起买机票来要麻烦得多。

我开始翻看当地报纸的"招聘广告",很快发现旅行社"只需要有经验的旅行代理人和航空公司的工作人员"。我一项条件都不符合。可是,就在我家附近的一家旅行社(天下有这么幸运的事情)有一个初级的空缺职位,负责接听电话,打印旅行线路,给票据打包等工作。老板交代得很清楚,干这份工作是没有机会晋升为旅行代理人,或者参加代理人培训的,但是我如果感兴趣,他们就安排面试。

I was interested.I was definitely interested! I interviewed and was hired. Bravo,at least I had my foot in the door.

After working on the packaging desk for nine months,I approached the agency owner,and again expressed my desire to become a travel agent.Fortunately,she made an exception and broke her "no experience no training"rules by enrolling me in a United Airlines computer training course.Thus,I realized my dream and became a full-fledged agent.

My confidence and self-worth increased with each error-free reservation and each satisfied customer.I was having a ball! I learned as much as possible about the foreign destinations I booked and got to know my clients well,so their special needs could always be met.I loved my work and took pride in it.I am proud to say,never once did I take the marvelous travel benefits I was receiving for granted.I did keep track of them,however,and received a great deal of satisfaction the year the value of my benefits exceeded my yearly salary.Now that is what I call a job! Way back when I began this career,I could not imagine myself working full time,but just as quickly couldn't visualize myself not working full time,for I was having the time of my life!

What a positive impact those middle-age "hot flashes"had on my life.Ultimately,I became a top-producing corporate international sales agent before my early retirement seventeen years later.I also experienced a world of travel,some shared with family and friends.Most importantly,I proved to myself I could do what I made up my mind to do,no matter how difficult or foreign the task.Yes indeed,life is beautiful and life can begin at forty-plus years of age.

Carolee Ware

我当然感兴趣了！我通过了面试，被录用了。好极了！至少我有一只脚已经跨进了大门。

做了9个月的给票据打包的工作之后，我找到旅行社的老板，再次表明了我想做代理人的愿望。有幸的是，她网开一面，打破"无经验者不可参加培训"的戒律，送我去参加了一个美国联合航空公司的电脑培训课程。于是，我实现了梦想，成了一个训练有素的旅行代理人。

每多一次万无一失的预定，每多一个心满意足的顾客，我的自信和自我价值就会增长一分。我非常快乐！我竭尽所能地了解我预定的异国目的地以及顾客，以便尽可能地满足他们的特殊需求。我热爱工作，也很自豪有这份工作。工作给我自己的旅行带来巨大的方便。我可以骄傲地说，我从来没把这种福气当运气。相反，我时刻记住这些好处。一年下来，当好处最终超过一年的收入的时候，我获得了极大的满足感。这样的工作才叫工作！刚开始当旅行代理人的时候，我不相信自己会全天地工作，可是不久之后，我就发现自己很难停止工作，因为工作已经成了生活。

"更年期"反应竟然对我产生了如此积极的作用。终于，17年后，在决定提前退休的之前，我已经成了业绩最好的国际团体销售代理。我也体验了旅行的世界，有时是和家人一起的，有时是和朋友一起的。最重要的是，我向自己证明了只要我下定决心做的事情，不管困难有多大，不管任务有多么陌生，我都可以做好。是的，生活是美好的，生活可以从40多岁开始。

卡罗里·沃尔

First-Year Working Woman

"Are you Joan Clayton?"A man's voice asked on the phone that early morning.

In late August,many teachers find greener pastures,and this superintendent had to have a replacement immediately.

Having graduated the previous May with a master's degree and honors in education,I thought I had arrived.I had applied everywhere within driving distance.There were no vacancies.All of that money my husband spent to get me through college just wasted,I thought.

"Well,get yourself over here,"the superintendent was saying. "We need an interview."

"I just washed my hair and it's in big ugly rollers."What is wrong with me?Why did I say that?I wanted the job!

"Well,take those rollers out.We like our teachers to look pretty."

I snatched my master's diploma as I went out the door.Since it was a hot summer morning,I drove the thirty minutes with all the windows down,hoping my long hair would dry.I stopped one block shy of the superintendent's office and took the rollers out.My hair fell down,limp,wet and looking like a straggled hound.

I made the best of it,introduced myself and shared my philosophy of teaching.After all,he was meeting the world's best teacher and every student would learn. Boy!Did I ever have stars in my eyes? World. You just wait.You haven't seen this working woman yet!

"You be here bright and early Monday morning for the first faculty meeting before the children arrive."The superintendent shook my hand and I thanked him with great enthusiasm.

"Yahoo! "I shouted when I got in the car.I couldn't wait to get home to tell my husband.

双语精华版·心灵鸡汤·

职场第一年

"你是琼·克雷顿吗？"那天一大早一个男人打来电话。

8月底，很多老师都另择高枝了。主管不得不火急火燎地找人替代。

5月份，我刚从学校毕业，拿到了教育专业的硕士学位和荣誉学生的头衔，满以为自己出师了。我在驾车可到的范围内四处求职，不料却没有找到空缺职位。丈夫供我上大学的钱都打水漂了，我心里想。

"那好，你自己过来吧，"主管说，"我们需要面试。"

"我刚洗头，头上还顶着难看的大卷发器。"我是怎么了？说这些干吗？我需要这份工作！

"那就取下来吧。我们欢迎漂亮的老师。"

我抓起硕士文凭，夺门而出。车在路上走了30分钟。那是夏天的早上，天气炎热。我想晾干头发，所以一路上车窗都开着。离主管办公室还差一个街区路程的时候，我把车停下来。摘下卷发器，头发立刻耷拉下来，很软，很湿。我的样子就像一条离队的猎狗。

不过我还是要力挽狂澜。先是一番自我介绍，接着又是一通自己的教学哲学。毕竟嘛，他面前的是全天下最优秀的教师，所有的学生都会因她受益匪浅。天啊！我的眼睛里有没有冒火花？天下人，你们等着看吧，这样优秀的职场女性你们还是从来未见过呢！

"周一清早过来。我们在孩子们来之前召开第一次教职工会议。"主管和我握了握手，我回赠给他热切的感激。

"万岁！"我钻进车里大喊。此刻的我归心似箭，急着去向丈夫报喜。

I arrived an hour early on that first Monday morning,eager to get my wonderful expertise rolling.

I had never seen so many children in one room … and still they came.By 10:30,surely every child had arrived.I counted the children,all thirty-nine of them.My well-thought-out and marvelously well-written lesson plans somehow didn't fit these third-graders.

"Now class,we are going to write about what we did this summer." I gave the writing papers to a student to pass out and right away he dropped them.I had both outside doors open because of the heat and no air conditioning.The breeze from outside blew the papers all over the room and thirty-nine children turned into ants,except ants don't talk!

When I finally got everyone settled and busy writing their story,I had another big surprise! Quite suddenly,for no rhyme or reason,Ben stood up in his chair desk,flapped his arms like a rooster and yelled at the top of his voice:"Err…err…err…err! "

They didn't tell me about this in college,kept going through my mind.My principal,seeing I had minor trouble（yeah … right）with discipline,brought me some little brochures.The titles read *"Tips on Discipline"*.One of the tips suggested:"When lining up the children,let all the children with blue eyes line up first,or all the children with brown eyes,etc."

The longest school week ever finally came to an end for this working woman.I breathed a sigh of relief when the three o'clock bell rang.Completely exhausted and worn to a frazzle,I went to the exit door and announced:

"All the children with two eyes may line up first! "Immediately a stampede occurred.I dodged just in time.As the last student went out the door,he exclaimed:"Teacher,you get sillier by the day! "

In my second week of teaching,I lost what common sense re-mained.I thought a quick way of checking math papers included a long line of children waiting at my desk for their turn.This fiasco turned into a zoo,too.Did I actually think thirty-nine kids were going to wait quietly in line? The last little girl in line handed me a blank paper and asked:

开学第一个周一的早上,因为迫不及待地想将过人的才华一显身手,我早到了一个小时。

我从没见过一间屋子里有这么多孩子啊……而且还有不断进来的。10:30时,约摸所有的孩子都到齐了,我开始点人数,总共39人。可是我那构思缜密、精心打造的教学计划却并不见得适合这些三年级的小朋友。

"好了,同学们,我们来描写一下暑假的经历。"我把作文纸交给一个学生,让他来发,可是他没接稳,纸掉了。教室里很热,没有空调,两扇门都大开着。小风从外面吹进来,把纸吹得到处飞。39个孩子全部都成了忙碌的小蚂蚁,不同的是蚂蚁不说话!

好不容易全班同学都安静下来了。开始写故事的时候,又发生了一件特别离奇的事。突然之间,一个叫"本"的小孩莫名其妙地从课桌边椅子上站了起来。模仿公鸡两只胳臂向后一撇,扯着嗓子就叫:"喔……喔……喔!"

大学里可没教过怎么应对这样的情况,我的脑子里当时就这一个想法。校长知道我在管纪律方面遇到了小麻烦(没错……是这样),给我送来了一本小手册,书名是《纪律管理技巧》。其中我看到这样一条:"给孩子们排队的时候,可以让所有蓝眼睛的孩子先站出来,也可以让棕眼睛的孩子先站出来。"

本人在学校度过的最漫长的第一周终于画上了句号。3点钟的铃声响起,我长长地吐了一口气。真是累得精疲力竭、人仰马翻啊。我走到门口宣布:

"所有长了两只眼睛的孩子先站出来!"话音刚落就出现了群兽惊逃的场面,幸亏我躲闪得及时。最后一个学生出门的时候,冲着我喊:"老师,你越来越傻了!"

在任教的第二周,我干脆连常识都忘了。我以为让一大堆孩子都到讲台来排队,可以加快数学试卷的阅卷速度。这次溃败使教室再次变成了动物园。我难道真的相信39个孩子会安安静静地来排队?排在队尾的小女孩交的竟然还是空白卷。她问我:"老师,卷子上

"Teacher,do we put our name on our paper?"

I was still hanging in there at Christmastime,but I panicked when told I would be presenting the Christmas program for the grade-school parents.I decided to have the children do a rhythm-band number.It went pretty well,I thought.When the performance ended,I instructed the children to pass their instruments down to me,cautioning how careful and quiet they must be,and they turned into little angels.As we quietly exited the gym,the children followed right behind me.My arms,being full of bells,tambourines and noisemakers gave way and all the instruments toppled to the floor with the thunderous sound of an earthquake.The zoo was back! Children came from everywhere,grabbing this and that,shouting "I got it! No,that's mine.I saw it first! Get out of my way! "The parents hid their faces,trying not to laugh.About this time,I would have made a great candidate for an aspirin commercial.Whatever happened to the world's-best-teacher-working-woman?

Back in our room,one oversized plump boy popped up and down in his seat.I asked what he was doing.He replied:"I'm popping them mustard packs I got at the show last night.Don't it smell good?"

When May rolled around,I felt both happy and sad.Happy that in spite of all my "boo-boos",these children had won my heart.I found myself planning for next year.A lot of new ideas and strategies beckoned me.

The students' achievement scores during my first year as a working woman were extraordinarily good.My students had learned in spite of me,but I had learned more than anyone!

My first year as a working woman,despite the many "boo-boos", turned into a thirty-one year teaching career,and I wouldn't have missed it for the world!

Joan Clayton

写我们的名字吗？"

到圣诞节边上我还在顽强地坚守着。可是为小学生家长们表演圣诞节目的任务一到，我立刻惊恐万分。我决定让孩子们练习打击乐的曲目。计划进展得还挺顺利，我暗自想。演出结束后，我让孩子们把乐器传给我，并且交代他们，传递的时候务必要小心，要保持安静。他们变成了听话的小天使。我们安静地退出体操馆，孩子们紧跟着我。抱着那么多铃铛、铃鼓和其他打击乐器，我的胳臂很快就吃不消了。所有的乐器全部栽到地上，一时间震耳欲聋，好似地震来了。动物园的一幕又回来了！孩子们从四面八方赶来，有的抢这个，有的抢那个，还大声地叫喊着："我拿到了！不，那个是我的。我先看到的！你走开！"家长们转开脸，强忍着没笑。看来我完全可以给阿司匹林做电视广告了。这位世界上最优秀的教师和职场女性究竟是怎么了？

回到教室，一个小胖子男生在位子上跳上跳下。我问他在做什么。他回答说："我把昨天晚上看表演时吃的几包芥末都抖出来。味道不错吧？"

当一转眼又到了5月份的时候，我感到既开心又伤心。开心的是，尽管我惹出了不少让人啼笑皆非的笑话，我的心却深深地爱上了这些孩子。我已经在着手准备第二年的工作了。很多新鲜的构思和方法在向我招手。

上班的第一年，学生们的成绩就非常优秀。尽管我的表现不尽如人意，孩子们还是学到了东西，不过我学到的最多！

第一年工作当中的那么多的"笑话"并没有影响到我，相反，它让我决定把31年的生命都献给了教育事业，而且决不后悔！

琼·克雷顿

So…What Do You Grow?

We are not rich by what we possess but rather by what we can do without.

Immanuel Kant

Sandy lives in an apartment so small that when she comes home from shopping at Goodwill, she has to decide what to move out to make room for her purchases. She struggles day-to-day to feed and clothe herself and her four-year-old daughter on money from freelance writing and odd jobs.

Her ex-husband has long since disappeared down some unknown highway, probably never to be heard from again. As often as not, her car decides it needs a day off and refuses to budge. That means bicycling (weather permitting), walking or bumming a ride from friends.

The things most Americans consider essential for survival—a television, microwave, boom box and high-priced sneakers—are far down Sandy's list of "maybe someday" items.

Nutritious food, warm clothing, an efficiency apartment, student loan payments, books for her daughter, absolutely necessary medical care and an occasional movie matinee eat up what little cash there is to go around.

Sandy has knocked on more doors than she can recall, trying to land a decent job, but there is always something that doesn't quite fit— too little experience or not the right kind, or hours that make child care impossible.

播撒爱的种子

富裕并不在于我们占有多少财产,而是看生活中有多少是不可或缺的。

伊马纽尔·康德

桑迪住的公寓太小。她从良愿超市购物回来之后,就得决定哪些东西该搬出去,才能把新买的东西放进去。她是自由职业作家,靠写稿子和打零工挣钱勉强给自己和4岁的女儿解决衣食问题。

前夫很久以前就在人间蒸发了,可能以后也永远不会有他的音信了。她的汽车又犯了老毛病,自作主张给自己放一天假,一步不肯走。就是说,她就要骑自行车(天气允许的话)、步行或者找朋友蹭车了。

大多数美国人观念中的生存必需品——电视、微波炉、录音机和高价的运动鞋——都坠在桑迪的"可能购买"的购物清单下面。

营养食品,御寒的衣服,五脏俱全的小套公寓房,归还学生贷款,为女儿买书,最基本的医疗保健费用和偶尔的午后电影等,仅这些就吞掉了她那点儿仅够周转的现金。

为了找一份体面的工作,桑迪已经记不清自己敲过多少门。找到的总是些不适合她干的工作——要不就是她的经验不足,要不就不是她想要的类型,再或者就是工作时间不适合,没法带孩子。

Sandy's story is not unusual.Many single parents and older people grapple with our economic structure,falling into the crevice between being truly self-sufficient and being sufficiently impoverished to gain government assistance.

What makes Sandy unusual is her outlook.

"I don't have much in the way of stuff or the American dream," she told me with a genuine smile.

"Does that bother you? "I asked.

"Sometimes.When I see another little girl around my daughter's age who has nice clothes and toys,or who is riding around in a fancy car or living in a fine house,then I feel bad.Everyone wants to do well by their children,"she replied.

"But you're not bitter? "

"What's to be bitter about? We aren't starving or freezing to death, and I have what is really important in life,"she replied.

"And what is that? "I asked.

"As I see it,no matter how much stuff you buy,no matter how much money you make,you really only get to keep three things in life,"she said.

"What do you mean by 'keep'? "

"I mean that nobody can take these things away from you."

"And what are these three things? "I asked.

"One,your experiences;two,your true friends;and three,what you grow inside yourself,"she told me without hesitation.

For Sandy,"experiences" don't come on a grand scale.They are so-called ordinary moments with her daughter,walks in the woods,napping under a shade tree,listening to music,taking a warm bath or baking bread.

Her definition of friends is more expansive."True friends are the ones who never leave your heart,even if they leave your life for a

CHICKEN
SOUP

双语精华版·心灵鸡汤·

桑迪的故事绝不是特例。很多单亲父母或者是老年人都在我们的经济结构里艰难地生存着。他们既没富到真正地自给自足，又还没穷到够资格领取政府补助，偏偏落在政策的夹缝里。

　　使桑迪与众不同的地方是她的人生观。

　　"从财产和美国梦的方面讲，我拥有的不多。"她说着，露出真心的微笑。

　　"那你不心烦吗？"我问。

　　"有时候。当我看到和我女儿同龄的孩子有漂亮的衣服，有好玩的玩具，或者坐高档的车子，住豪华的房子，我就会感觉很糟糕。所有的人都想对孩子好一些。"她回答道。

　　"但是你不生气吗？"

　　"为什么生气？我们没有饿死，也没有冻死。我拥有生命中最重要的东西。"她答道。

　　"那是什么呢？"我问。

　　"在我看来，不管你买多少东西，不管你赚多少钱，生活中你必须要保住这三样东西。"她说。

　　"'保住'是什么意思？"

　　"我是说，这些东西都是别人从我这儿拿不走的。"

　　"是哪三样东西呢？"我问。

　　"一是个人经历；二是真心的朋友；三是你在心里种下的种子。"她毫无保留地告诉了我。

　　对桑迪来说，"经历"不是指惊天动地的事情，而是指与女儿一起、在树林里散步、在树荫下小睡、听音乐、洗热水澡、烤面包等所谓的平凡时刻。

　　她对朋友的定义更加宽泛。"真正的朋友是那些即使离开一段时间，也会常驻在你心中的朋友。就算他们离开你的生活很多年，再

while.Even after years apart,you pick up with them right where you left off,and even if they die,they're never dead in your heart,"she explained.

As for what we grow inside,Sandy said, "That's up to each of us, isn't it? I don't grow bitterness or sorrow.I could if I wanted to,but I'd rather not."

"So what do you grow? "I asked.

Sandy looked warmly at her daughter and then back to me.She pointed toward her own eyes,which were aglow with tenderness,gratitude and a sparkling joy.

"I grow this."

Philip Chard

Submitted by Laurie Waldron

见面时依然是非常要好。就算他们离世了,他们也会永远活在你心里。"她说。

至于我们在内心种了什么,桑迪说:"那就是因人而异,是不是?我不会种下仇恨和悲伤的种子。如果我想的话,我可以这么做,但是我不愿意这么做。"

"那你种什么?"

桑迪充满爱意地看着女儿,然后转过身来。她指着自己的眼睛。她的眼睛闪耀着温柔、感激和激扬的欢乐。

"我种的就是这个。"

菲利浦·查德

劳利·沃尔德隆　整理

THE WIZARD OF ID

Just the Way You Are

My friend Mark Tucker produces and delivers multimedia slide presentations to audiences across the country.

One night, following one of his shows on the East Coast, a woman came up to him and said, "You know, you really should be using my son's music in your show."

So Mark started to give her the usual rap. First, her son should make a demo tape. It didn't have to be professional, he explained. In fact, her son could just go into his bedroom and play some simple chords on his guitar—just enough to give Mark an idea of the type of music he played.

After he had explained the whole process, the woman gave him a funny look and said, "Well, my son is Billy Joel."

As soon as he had recovered from the shock, Mark quickly assured her that her son would not need to send a demo tape! He then listened as this woman urged him to consider using one particular song her son had written. She felt it contained a positive message about self-worth that would fit Mark's work beautifully. And she went on to describe how the seeds of that song had been planted in early childhood.

As a young boy, she explained, Billy Joel often wanted to be someone else, someone different from who he was. It seems he was teased a lot because he was shorter than the rest of the kids. It was common for him to come home from school or play and complain that he wasn't good enough. And he truly believed that if he could be just a little taller, then he'd be okay.

His mother, of course, never believed for a minute that her son was

爱的就是你

我的朋友马克·塔克的工作是制作并且面向全国观众播放多媒体幻灯片。

一天晚上,在他制作的关于东海岸的幻灯片放映完之后,一位女士走上来,对他说:"你真该在节目当中用上我儿子的音乐。"

马克于是和往常一样,讲了一大通指令。首先,她儿子应该先录制一份样带。他解释说,样带不必很专业,用吉他弹奏几个简单的和弦就可以了,在卧室里录制的都行——有了这些,马克就可以知道他演奏的音乐是哪种类型的了。

等他说完整个流程,那位女士脸上露出了滑稽的表情。她说:"噢,我的儿子是比利·乔。"

马克好不容易从震惊中回过神来,他赶紧向那位女士保证,她的儿子不需要再寄样带过来了!然后就认真地听女士极力推荐她儿子的一首歌。她认为那首歌传递了关于自我价值的正面的信息,与马克的节目是天作之合。然后,她又说那首歌的种子萌芽于比利幼年时的经历,并且详尽地描述了这段经历。

她说比利·乔年轻的时候总是希望自己是别人,是一个与自己不一样的人。因为他的个头比别的孩子矮小,可能经常遭到戏弄,所以放学或者玩耍回来抱怨自己不够好是常有的事情。他真心地相信,只要个子能长高一点,他就会好起来。

他的母亲当然从来都相信他是完美的。所以,每次他表现出对

anything less than perfect.So every time he expressed something negative about himself, she said to him, "Don't worry—it doesn't matter.You don't have to be like anyone else because you're already perfect.We're all unique, we're all different.I love you just the way you are."

Remember that old expression about words coming back to haunt you? In this case, the words of a mother who unconditionally loved her son came back many years later in the form of a song.You see, as Billy Joel grew up, he learned who he was and he found his dream of creating music for the world.And millions of people got to hear with their hearts, as his mother did, the words of his Grammy Award-winning song:

> *Don't go changin'*
> *to try and please me...*
> *I love you just the way you are.*

Jennifer Read Hawthorne

自己不满意的时候,母亲都会告诉他:"别担心——没有关系。你不需要成为别人,因为你已经够完美了。我们都是独一无二的,我们都是与众不同的。我爱的就是现在的你。"

记得人们常说有些话会终生伴随你吗?在这个故事里,母亲无条件地爱着儿子,她的话多年以后被记录在儿子创作的歌曲里。你可以看出,比利长大后,明白了自己是谁,他发现自己的梦想是为世界创作音乐。他的母亲和上百万的听众用心聆听着这首获得格莱美大奖的歌曲:

> 不要因为让我高兴
>
> 而改变自己……
>
> 我就爱现在的你。

詹尼弗·瑞德·霍桑

Just Say Yes

Life is either a daring adventure or nothing at all.

Helen Keller

I'm a standup comic.I was working at a radio station in New York, doing the weather as this character called June East(May West's long-lost sister).One day, a woman from *The Daily News* called and said she wanted to do an article on me.When she had finished interviewing me for the article, she asked, "What are you planning to do next? "

Well, at the time, there was absolutely nothing I was planning on doing next, so I asked her what she meant, stalling for time.She said she really wanted to follow my career.Here was a woman from *The Daily News* telling me she was interested in me! So I thought I'd better tell her something.What came out was, "I'm thinking about breaking the Guinness Book of World Records for Fastest-Talking Female."

The newspaper article came out the next day, and the writer had included my parting remarks about trying to break the world's Fastest-Talking Female record.At about 5:00 P.M. that afternoon, I got a call from *Larry King Live* asking me to go on the show.They wanted me to try to break the record, and they told me they would pick me up at 8:00—because they wanted me to do it *that night*!

Now, I had never heard of *Larry King Live*, and when I heard the woman say she was from the Manhattan Channel, I thought, *Hmmm, that's a porn channel, right*? But she patiently assured me that it was a national television show and that this was a one-time offer and opportu-

先说行

生活是勇敢的冒险，否则你将一事无成。

海伦·凯勒

　　我是个单口喜剧演员，在纽约的一家电台工作，以June East的艺名（May West 失散多年的姐妹）播报天气预报。有一天，《每日新闻》杂志社的一位女士打来电话，说她想为我写篇文章。在结束了对我的采访之后，她问："你下一步要做什么？"

　　可是，在那个时候，我对下一步做什么毫无打算。所以，就反问她是什么意思，以此来拖延一些时间。她说她真想从事我的职业。她在《每日新闻》工作，却告诉我她对我的工作感兴趣！所以我想不妨向她多透露一些。于是从我的嘴里冒出这样一句话："我想打破吉尼斯全球女性最快语速的记录。"

　　第二天的报纸就登出了那篇文章，作者把我分别的时候说的打破女性最快语速的世界记录的想法也写了进去。当天下午5点钟，我接到拉里·金直播节目的电话邀请。他们希望我上他们的节目，尝试打破该项记录，并且告诉我，他们会在8点的时候来接我——因为他们希望我当晚就去！

　　可是我从来没有听说过拉里·金直播节目。当我听到那位女士说她是曼哈顿频道的，我想，嗯，那是个黄色频道吧？但是她不厌其烦地向我保证，这是一个全国性的电视脱口秀节目，而且他们只会

nity—it was either that night or not at all.

I stared at the phone.I had a show that night in New Jersey,but it wasn't hard to figure out which of the two engagements I'd prefer to do. I had to find a replacement for my 7:00 show,and I started calling every comic I knew.By the grace of God,I finally found one who would fill in for me,and five minutes before the deadline,I told *Larry King Live* I could make it.

Then I sat down to figure out what on earth I was going to do on the show.I called Guinness to find out how to break a fast-talking record.They told me I would have to recite something from either *Shakespeare* or the *Bible*.

Suddenly I started saying the ninety-first Psalm,a prayer of protection my mother had taught me.*Shakespeare* and I had never really gotten along,so I figured the *Bible* was my only hope.I began practicing and practicing,over and over again.I was both nervous and excited at the same time.

At 8:00,the limousine picked me up.I practiced the whole way there,and by the time I reached the New York studio,I was tongue-tied. I asked the woman in charge,"What if I don't break the record? "

"Larry doesn't care if you break it or not,"she said."He just cares that you try it on his show first."So I asked myself,*What's the worst that can happen? I'll look like a fool on national television*! *A minor thing*,I told myself,thinking I could live through that.And what if I broke the record?

So I decided just to give it my best shot,and I did.I broke the record,becoming the World's Fastest-Talking Female by speaking 585 words in one minute in front of a national television audience.(I broke it again two years later,with 603 words in a minute.)My career took off.

People often ask me how I did that.Or how I've managed to do many of the things I've done,like lecturing for the first time,or going

邀请我一次——要么今晚就去,要么过了这村没了这店。

我瞪着电话机。当晚,我在新泽西州有个演出,但是在两个预约当中不难做出取舍。我得找个人代替我去参加7点钟的演出。于是我开始给所有认识的喜剧演员打电话。上帝保佑,我在最后期限前5分钟,找到了一个候补人选。我告诉拉里·金我可以到场。

然后我坐下来思考我要在节目中表演什么。我给吉尼斯打电话,咨询他们打破语速记录要做些什么。他们告诉我,可以朗诵莎士比亚的作品或者是《圣经》。

我不禁吟诵起了第91首赞美诗,那是母亲教我的一首护身祷文。我和莎士比亚向来无缘,所以我琢磨着,圣经应该是我唯一的救命稻草。我一遍又一遍地反复练习,那一刻紧张和兴奋混在一起。

8点的时候,有轿车来接我。一路上我都在练习。到达纽约演播室的时候,我的舌头都练僵了。我问负责的那位女士:"我要是不能打破记录怎么办?"

"拉里并不在乎你能不能打破记录,"她说,"他只是希望你上他的节目来尝试一下。"我心里暗想:最糟糕的后果是什么呢?大不了是全国观众面前的一个呆瓜!小事一桩,我这样告诉自己,我想我能接受这样的结果。要是打破了记录呢?

所以我决定破釜沉舟,并且付诸实践。我打破了记录,当着全国观众的面一分钟内说出了585个字,成了世界上语速最快的女性(两年后,我再次打破记录,一分钟说了603个字)。我的事业获得了腾飞。

人们经常问我,是如何做到这一点的,或者做到其他很多事情

on stage for the first time, or bungee jumping for the first time. I tell them I live my life by this simple philosophy: I always say yes first; then I ask, *Now, what do I have to do to accomplish that?*

Then I ask myself, *What is the worst thing that can happen if I don't succeed?* The answer is, I simply don't succeed! And what's the best thing that can happen? I succeed!

What more can life ask of you? Be yourself, and have a good time!

Fran Capo

的,诸如第一次做讲座、第一次登台、第一次蹦极。我告诉他们,我的生活遵循着这样一条简单的哲学:我总是先说行;然后再问,为了实现这个目标,我要做些什么?

接着,我问自己,如果我不能成功,最糟糕的结果会是什么?答案是:我失败了!最好的结果是什么?我成功了!

生活对你还有什么要求呢?做你自己,享受人生!

弗朗·卡波

"It was a purely professional decision, Harris. I hope my firing you won't affect our marriage in any way."

Reprinted by permission of Harley Schwadron.

May Basket

Forgiveness ought to be like a cancelled note—torn in two,and burned up,so that it never can be shown against one.

Henry Ward Beecher

"Hey,do you know what? Today is May Day!"my sister announced. "Do you remember the May Day baskets we used to make with colored paper and paste?"

Childhood memories and warm feelings engulfed me as I recalled that my sisters and I would run around our neighborhood delivering the not-so-perfect baskets brimming with spring flowers.We would place the handmade treasures on a doorstep,knock on the door,then scurry away as fast as our legs could carry us.It was delightful to peer around a bush and watch our friends open their doors and pick up the colorful gift, wondering who had left it out for them.

I distinctly remember the May Day of the year that I was in fifth grade.That year I was faced with a challenge involving one of my dearest friends.She lived right across the road from our family,and we had walked together to school nearly every day since first grade.

Pam was a year older than I,and her interests were starting to change from the interests that we had shared together.A new family had recently moved into our small town,and Pam was spending more and more time at their house.I felt hurt and left out.

When my mother asked me if I was going to take a May Day basket to Pam's house,I responded angrily,"Absolutely not! " My mom

五月的花篮

"喂,你知道么?今天是五月节!"我的姐姐宣称道。"你还记得我们曾经用彩纸和糨糊做成的五月花篮吗?"

当我回想起我的姐妹们和我跑遍附近的邻居家,为他们送去用春天盛开的鲜花点缀的并不是很完美的花篮时,那些儿时的记忆与温馨的感觉淹没了我。我们会把这些手工制作的财宝挂到门环上,敲敲门之后,就以最快的速度跑到一边。躲到灌木丛后面,偷偷看着我们的朋友打开房门,捡起色彩斑斓的礼物,猜测着是谁送给他们的礼物时令我们感到开心。

我清楚地记得我上五年级那一年的五月节。那一年我要面对一个挑战,就是开我一个最好朋友的玩笑。隔着一条街,她就住在我家对面,自打一年级开始,我们就几乎每天一起步行去学校。

帕姆比我大一岁,她所感兴趣的东西发生了改变,已经不同于我们曾经共同感兴趣的东西。我们小镇上新搬进来一家人,帕姆待在他们家的时间越来越长,我越感到自尊心受到了伤害和背叛。

当我妈妈问我五月节时我是否会给帕姆家送一个花篮时,我气急败坏地说:"决不!"妈妈停下了她手里的活,蹲了下来把我抱在了

stopped what she was doing,knelt down and held me in her arms.She told me not to worry,that I would have many other friends throughout my lifetime.

"But Pam was my very best friend ever," I cried.

Mom smoothed back my hair,wiped away my tears and told me that circumstances change and people change.She explained that one of the greatest things friends can do is to give each other a chance to grow,to change and to develop into all God wants each of them to be.And sometimes,she said,that would mean that friends would choose to spend time with other people.

She went on to say that I needed to forgive Pam for hurting me and that I could express that forgiveness by giving her a May Day basket.

It was a hard decision,but I decided to give Pam a basket.I made an extra special basket of flowers with lots of yellow because that was Pam's favorite color.I asked my two sisters to help me deliver my basket of forgiveness.As we watched from our hiding place,Pam scooped up the flowers,pressed her face into them and said loudly enough for us to hear, "Thank you,Susie,I hoped you wouldn't forget me! "

That day,I made a decision that changed my life: I decided to hold my friends tightly in my heart,but loosely in my expectations of them, allowing them space to grow and to change—with or without me.

Sue Dunigan

怀里。她告诉我不要担心,在我的一生中我还会有其他很多朋友。

"但是帕姆是我最好的朋友呀。"我哭着说。

妈妈抚摸着我的头发,拭去我的泪水,告诉我说环境会改变,人也会改变。她解释说朋友之间能够做得最重要的事情之一就是让彼此都有成长的机会,有改变的机会,有成为上帝所希望你们每一个人应该成为的那种人的机会。有时候,她说,就意味着朋友会选择与别的人在一起。

她接着说我需要宽容地对待帕姆伤害我自尊心一事,并且我可以通过送给她一个五月花篮来表示我的宽容。

那是一个艰难的决定,但是我还是决定给帕姆一个花篮。我做了一个特别的花篮,有很多黄色的花儿,因为帕姆最喜欢的颜色就是黄色。我请求我的两个姐姐帮我把这个宽容之篮送给帕姆。从我们躲藏的地方看到帕姆捧起花儿,把她的脸埋进花儿里,然后用大得我们能够听见的声音喊道:"谢谢你,苏茜,我希望你不会忘记我!"

那一天,我做了一个改变我一生的决定:我决定只将我的朋友们深深地留在心底,但是对他们也只抱有不多的期许,给他们空间去成长、去改变,不论是有我还是没有我在他们身边。

苏·邓尼格安

Love Beyond Tears

CHICKEN SOUP

Some people come into our lives and quickly go.Some people stay for a while and leave their footprints on our hearts,and we are never,ever the same.

Flavia

Julie was five years old when we first met in 1967. "This is Julie. She's my friend."My daughter,Susan,introduced us one morning after kindergarten.

The girls became fast friends.They were inseparable,singing silly songs as they squeezed into one overstuffed living room chair laughing until tears streamed down their faces.

Julie's mom and I took turns transporting the toothless and giggly twosome back and forth from our home to theirs.But the trips ended when my Susan was stricken with a brain tumor in 1969 at the age of seven.

During Susan's twenty-one month illness,Julie never stopped visiting.The girls played finger games when Susan's eyesight dimmed.Julie flipped phonograph records and kept right on singing with Susan,never asking why Susan no longer raced through the house,spun the hula hoop,attended ballet classes or ice-skated.Whenever Susan phoned to invite her friend for dinner,Julie jubilantly arrived to share a meal at Susan's bedside.

In June 1971,Susan died.Julie visited a few weeks later to spend time with our family,but her best friend was gone.Seeing the sadness in Julie's eyes,I told her that Susan loved God and was probably singing with the angels in heaven.

超越泪水的爱

> 有些人走进我们的生命,又匆匆离去。有些人停留了一会儿,在我们的心里留下了足印,因此我们不再和以前相同。
>
> 佛拉维亚

1967年我们第一次见面时,茱莉才5岁。"这是茱莉,是我的朋友。"一天早上,幼儿园放学后,我的女儿苏珊这样把她介绍给我们。

女孩子们很快就成了朋友。她们形影不离,一起挤进卧室中那个厚厚的沙发时,她们唱着"无聊"的歌曲直到自己笑得眼泪直流。

我和茱莉的妈妈轮流把这两个牙还没长齐的叽叽喳喳的家伙在我们两家之间来来回回接来送去。但是1969年,苏珊7岁的时候得了脑瘤,这种旅行终止了。

在苏珊生病的21个月间,茱莉从没有停止探望。当苏珊的视力变模糊时,她们就一起玩手指游戏。茱莉翻动着留声机唱片,跟着苏珊一起歌唱,她从不问苏珊为什么再也不在屋里跑来跑去,为什么不再玩呼拉圈,为什么不再参加芭蕾舞蹈课或者滑冰课,无论什么时候苏珊打电话邀请她的朋友一起吃晚餐,茱莉总是欢欣雀跃地到来,在苏珊的床边陪她一起吃饭。

1971年6月,苏珊病逝。几个星期后,茱莉来到我们家并跟我们住了一段时间,但是她最好的朋友却已经离去。看到她眼里的悲伤,我安慰她说苏珊爱上帝,或许她正在与天堂里的天使一起歌唱呢。

Julie continued to drop by occasionally.On my first Mother's Day following Susan's death,Julie popped in with a red rose.A tradition was started that Sunday in 1972.Julie has never missed giving me a rose and special card on Mother's Day.

That isn't all.Throughout her school years,Julie invited me and my husband,Phil,to important class activities.At graduation,I watched her receive her diploma and knew Susan was there in spirit with her classmates.And when Julie,a member of the yearbook staff,handed me the 1980 yearbook,I opened it to find a dedication to Susan.

Before long,Julie was engaged and planning her wedding to Rob.I was not forgotten.At her shower,Julie's sister,Allison,quietly whispered, "If Susan were here,she'd be up front with Julie."

Another surprise awaited me on Julie and Rob's wedding day.I responded to Julie's telephone request to come to her home.She was waiting for me with a photographer.As she pinned a corsage on my dress and the camera clicked,she invited Phil and me to sit behind her parents in church.

And when Julie and Rob bought their home in Gardner,Massachusetts,of course,we were invited over.

Julie and I have become good friends.Our paths cross,part and unite again.Although we both lead busy lives, when we get together,it's like we never missed a moment.We meet for lunch and enjoy catching up on each other's lives.Julie asks about Phil,our son,Michael,and daughter, Kristin,their spouses and our delightful grandchildren.I listen as she fills me in on her mom and dad,her two sisters,Allison and Tammy,and their families.

Julie,like the five-year-old I first met,can still enthusiastically bring happiness into a dull day.She never fails to mention Susan and the meaning of their deep friendship at such a young age.She remarked,"I never knew Susan was that sick."

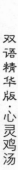

茱莉仍然时不时地来我们家。苏珊去世后的第一个母亲节,茱莉突然来到了我们家,带着一朵鲜红的玫瑰。从那个1972年的星期天起,一个传统就开始了。茱莉从没有忘记在母亲节这一天送我一枝玫瑰和一张纪念卡。

那还不是全部。在她整个上学期间,茱莉邀请我和我的丈夫菲尔参加了很多班级的活动。毕业那天,我看着她接过毕业证书,我知道,苏珊的在天之灵与她的同学们在一起。茱莉当时已经是一个年鉴的工作人员了,递给我一本1980年年鉴,我打开它,发现上面写着"致苏珊"。

不久,茱莉订婚了,并且筹备她同罗伯的婚礼。我是不会被遗忘的。在为庆祝她即将做新娘而举行的聚会上,茱莉的姐姐爱莉森轻声地说:"如果苏珊还在,她肯定会同茱莉一起站在前面。"

茱莉同罗伯婚礼的那一天,另一个惊喜在等待着我。我应茱莉在电话中的邀请赶到了她的家。她正同一个摄影师等着我。当她把一枚胸针别到我的衣服上时,相机的快门闪动。她邀请菲尔和我坐在教堂里她父母的身后。

当茱莉和罗伯在马萨诸塞州的佳得买房子时,我们也理所当然地被邀请了过去。

茱莉和我成了好朋友。我们的轨迹交错、分开,又重合。尽管我们都忙于生计,但是当我们重逢时,就像我们彼此之间从没有分开过。我们一起吃午饭,享受着追赶彼此生活的乐趣,茱莉会问一些关于菲尔,我们的儿子麦克尔,我们的女儿克里斯汀,还有他们的妻子和丈夫,还有我们那些讨人喜欢的孙子们的事情。我倾听她告诉我的关于她的父母、她的两个姐姐爱莉森和泰米,以及她们家庭的事情。

茱莉,就像是我在她5岁时第一次遇见她的那样,总是能够以她的热情给人阴郁的一天带来幸福快乐。她从没有忘记提及苏珊,还有她们在那个小小的年纪所建立起来的深厚情谊的意义。她在谈到苏珊时说:"我从不知道苏珊病得那么严重。"

I asked why she continued to visit. "After all, you were only nine when Susan died."

"I felt like I belonged in your house. I was always there with Susan. My mother never told me to come; it was what I wanted to do."

Julie isn't afraid to say, "I know whenever I'm going through a hard time, Susan is up there for me."

Julie continues to enrich my life. Over the telephone, I learned of her pregnancy. "If it's a girl, I'd like to use the name Susan for her middle name," Julie announced.

This time, I burst into tears. How did Julie know I secretly prayed for Susan's name to be carried on?

Carley Susan Walsh was born October 10, 1997. When I cuddled her in my arms, I felt such love.

For seven years now, I've enjoyed all the hugs and kisses just like my other grandchildren. To Carley I am Granny Phyllis. I'm always invited to her ballet recitals, birthday parties and all the highlights in her life. Julie's joyful, gentle, loving spirit and compassionate heart never stop touching my life.

Today, I remember two five-year-old girls, Susan and Julie, whose paths crossed, then divided, but in truth, never really separated. Through their lives, God has taught me lessons I might never have understood otherwise.

I believe God, in his ultimate plan, brought Julie into my life to walk beside me, to share, care and remind me that God never leaves us comfortless.

Phyllis Cochran

双
语
精
华
版
·
心
灵
鸡
汤
·

我问她为什么一直要来我们家，"毕竟，苏珊去世的时候你才9岁。"

"我感觉自己就属于你们家。在那里我总是与苏珊在一起。我的妈妈从没告诉我不要去，去你那里是我想做的事情。"

茱莉毫不犹豫地说："我知道，无论什么时候我遇到了困难，苏珊都与我在一起。"

茱莉继续让我的生活丰富多彩。在电话里，我知道她怀了孕。"如果是个女孩，我想用苏珊作为她中间的名字，"茱莉宣布道。

这一次，我潸然泪下。茱莉是怎么知道我暗地里祈祷着苏珊的名字能够延续下去？

卡雷·苏珊·沃尔在1997年10月出生，当我把她抱在怀中时，我感到了深深的爱意。

7年过去了，我一直享受着像对待自己的孙儿一样拥抱、亲吻所带来的快乐。对卡雷来说，我是她的菲利斯奶奶，我常常被邀请去参加她的芭蕾舞表演、生日聚会，以及其他她生活中的重要活动。茱莉的快乐、温柔、爱心和同情心一直在滋养着我的生命。

如今，我记得两个5岁的小女孩，苏珊和茱莉，她们的生命轨迹交错、分开，但是事实上，她们从不曾分离。通过她们的生活，上帝教会我懂得了或许我从不会了解的东西。

我相信上帝，在他最重要的计划里，把茱莉安排进我的生活，陪着我一路走下去，安慰我，提醒我上帝永远不会给我们不安与痛苦。

菲利斯·科奇瑞

Opening Doors

The doors we open and close each day decide the lives we live.

Flora Whittlemore

There are thirty-two pairs of teenage eyes on me,and I'm beginning to sweat.It's Career Day here at Denver's Kennedy High School,and I'm speaking about my job as an international journalist.

So far,my speech hasn't gone too well.The young man in the back corner is asleep,and a girl in the front row is playing games on her cell phone.Most of the others have a glazed look in their eyes.

Desperate,I plunge further into my talk,describing assignments in Thailand,interviews in England and stories in Singapore.

But I may as well be speaking of the moon.For most of these students,the rest of the world is a far-off place.They have little exposure to it,and frankly,they're not all that interested.

And who can blame them? I once felt just as they do.

After all,when you grow up in the middle of a big,powerful country,where exposure to other lands and ways of life are somewhat limited,it can lead you to believe that the rest of the world is just like the one in which you grew up. So what reason is there to explore new places? I had little interest in other countries and cultures.

Then I met Melanie.

We all have people who come into our lives who influence or change us,somehow.For me,one of those people was a twenty-year-old girl from Iowa.

放眼大千世界

我们每天开启、关闭的门都与我们的生活息息相关。
弗劳拉·惠特莫尔

　　有32对青少年注视着我，这让我开始冒汗。今天是丹佛肯尼迪高中的职业教育日，我，作为一个国际记者，要对他们讲讲关于我的工作的事情。

　　就目前来说，我的演讲进行得并不是很顺利。后面角落里的小伙子睡得正香，前排的一个小姑娘正沉迷于手机游戏，大部分学生眼中都弥漫着迷茫。

　　孤注一掷的，我开始更加投入地进行我的演讲，我向他们描绘了在泰国的各种采访任务、在英国的各类访谈，以及在新加坡发生的各种故事。

　　但是，我可能是在对牛弹琴，对绝大部分学生而言，其他的世界离他们太过遥远。他们对外界几乎一无所知，坦率地说，他们压根就不感兴趣。

　　但是谁又能责怪他们呢？ 我曾经也同他们一样。

　　毕竟，当你在一个广阔而强大的国家中长大，而这个国家在某种程度上来说与世界的其他地方和别的生活方式接触非常有限，这就会令你相信在世界其他地方，一切都与你所生长的这个地方没什么两样。那么有什么理由去了解新的世界呢？我对其他国家和文化几乎没有什么兴趣。

　　后来我遇见了麦兰尼。

　　生命中我们都会遇见一些人，他们能够影响并改变我们的生活。对于我来说，这些人当中的一个就是来自衣阿华州的20岁的小姑娘。

I was attending college in Indiana that year,and I met Melanie on the school's softball team.In truth,we really didn't play much,but sat out game after game with injuries.While our team sailed on to victories without us,Melanie and I sat on the bench and talked.Eventually,we became roommates.

Melanie was different from anyone I had ever known.She made me laugh with her witty sense of humor,but most of all,she was a story-teller.Her tales were different,though,for she had actually been outside the country.

Day after day,she wove stories of places I had never imagined.She talked of dreamy Austrian villages and narrow,ancient streets.She told of tall,handsome Dutch boys and the thrill of cruising down the autobahn.

At first,I feigned disinterest,but eventually,I began to listen,picturing this world that she painted with words.Gradually,Melanie wore me down.

"Okay! " I said one evening after a long story regaling the thrills of travel."I give up! I want to see this for myself.Let's go! "

And so we did.

Culture shock set in as soon as we set foot in Rotterdam on that weeklong trip during semester break.Surrounded by the staccato sounds of Dutch,I felt like a fish out of water.I wanted to rush back to the plane and head for the familiarity of home.

But I was stuck here,so I followed Melanie through the streets of Rotterdam.She laughed and talked with everyone she met,not afraid of the new things she saw.Slowly,I began to view this new world through her eyes.My discomfort first turned to curiosity,then real interest.

We spent New Year's Eve in Rotterdam,and I watched in awe as the local residents poured into the streets that night,lighting monstrous fireworks,drinking warm drinks and greeting one another(and me!) with two-cheeked kisses.

那一年我正在印第安纳读大学,在学校的垒球队里我认识了麦兰尼。实际上我们打球打得并不多,只是在比赛之后同伤员们坐在一块儿。当我们队一路扬帆取得胜利时,我们并不在其中,麦兰尼和我坐在长椅上聊天,最终,我们成了室友。

麦兰尼不同于我所认识的其他任何一个人。她用她富有智慧的幽默感令我发笑,但是最主要的是,她是一个会讲故事的人。她的故事与众不同,因为她确确实实去过别的地方。

日复一日,她编织着各种地方的故事,都是我从不曾想象过的。她告诉我关于梦幻般的奥地利村庄和狭窄、古老的街道。她告诉我关于高大、英俊的荷兰小伙子以及在德国高速公路上飙车的刺激。

起初,我装作对她的那些故事毫无兴趣,但是最终,我开始聆听,开始想象她用语言所描述的世界是个什么样子。渐渐地,麦兰尼让我彻底折服。

"好吧,"一天晚上,当麦兰尼说完了一个享受旅行的刺激的故事之后,我说,"我服了,我想亲眼看看,我们出发吧!"

于是我们就这么做了!

在那个学期休假期间,我们做了一次为期一周的旅行,文化震撼在我们踏上鹿特丹的那一刻就袭来。被断断续续的荷兰语所包围,我觉得自己仿佛是一条离开了水的鱼儿,恨不得立即冲回机舱,一头扎回熟悉的家乡。

但是我已经来到了这里,于是我跟着麦兰尼穿行在鹿特丹的大街小巷。对于她所遇见的每一个人,她都微笑并与他们交谈,一点也不害怕所看见的新事物。渐渐地,我开始通过麦兰尼的眼睛来观察这个新世界。我的不适开始转变为好奇,最后变为了真正的兴趣。

我们在鹿特丹过新年除夕,我惊奇地看到当地居民在夜间涌入街道,点燃绚烂的焰火,喝着热饮,互相亲吻,彼此问候着(也包括我)。

Right then,even though I couldn't understand a word spoken around me,I smiled with glee.This once strange land that had felt like Mars suddenly turned into heaven on Earth.

From there,Melanie and I rented a little Peugeot and headed out through Europe.We fumbled our way through the countryside,getting lost,but always stopping to ask cute boys for directions.We ran into difficulties with the new languages and cultures,of course,but Melanie just laughed and considered it an adventure.

We drove through Holland and Germany,but it was Austria that stole my heart.The beauty of the Alps surrounding Salzburg took my breath away;and in the cozy cafés that are such an integral part of Austrian culture,I discovered a never-before-seen side of myself.I discovered the quiet joy of sitting all afternoon around a tiny table,drinking dark coffee with whipped cream and discussing the meaning of life with new friends.

Perhaps that is why we are drawn to travel; for leaving our homes and venturing into other parts of the world reveals a side of ourselves that we would never discover otherwise.In learning about others,we learn most about ourselves.

Vienna was the icing on the cake.Wandering with Melanie and my new Austrian friends at midnight down the cobblestone streets of this former imperial city,I could barely contain my delight.Something,I knew,had awakened deep inside of me.

Nine months after that first trek to Europe,I packed up my college boxes and moved to Austria,where I attended university before eventually returning home to the States.My life had turned down a whole new path.

Sadly,that path didn't include Melanie.She graduated and became a teacher.True to her love of adventure,she chose to work in a whole new city and culture: San Antonio,Texas.

就是那个时刻，尽管我不懂得身边的人所说的每一个字，但是却开心地笑了。这个在我看来曾经像火星一样神秘的国度突然间变成了地球上的天堂国度。

从那里，我和麦兰尼租了一辆标致汽车，开始了穿越欧洲的旅程。我们摸索着穿过乡村，迷失了方向，但总时不时停下来问一问可爱的男孩子们。当然，我们遭遇了新语言和新环境这样的困难，但是麦兰尼只是笑对这些，把这当成是一种冒险。

我们驾车穿过荷兰、德国，但是让我着迷的确是奥地利。环绕在萨尔茨堡附近的阿尔卑斯山脉的美景让我心醉；咖啡是奥地利文化不可分割的一部分，在一家温暖舒适的咖啡店里，我发现了自己以前不曾有过的一面。我发现了午后坐在一张小桌子边，喝着伴有奶油的黑咖啡，与新结识的朋友探讨关于生命的意义时所带来的那种宁静的快乐。

或许，这就是我们沉湎于旅行的原因。离开我们自己的家，去世界其他地方冒险会让我们发现关于自身从不曾注意过的另一面。在学会了解别人的同时，我们了解更多的是我们自己。

维也纳就像是蛋糕上的冰。走在鹅卵石铺成的街道上，同麦兰尼以及我们新结识的奥地利朋友在午夜时分漫步在这个曾经的皇家城市，我几乎无法抑制自己的喜悦之情。我知道，某种东西已经唤醒了我心底最深处的情愫。

距离第一次去欧洲的9个月后，我收拾起我上大学的东西，去了奥地利，在最终回到美国之前，我一直在那里的大学读书。我的生活开始了一条新的轨迹。

令人悲哀的是，这次旅行却没有麦兰尼。她毕业之后成为了一名教师。为了忠于她冒险的爱好，她选择在一个新的城市和一种新的文化环境下工作——得克萨斯州的圣·安东尼奥。

My fascination with exploring other cultures and destinations never left me either.I went on to become a journalist,and then an editor for an international travel magazine.

For almost a decade,Melanie and I lost touch.Then one day,a colleague asked me,"Why did you choose this career path?"

In my mind,I immediately saw an image of Melanie,chatting over dinner at the college cafeteria,telling me stories of worlds I had never known.It was time to track down my long-lost friend.

That evening,I looked up Melanie's parents on the Internet and called them.I learned that they were still living in Iowa and that my former roomie had gone on to become a principal,turning around entire schools with her passion for success and achievement.I grinned as I dialed her number.

With some friends,lost years just slip away and you're right back to your same relationship.That was how it was with Melanie and me. Within minutes,she had me laughing as we talked.Life was going well, and my friend was very successful."But I really miss having the chance to travel," she admitted.

So we remedied that.Every year,we meet up somewhere in the world and spend a week exploring.Last year,it was the Scottish Isles; this year,it will be Switzerland.Who knows where we'll end up after that?

Melanie is the reason I am standing in front of this classroom today.So I stop my speech,take a deep breath and try another angle. Forget stories of journalism; there are better tales to tell.

So I begin to talk of Dutch celebrations,of dreamy Austrian villages and the thrill of cruising down the Autobahn.And in the far corner,I see something stir.The boy in the back has woken up,and I can't help but grin.

After all,it only takes one person to open your eyes to the world.

Janna Graber

我对了解其他文化和国家的兴趣却没有消失,我后来成为了一名记者,之后成为一本国际旅游杂志的编辑。

几乎有10年,我同麦兰尼失去了联系。有一天,有位同事问我:"你是如何选择了这个职业的?"

我的脑海里立即浮现出一幅关于麦兰尼的景象:在校园的咖啡馆里,一边吃着晚餐,一边告诉我我从未听说过的世界上其他地方的故事。是该找到我这位很久不见的朋友的时候了。

那天晚上,我从互联网上查到了麦兰尼父母并给他们打了电话。从他们口中我得知他们依然居住在衣阿华州,而我的前室友已经成为了校长,她用她全部追求成功与成就的热情管理着学校。当我拨打她的电话时,我会心地笑了。

对于朋友之间来说,失去的岁月不过如白驹过隙,重逢会令你们立即回到当初的那种友谊之中。麦兰尼和我就是这样。短短几分钟,她就在言语中令我开怀大笑。生活进行得如此美妙,而我的朋友是如此的杰出。"不过我是确实错过了旅行的机会,"她坦诚地说。

于是我们决定弥补这些。每一年,我们都会在世界的某个地方见面并待上一个星期去四处观光。去年,我们到了苏格兰群岛,而今年我们会去瑞士。谁晓得我们的下一个目的地是哪里呢?

麦兰尼就是我今天站在讲台前的原因。于是我停下演讲,深深地吸了一口气,开始了另外一个话题。抛开记者的那些报道,告诉学生们一些更好的故事。

于是我开始谈起荷兰的庆典,梦幻般的奥地利村庄,在高速公路上飚车的刺激。于是,在那个角落里,我看到了一些动静。后排的那个男孩已经醒了过来,我不由得笑了。

别忘了,只需要一个人就可以让你开阔视野、认识世界。

亚娜·格拉贝尔

The Book of Friendship

Happiness isn't the easiest thing to find, but one place you're guaranteed to find it is in a friend's smile.

Allison Poler

December 24 arrived along with heavy snow that clung stubbornly to the roads. Highways closed and the authorities issued travel advisories throughout the day. Into the evening it fell, sealing in the somberness of the day.

Let it snow, I thought. It was my first Christmas Eve without my mother, and my sadness dampened the day's usual excitement. Any excuse not to leave the shelter of my small apartment seemed good to me.

The telephone rang. I ignored it and went to my bedroom to bury my face in the softness of my pillow, hoping to muffle out the incessant and demanding shrill, knowing it must be my friend Rebecca calling. It was eight o'clock and I was supposed to be at her house for dinner.

I'm doing her a favor by not being there, I thought to myself. How could I be joyful when I feel so lousy? I want to be left alone.

My eyes were red and sore from the tears that would not stop. My heart felt as heavy as the falling snow. My grief was piled as high as the snowdrifts.

How do I stop missing my mother?

I must have drifted off to sleep, for I awakened with a start. Someone pounded at the front door.

I tiptoed to the window and looked through the frosted pane. Seeing

双语精华版·心灵鸡汤·

友谊之书

　　幸福不是最容易被发现的东西,但是有一个地方可以保证你得到它,那就是朋友的微笑。

　　　　　　　　　　　埃里森·普勒

　　12月24日,天下起了鹅毛大雪,道路被盖了个严严实实。高速公路也关闭了,整整一天,官方都在发布关于出行的建议。雪一直下到晚上,一整天都是阴沉沉的。

　　就让雪一直下吧,我心里念叨道。这是我的第一个没有妈妈陪伴的圣诞夜,我的忧伤令往常这一天的快乐与兴奋消失无踪。任何理由让我不离开这个如同避难所的小小公寓对我来说都是不错的。

　　电话铃响了。 我没有理会,而是进了我的卧室,把脸深深埋在软软的枕头里,希望把这种不停歇的、苛求的刺耳声遮住。我知道那一定是我的朋友瑞贝卡打来的电话。时间已经是8点了,这个时候我应该是在他们家一起共进晚餐的。

　　不接电话就等于是帮她一个忙,我对自己说。在我感到极不舒服的时刻,又怎么能够快乐起来? 我想一个人待着!

　　因为不停地流泪,我的双眼又红又痛,我的心情也如飘落的雪花一样沉重,我的悲伤,也如同雪堆一样,越积越多。

　　我如何才能停止思念我的妈妈?

　　我一定是不知不觉睡着了,因为一个动静惊醒了我。有人在敲我家的前门。

　　我踮着脚尖走到窗户跟前,透过结满霜花的窗户向外看去。我

Rebecca's car parked out front,I padded back to bed and drew the covers over my head.

"Girlfriend! " she shouted. "I know you're in there.Answer the door! "

"Leave me alone! " I shouted back.

The floorboards creaked in the hallway.I heard paper rustling as she slid something under the door.

"Merry Christmas," she called out.

Not answering the door made me feel worse,if that was possible.I wasn't being fair to my best friend.Ever since grade school,we had been inseparable.Most people mistook us for sisters.Her father and sister died in a car accident when she was eight years old.As a result,her mother had to return to work,and Rebecca was pretty much left to fend for herself.She became a fixture at our house.

Still,my misery kept me from answering the door.

When I was sure she left,I retrieved the small square package. Wrapped simply in gold foil,it had no other decoration.Carrying it to the bench by the window,I sat down and unwrapped it: a gold pen and a journal.When I opened the front cover,out fell a bookmark with a note on it:

> *Dear Sister Friend,*
>> *My words won't heal the pain.But your own words can.*
>>
>> *Love,*
>> *Rebecca*

I stared at the blank pages,not wanting to spoil the pure whiteness with empty phrases.A single tear fell and the page absorbed it.I wrote my name on the first page and looked at it for a long time.

Out of the corner of my eye,I caught some movement on the

看到瑞贝卡的车子停在屋前,我回到床前,用东西蒙住了我的头。

"朋友,"她喊道,"我知道你在里面,开门呀。"

"不用管我,让我一个人待着!"我喊道。

门厅的地板发出吱吱的声音,我听到她通过门下的缝隙塞进纸张的沙沙声。

"圣诞快乐!"她高声说。

没有给她开门令我感觉更加糟糕,如果可能我是会开的。我这样对待我的朋友很不公平。从小学开始,我们就不曾分开过。绝大部分人都会把我们当做亲姐妹。当她8岁的时候,她的爸爸和姐姐被一次车祸夺去了生命,因此,她的妈妈不得不回来重新工作,而瑞贝卡常常被留下来自己照顾自己。她成为我们家的一分子。

尽管如此,我的悲伤还是阻止我给她开门。

当我确信她离开后,我找到了一个方形的包裹,包裹除了用一张金色纸包着外,没有其他的点缀。我拿着它走到窗边的长椅那儿,坐了下来,然后拆开了包裹:里面是一支金笔和一本日记本。当我翻开封面时,一张书签飘了下来,上面写着:

亲爱的姐妹、朋友,

我的话无法治愈你的悲伤,但是你自己的语言可以做到。

爱你的,
瑞贝卡

我凝视着空白页,不想用我空洞的语言来破坏这片纯白。一颗泪珠落在本子上,被纸吸干。我把自己的名字写在了第一面上,然后盯着它看了很久很久。

透过眼角的余光,我发现窗外有什么东西在移动。一只猫蜷坐

windowsill outside.A cat sat crouched,waiting to pounce on a sparrow that just landed in search of some seed I sprinkled there earlier in the day.Every time the cat pounced,the sparrow flew away,returning only moments later to eat the rest of the seed.I am a terrible artist,however,to my bewilderment,I sketched several pictures of the bird,as it flew away and returned again.Next I drew the cat,poised and ready to attack its prey.

When the cat finally gave up on the sparrow and darted to another ledge,I surveyed my drawings.

Am I the sparrow or the cat? I wondered.I wrote the question beside the drawings,then closed the journal.

Over the following months,my stormy emotions took refuge within the pages of the book.Tears fell on the paper as often as words.

Prayers tearfully written,faith renewed.The storm ebbed as each image and word touched the pages.

I was the sparrow,foraging for answers and oblivious to the threat of being swallowed by grief.

As my heart healed,so did my understanding of the incredible friendship Rebecca and I shared.This journal was,in essence,an extension of her friendship.Even though I pushed her away at a very difficult time, she found a way to help me communicate my grief,by giving me this "surrogate" friend.

One night,I picked up the phone and dialed her number.

"Looks like the snow is melting," I said.

Spring was just around the corner.

S.A.(Shae) Cook

在那里,等着向一只小麻雀发起突袭,那只小麻雀刚刚落地,正在寻找着我今天早些时候撒下的种子。每次猫向麻雀发起攻击,麻雀就飞开,然后一小会之后再飞回来,继续吃剩下的种子。我是一个糟糕的画家,但是,使我困惑的是,在鸟儿飞去飞回的时候,我竟然能够画出几张它的素描。接着我画了猫,泰然自若,对它的猎物虎视眈眈。

当猫最终放弃捕捉麻雀,向另外一个窗台飞快地跑去,我审视了一下自己的杰作。

我是那只猫还是那只麻雀呢?我困惑不解。我把问题写在那些素描边上,然后合上了日记本。

在接下来的几个月里,我汹涌澎湃的思绪在日记本里找到了避难的港湾,泪水经常和着文字滴入纸间。

祈祷被含泪写下,信仰也再次归来。当每一幅画、每一个字在纸间流淌,暴风骤雨般的情感也开始平息。

我就是那只麻雀。四处寻找着答案,并且忘记了被悲伤吞噬的危险。

当我从悲痛的心情中恢复过来,我对和瑞贝卡之间的令人难以置信的友谊的理解也同样恢复了过来。这个日记本实质上就是她友谊的延伸。尽管在那个极度困难的时候我拒绝过她,但是她却找到了一个途径让我同自己的悲伤交流、沟通——送给我这个"替身"朋友。

一天夜里,我拿起电话,拨通了她的电话。

"看起来冰雪正在融化。"我说。

春天就要来临了。

S.A.(雪) 库克

The Tablecloth

Friends are together when they are separated, they are rich when they are poor, strong when they are weak, and a thing even harder to explain—they live on after they have died, so great is the honor that follows them, so vivid the memory, so poignant the sorrow.

Cicero

Last year, my mother, Rose, lost her best friend of fifty years, Rosa, to cancer. Over a lifetime, Mom and Rosa forged a relationship that transcended the two of them, tightly intertwining their families as well. The two women knew and understood each other thoroughly and plainly, and deeply valued each other's company and wisdom.

Their friendship began when they were young brides, inviting each other to barbecues and cocktail parties where they tried out and polished their cooking skills. A few years later, each became pregnant, beginning parallel journeys of motherhood. As the years passed, together they experienced the normal ups and downs of raising a family, providing one another with daily comfort, encouragement and companionship.

When Rosa's cancer was diagnosed, my mother was her greatest cheerleader. Galvanized by fear and a loss of control, Mom organized meals, shuttled Rosa to doctor appointments, ministered to Rosa's husband and grown children, and when possible, translated medical lingo to a bewildered family. My mother, a quintessential helper, gave Rosa and her loved ones much-needed support, gratified to be the scaffolding on which her fragile friend leaned.

未织完的台布

即使分离，朋友依然在一起；即使贫穷，他们依然富有；即使羸弱，他们依然强壮。更难以解释的就是，即使它们逝去，却依然活在我们心里，与他们相随是至上的荣耀，关于他们的记忆是如此的鲜活，而悲哀又是如此的强烈。

西塞罗

去年，我的妈妈罗斯失去了她相交了50年的最好的朋友——罗莎，因为癌症去世了。在长达一生的时间里，妈妈和罗莎铸就了超越她们两人的、紧密地相互交错的家庭的友谊。两位女士彼此相知，并且非常珍惜对方的陪伴与智慧。

当她们还是新娘时，友谊就开始了，她们相互邀请去吃烧烤，并且参加鸡尾酒会，在那里他们尝试并提高她们的烹饪技术。几年之后，她们都怀了孕，同时开始了做母亲的日子。又是几年过去了，她们一同经历了维持家庭生活所有的起起落落，每一天她们彼此都会给对方安慰、鼓励以及友情的问候。

当罗莎被确诊得了癌症时，我妈妈是她最伟大的拉拉队长。由于担心而引起的激动和失控，妈妈安排了所有的饭食，护送罗莎往返于家和医院之间，安排好罗莎的丈夫和孩子们，如果可能，还向不知所措的家庭成员们解释那些医疗术语。我的妈妈，一个模范的助人为乐者，给了罗莎和她所爱的人最需要的支持，成为她虚弱的朋友得以依靠的支撑，这让她很满足。

Rosa's prognosis was poor from the start,and within a year,she died.As arrangements for the funeral were made,Mom,herself grief-stricken,played a critical role stabilizing Rosa's family and assisting with important decisions.The fact that she was needed was,of course,good therapy as she struggled through her own emotions.

Shortly after Rosa passed away,her bereaved husband,Jean,called my mother on behalf of their daughter,Marsha,who lived out of town. "Rose," he said,"when Marsha was here for the funeral she turned the house upside down looking for a tablecloth she said Rosa had been working on,embroidery or something.I have no idea where it is,and Marsha is devastated about it.I think Rosa was working on it for her.Do you have any idea where she might have put it?"

The next day,my mother,her heart heavy with loss,pulled up in front of her friend's house.Walking into the dining room,fifty years of knowing Rosa's habits her guide,she opened the bottom drawer of the china cabinet,revealing the tablecloth and napkins Marsha was searching for.Unfolding the embroidered cloth,she said to Jean,"I remember Rosa telling me about this cloth before she became sick.She was working on it for Marsha,but it looks like she finished only half of it before she had to give it up.Do you mind if I finish it?"

My mother carried the cloth home and lovingly studied her friend's handiwork. With tears in her eyes but with a sense of renewal, she threaded the embroidery needle tucked into the fabric and began to sew.For days,she embroidered,each stitch fortifying and healing her.

The tablecloth finished and ironed,Mom draped it over her lap,examining the commingling of her stitches with Rosa's,contemplating the weight of their joint effort and thinking how true it is that the whole is much more than the sum of its parts.With great care,she swaddled the cloth in tissue,placed it in a box and mailed it to the daughter of her best friend.

Bohne G. Silber

罗莎的预兆从开始就不好，一年之内就病逝了。在做葬礼准备时，我的妈妈尽管自己深受悲伤的打击，但是在稳定罗莎家庭上起了重要的作用，并且提供给他们一些重要的建议。当然，事实上在她与自己的感情做斗争的时候，她也需要一个良方来解除自己的悲伤。

就在罗莎去世后不久，她的孤独的丈夫吉恩代表他住在城外的女儿玛莎打电话给我妈妈："罗斯，玛莎在这边参加葬礼的时候，在房子里翻箱倒柜地找一块桌布，她说罗莎一直在编织它，刺绣或者什么东西的。我不知道它在哪儿，玛莎为此快疯了。我想罗莎一定是为她编织的。你知道罗莎会把它放在什么地方呢？"

第二天，我的妈妈带着沉重的心情，把车停在了她朋友的房子前。走进餐厅，凭借着50年来她所知道的罗莎的习惯，妈妈打开了一个中国式橱柜最底下的抽屉，找到了玛莎所寻找的桌布和餐巾。打开绣着花边的桌布，妈妈对吉恩说："我记得罗莎生病之前告诉过我，她在给玛莎织桌布，但是看起来在她不得不放弃之前，只织好了一半，你会介意由我来把它织完么？"

妈妈把那块桌布拿回了家，并且满怀深情地研究她的朋友的编织手法。泪水涌进她的眼里，但是带着一种焕然一新的感觉，她将线穿进绣花针，开始编织。一连几天，她不停地绣着，每一针每一线都让她自己变得坚强，让她从痛苦中走出来。

编织完桌布之后又用熨斗熨过，妈妈把它平铺在膝盖上，检查她同罗莎的针脚混合处，思量着他们共同努力编织的东西的分量，思考着这块完整的桌布的意义要远远大于它所有的部分。小心翼翼地，她用丝巾把桌布包扎起来，把它放进一个盒子里，邮寄给了她最好朋友的女儿。

伯尼·G. 西尔伯

My Butterfly Friend

Carol and Fred were newcomers to our church.I wanted her to feel welcome,so I invited her to attend the monthly ladies' luncheon with me.She hesitated. "I have a rare heart disease that can only be treated with experimental medication.I never know when I'm feeling up to doing something.I'd really like to,but I'd better not plan on it.I'm sorry."

I was disappointed.I had immediately liked her and I wanted to get to know her better.She had such beautiful sparkling blue eyes and a smile that belied the fact that there was anything physically wrong with her.

As the months went by,we greeted each other in church,but every time an invitation was extended to do something,she refused.Still,Carol remained on my mind and in my heart,so I decided to try once more. This time,I invited her to attend a *Bible* study with me at another friend's home. "I don't even know if I could concentrate on the lesson. The heart medication slows everything down." Then,softly,she added, "I think I'd like to try."

As the weeks went by,Carol began to respond to the love shared at the study,and she participated more and more.Even when she wasn't feeling her best,she made the effort to attend,and we began to see a transformation.God was touching her heart,physically and spiritually.

One morning as we visited in the church foyer,my friend Darlene said, "Let's invite Carol to our pajama party!"This fun routine shared by Darlene and me had begun as a way to cure my loneliness when my husband was away on business trips.It seemed we never had enough time together,and there was always so much to talk and pray about.We

好友如蝶

卡罗尔和弗雷德是新近加入我们教堂的人。我想让她感到在这里受到欢迎,因此邀请她与我一起参加每月一次的女士午餐会。她犹豫不决:"我得了一种罕见的心脏病,只能通过手术治疗。我不知道自己什么时候能够做些什么事情。我是真的想参加,但是我最好还是不去了。我很抱歉。"

我感到失望。我立即喜欢上了她并且想了解她更多一些。她有着一双美丽明亮的蓝色双眼、迷人的微笑,掩盖了她身体上的不足之处。

几个月过去了,我们在教堂里互相问候,但是每次邀请她出去做些什么事情的时候,她总是谢绝了。尽管如此,卡罗尔还是一直在我的脑海里和心里挥之不去,于是我决定再试一次。这一次,我邀请她与我一起在一个朋友家学习《圣经》。"我不知道自己是否能够全神贯注于学习课上,对心脏的治疗让一切都慢了下来。"接着,她轻声地补充说道,"我想我可以试试。"

几个星期过去了,卡罗尔开始回应我们在学习过程中分享到的爱,而且她也越来越多地参加进来。甚至是在她感觉不是很好的时候,她也努力参加,我们开始看到了一个转变。上帝正在触动她的心,从她的身体到她的精神。

一天早上,当我们去教堂休息室时,我的朋友戴莲娜说:"我们邀请卡罗尔参加我们的睡衣晚会吧!"这个我和戴莲娜之间有趣的日常聚会是在我丈夫出差途中去世后开始的,是为了解除我的孤独。看起来我们从不曾有足够的时间待在一起,而且总是有很多东

女性系列／聆听花开的声音

invited Carol and were surprised and delighted when she said, "That sounds like fun! I'd love to come! "

She came through my door the next week with her arms loaded, then went back to the car to get her pajamas,pillow,comforter,teddy bear and everything else she needed to feel at home away from home.The three of us talked until the wee hours of the morning,and after a late breakfast,continued to talk on into the afternoon,still in our pajamas.

Many more pajama parties followed.Each time,the guest room Carol occupied became more and more like home,until she finally left her pillow,comforter and all the other things for the next time.Like a butterfly,she emerged from her cocoon.

Miraculously,more adventures began.We started going on little out-ings,then bigger and bigger ones.The highlight of our escapades was the three of us taking an overnight trip to attend Oprah.Eventually,trips to Disney World on her own were second nature to her.

But when her daughter called announcing Carol's impending grand-motherhood,some of Carol's old doubts resurfaced: "Can I be the kind of grandma I want to be? I want to have fun with my babies.I want to baby-sit for them,rock them,hold them and play with them."Carol's concerns about being physically able to care for her new grandson soon faded.The joy of holding him filled her heart to overflowing and her caregiving took over.And with the second grandchild,her heart's capacity and her ability doubled.

Last week she called,exclaiming,"I'm going to Europe! Five days in Paris and five days in Austria to celebrate Holly and Andy's anniversary.They want me to come to watch the grandkids while they enjoy evenings out.My doctor has given me permission to go! Can you believe it?"

I do believe it.Girlfriends and pajama parties are the best medicine.

Karen R. Kilby

西要去谈论和祈祷。我们邀请了卡罗尔参加这个聚会，并且当她说出"听起来很有趣，我很想去"时感到惊讶万分和高兴。

在下个星期，卡罗尔来到了我的门前，捧满了东西，然后她回到车子那里取了睡衣、枕头、盖被、泰迪熊和一切能够让她在远离家门时还能让她有家的感觉的东西。我们3个一直聊到凌晨，吃了宵夜之后，我们又继续聊到第2天的下午，就这么一直穿着睡衣。

之后我们又举行了很多次睡衣派对，一次接着一次。卡罗尔在客厅所占据的位置越来越像是她的家了，直到最后她把枕头、盖被等所有东西都留在我这儿以便下次再用。像是一只蝴蝶，她已经破茧而出。

不可思议的是，我们开始了更多的冒险。我们开始做一些小的远足活动，然后活动越来越大。我们最重要的一次"壮举"就是我们3个来了一次彻夜之旅去参加Oprah的访谈节目。最终，自己做一次迪斯尼乐园之旅成为卡罗尔的第二个需求。

但是当卡罗尔的女儿打电话告诉她她即将做祖母时，卡罗尔曾经有的一些迟疑又浮现出来："我能够成为一个好祖母吗？我想同孩子们一起玩乐，我想照看他们，轻轻晃着他们，抱着他们，跟他们一起做游戏。"卡罗尔对自己的身体状况是否能够照顾她孙子的担心很快就消失了。抱着孙子时的喜悦充满了她的心灵，使她精力充沛，当她有了第二个孙子时，她心脏和身体的承受能力都提高了一倍。

上星期，她打电话过来宣称："我要去欧洲了！在巴黎待5天，在奥地利待5天，庆祝霍利和安迪的周年纪念日。他们希望我跟过去，这样晚上他们出去的时候我可以照看孙子们。我的医生允许我去！你能够相信吗？"

我当然确信无疑。女友和睡衣派对是最好的药！

卡伦·R.基尔比

Discovery Toys

CHICKEN SOUP

If I were asked to give what I consider the single most useful bit of advice for all humanity,it would be this:Expect trouble as an inevitable part of life,and when it comes,hold your head high.Look it squarely in the eye,and say,"I will be bigger than you.You cannot defeat me."

Ann Landers

Twenty-five years ago,twenty-nine-year-old Lane Nemeth went toy shopping for her newborn daughter.She wanted simple,sturdy toys,like the ones in California,day-care center where she worked.But the local stores carried what she considered plastic junk.

The more annoyed she got,the more she became convinced she could do better.She knew what kids liked and what mothers wanted. Friends gently pointed out the obvious—nothing in her background qualified her to run her own business.

But Nemeth's father and husband thought she was on to something. They suggested the Tupperware approach:Sell toys at home-based demonstration parties.

Nemeth bought toys from her day-care center's suppliers and asked friends to hold toy parties.Encouraged by their modest success,she borrowed $5,000 from her grandmother to purchase select merchandise from Israel.Discovery Toys was born.

Nemeth converted her garage into a warehouse.Since she couldn't afford a staff,she offered three friends a title—"educational consultant"—and gave them a percentage of every sale they made.

Her enthusiasm was infectious.In the first year she grossed $20,000—enough to risk quitting her job.With a little more money

双语精华版·心灵鸡汤·

"发现"牌玩具

假如有人让我给全人类提出一条最有用的忠告，我会说：认定困难是生活不可或缺的一部分。遇到困难的时候，高高地昂起你的头，盯着它的眼睛说："我比你大。你赢不了我。"

安·兰德尔斯

25年前，29岁的莱恩·内密斯去为刚出世的女儿买玩具。她想买些简单结实的玩具，只要与她的工作地点（加利福尼亚州的日间护理中心）的那些玩具一样就好。可是，在她眼里，当地玩具店卖的净是些塑料垃圾。

她越是气愤，就越是有信心自己在这方面能够做得比别人好。她清楚孩子们喜欢什么，母亲们想要什么。朋友们委婉地指出一个显而易见的问题——她丝毫不具备独立创业的背景。

可是内密斯的父亲和丈夫觉得她有她的优势。他们建议采用特百惠的办法：在家里举办玩具展示派对，在派对上销售玩具。

内密斯从日间护理中心的供货商那里买进玩具，邀请朋友举办玩具派对。初步的胜利使她获得鼓舞，她又从祖母那儿借了5000美元，购进了产自以色列的高档货。"发现"牌玩具诞生了。

内密斯把车库变成了大仓库。雇不起员工，她就给3位朋友授予了"教育顾问"的头衔——并且把所有卖出商品的所得按比例分成。

她的热情很有感染力。第一年她的总收入是2万美元——意味

borrowed from her family,she leased a small warehouse in Concord in August 1978 and set herself the goal of selling $100,000 worth of toys by the end of the year.

Business was so good that most of her inventory was depleted by October.She would not be able to fulfill her Christmas orders. "It was horrifying,"she says. "I'd get an order for forty toys and only be able to send two."

The following year Nemeth was determined never to be caught short of toys again.She leased a larger warehouse and crammed it with toys.Sales broke $1 million.But at year's end she still had excess inventory and was $100,000 in debt.No bank would lend her more money,so she borrowed from a finance company at 27 percent interest.

Six months later,in even bigger financial trouble,Nemeth got a call from a venture capitalist in San Francisco.The man had gone to a Discovery Toys demonstration and had been so impressed that he offered to bail Nemeth out.She sold him 20 percent of the company.

Business picked up,and she expanded her operation again.But increased debts drove her to the brink of bankruptcy.

For the first time,Nemeth considered giving up."I always thought of Discovery Toys as my other child,"she says. "So I said to myself, 'If this were my daughter,and she were seriously ill,what would I do?' When I looked at it that way,it became clear."

Nemeth cut her payroll and found a bank to help.By 1985 Discovery Toys reached $37 million in sales.In 1989 it sold $100-million worth of games,books,toys and audio tapes through a nationwide part-time sales force of 48,000.

Nemeth's most important lesson? "Mistakes are fine.Just don't make the same one twice."

Doug Garr

[EDITORS' NOTE:Discovery Toys made $39.8 million in sales in 2002.]

着可以冒险辞职了。她又从家里借了一点钱,1978年的8月开始在康科德长期租用了一处小仓库,并且为自己定下了年底销售价值10万美元玩具的目标。

生意真是不错,大多数存货到10月就销售一空。眼看圣诞节的订单完成不了。"太可怕了,"她说,"有个客户本来要订40件玩具,我只能给出两件。"

第二年,内密斯决定再也不要出现供货不足的情况。她又租用了一间更大的仓库,里面是堆积如山的玩具。当年销售量超过了100万美元。可是,到年底,她还有过量存货,负债10万美金。没有一家银行愿意借钱给她,所以她就以27%的利率从一家金融公司借了些钱。

6个月之后,她的财政问题更加严峻。这时,她接到了旧金山一位风险资本家的电话。原来他去参加了一个"发现"牌玩具的展销会,展销会让他念念不忘,他愿意出手相助。内密斯把公司的20%股份转让给了他。

生意好起来,她又开始扩大了规模。但是越来越多的债务把她逼到了破产的边缘。

内密斯第一次有了要放弃的想法。"我经常把'发现'牌玩具当成我的另外一个孩子。"她说。"所以我对自己说,'假如这是我的女儿,她现在得了重病。我该怎么办?'当我这样想的时候,答案就显而易见了。"

内密斯裁减员工,并且向一家银行求助。1985年,"发现"牌玩具销售额达到了3700万美金。1989年,通过遍布全国的48 000名兼职销售人员卖出了价值1亿美金的游戏、书籍、玩具和录音带。

从内密斯身上能学习到的最重要的东西是什么?"犯错误没问题。只是不要重复犯相同的错误。"

道·伽

【编者按:2002年,"发现"牌玩具销售额达到了3980万美金。】

The Pirate

We don't see things as they are, we see them as we are.

Anals Nin

CHICKEN SOUP

One day Mrs. Smith was sitting in her doctor's waiting room when a young boy and his mother entered the office. The young boy caught Mrs. Smith's attention because he wore a patch over one eye. She marveled at how unaffected he seemed to be by the loss of an eye and watched as he followed his mother to a chair nearby.

The doctor's office was very busy that day, so Mrs. Smith had an opportunity to chat with the boy's mother while he played with his soldiers. At first he sat quietly, playing with the soldiers on the arm of the chair. Then he silently moved to the floor, glancing up at his mother.

Eventually, Mrs. Smith had an opportunity to ask the little boy what had happened to his eye. He considered her question for a long moment, then replied, lifting the patch, "There's nothing wrong with my eye. I'm a pirate!" Then he returned to his game.

Mrs. Smith was there because she had lost her leg from the knee down in an auto accident. Her trip today was to determine whether it had healed enough to be fitted with a prosthetic. The loss had been devastating to her. Try as she would to be courageous, she felt like an invalid. Intellectually, she knew that this loss should not interfere with her life, but emotionally, she just couldn't overcome this hurdle. Her doctor had suggested visualization, and she had tried it, but had been unable to envision an emotionally acceptable, lasting image. In her mind she saw

"海盗"

> 我们看到的事物并不是它们本来的样子,而是我们自己的投影。

艾阿纳斯·宁

一天,史密斯太太正坐在医生的候诊室里,医院里进来了一个小男孩和他的母亲。小男孩一只眼睛戴着眼罩。这引起了史密斯太太的注意。她目视着他随着母亲,在旁边的椅子上坐下来,心里禁不住感叹,失去了一只眼睛的孩子,竟然还能如此镇定自若。

那一天诊所里很忙,史密斯太太因此有机会与孩子的母亲攀谈起来。小男孩玩着自己的玩具士兵。刚开始,他安安静静地坐着,把士兵放在椅子扶手上玩。后来又一声不响地把它们移到地面上,还抬头看看妈妈。

终于, 史密斯太太有机会亲自向小男孩询问起眼睛的情况来。只见他想了半天,然后掀起眼罩,回答道:"我的眼睛没毛病。我是海盗!"之后,又接着玩起来。

史密斯太太是因为在车祸中失去了一只腿膝盖以下的部分才到医院来的。而今天这趟来,是为了确定恢复的情况,看看是否可以安装义肢。残疾对她产生了几乎是致命的打击。虽然她努力地想要勇敢地面对,可心里还是觉得自己是个没用的人。理智上她知道决不可以让失去的半条腿影响她的生活,可是情感上,这却是一条难以跨越的沟壑。医生建议她试试意念想象法。她尝试过,可是始终想象不出一个情感上能接受的、持久的形象。在她的脑海里,她就是一

女性系列／聆听花开的声音

herself as an invalid.

The word "pirate" changed her life.Instantly,she was transported. She saw herself dressed as Long John Silver,standing aboard a pirate ship.She stood with her legs planted wide apart—one pegged.Her hands were clenched at her hips,her head up and her shoulders back,as she smiled into a storm.Gale force, winds whipped her coat and hair behind her.Cold spray blew across the deck balustrade as great waves broke against the ship.The vessel rocked and groaned under the storm's force. Still she stood firmly—proud,undaunted.

In that moment,the invalid image was replaced and her courage returned.She regarded the young boy,busy with his soldiers.

A few minutes later,the nurse called her.As she balanced on her crutches,the young boy noticed her amputation. "Hey lady,"he called, "what's wrong with your leg? "The young boy's mother was mortified.

Mrs. Smith looked down at her shortened leg for a moment. Then she replied with a smile, "Nothing.I'm a pirate,too."

Marjorie Wallé

个废人。

可是,"海盗"这个词改变了她的生活。瞬间,她被带到了另外一个地方。她看见自己站在海盗船上,穿着打扮和朗·约翰·斯尔维尔一样。她岿然不动地立在那儿,双腿岔开——一只腿装上了义肢。双手紧握,放在腰上,头高昂着,肩膀向后,笑望风雨。大风把她的衣衫、头发都吹到身后。巨大的海浪撞到船身上,冰冷的浪花溅到甲板的栏杆里。船身摇晃着,在风雨的淫威下呻吟着,可是她依然屹立在那里——充满自豪,无所畏惧。

就在那一刹那,残疾人的形象被替换了,她重新鼓起了勇气。她注视着一旁还在摆弄玩具士兵的孩子。

几分钟之后,她接到了护士的电话。当她借助拐杖平衡好身体的时候,小男孩注意到了她截肢的腿。"喂,女士,"他喊道,"你的腿怎么了?"小孩的母亲吓呆了。

史密斯太太低下头,注视截断的腿片刻,微笑地回答道:"没事。我也是海盗。"

玛乔里·沃雷